The Bard of Bowell

• • •

W. P. Peart

ISBN: 1495274624
ISBN 13: 9781495274626
Library of Congress Control Number: 2014901213
CreateSpace Independent Publishing Platform
North Charleston, South Carolina

For Marjorie,
My Rosalind

I

As he stood on top of the septic tank, the concrete cap split down the middle and Henry Miller was suddenly standing nipple-deep in a pool of turds and brown sludge. Stunned for a few seconds, he slowly became aware that his left hip must have smashed into the baffle wall that separated the tank into two equal compartments.

Oh God, I hope I didn't break the skin, he thought. But it hurt like hell. "Nora!" he shouted. And louder still, "Nora! Come here! I'm in trouble!" His glasses had twisted on his head and hung askew from his nose. He lifted his hands to adjust them but stopped, seeing the filth on his fingers.

His wife ran around the corner of the house and came to a sudden stop when she saw Henry's shoulders and head rising out of the stinking cesspit. She started to hoot, realized her error, clapped a hand across her mouth, but couldn't gain control. She bent over in a fit of hysterical laughter. Finally, she said to her husband, "What do you want me to do?"

"Bloody well get me out of here."

"How? I'm not strong enough to pull you out. Can't you just climb out?"

"This stuff is like grease. If I try to get a grip I just slip back. And the stink is bloody awful."

While they mused about a possible solution, their neighbour, Elmer Knobber, wandered over. Elmer had owned the old farm house that Henry and Nora had bought recently and had moved into a tiny bungalow just over the property line. Elmer was ever curious about the activities of these young city folks who had become his new neighbours. And their goings-on caused him significant puzzlement. As always he made an appreciative survey of Nora's trim figure, her freckle-specked cheeks and nose and the blond ponytail that bobbed at the nape of her slender neck. Then he turned his gaze perplexedly at Henry, at least that part that he could see, and asked, "Did you intend to do this?"

"Not actually, Elmer. My original intent had been to dive in head first. But the cap broke just as I was getting into my stance."

Nora began to snort with laughter again and decided her safest recourse was to absent herself from the scene of action. "I'll get the hose ready behind the house. Take your clothes off beside the woodpile and I'll wash you down when you get out of here. And I'll tell the kids to stay inside." Her gales of mirth could be heard as she disappeared back around the corner of the house.

Henry now looked at Elmer and Elmer looked back. Finally, Henry said, "Elmer, could you give me a hand out of here?"

Elmer tipped his John Deere tractor cap back on his head, hooked his thumbs into the braces of the denim overalls that did little to disguise his large belly, considered Henry's request, and finally said, "Oh, no. I don't think I want to do that. I'll get crap all over my hands."

More silence ensued. "Can you think of a way to get me out of here."

"Probably." More silence. "I could get a long rope, wrap it around one of those big maples and toss the end in to you. You could pull yourself out."

"Well, why don't we just do that?" said Henry.

• • •

The morning had started well. They had breakfasted with the two children, who had finished quickly so that they could go outside to play and explore the vast new surroundings in which they found themselves. Their house sat on four acres and Elmer's two hundred acres of farmland surrounded them on three sides. For the kids it was a continent in size.

The house itself was built on a basic Georgian plan, with four large rooms and a hallway downstairs and four bedrooms upstairs, again with a central hall. The ceilings were ten feet in height downstairs and nine feet high on the second floor. The foundation was constructed of solid limestone blocks to a thickness of three feet and rose eight feet from bedrock to support the first floor joists. At this point the walls outside were of red brick, and inside of very worn plaster. The house was forty feet in length on each of its four sides. Gingerbread adorned the facia and posts of the porches.

"What are your plans for today?" Nora had asked.

"Well, we have to do something about the cistern if we want to have enough water. So we'll have to hire a stone mason to build us a new one. And I'll have to tear apart the old rotten one and get it out of the cellar. And I've got to replace all of the eavestroughing around the entire perimeter of the house because the stuff that's up there is totally worn through. And we have to make sure we have enough wood for winter. So I guess I won't be at a loss for meaningful occupation."

"I'm wondering if we made a mistake in paying cash for this place? We must be starting to get down in cash flow. And we probably should be hiring guys to do a lot of this work for us."

"Nah. I can do most of this stuff myself. And we still have about twenty thousand."

"When does your first pay cheque come in?"

"Not 'til the end of September, three weeks after I start teaching."

"That's almost two months away."

At that moment their elder daughter, Annie, came into the kitchen and announced, "Daddy, there's a hole in the front yard."

"Oh, Lord, I hope there are two of them."

"Why?" asked Nora.

"Because groundhogs always build their tunnels with two holes so that they'll have an escape route. If there's only one hole we're in shit."

There was only one hole. Henry tapped a piece of half-inch i-bar into the ground adjacent to the solo hole and quickly hit concrete. "Yeah, there's likely a piece out of the septic cover. I'll shovel the dirt off and we can see what's going on." Thirty minutes later the tank's surface was completely exposed and Henry stood proudly on top of the unit right next to the offending aperture.

• • •

After he had been hosed off, Henry turned to his befouled clothes, soaked them, sprayed them some more and left them spread out on the woodpile. Then he went inside, showered in water as hot as he could tolerate, put on some clean duds and joined Nora in the kitchen. It was only 11:30 but she opened him a beer. "You may need this."

"Elmer gave me the name of the septic pumper that he uses, so I'd better phone him. And I just remembered. I have a meeting at the school tomorrow. With Jean. I guess I'm finally going to find out what my timetable is going to be."

"Are you nervous?"

"Not really. I do know that they don't have any graduate classes, so it'll be all undergrad. And they're just kids. So how tough can that be?"

Henry gloried in the drive into town. It took a mere twenty-five minutes. If he were to go any farther he'd drown in Lake Ontario. And the traffic on the excellent two-lane highway varied from light to non-existent. As he cruised through the gently rolling farmland, he took pleasure in the grazing animals, cows, sheep and even scratching chickens that were evidently intelligent enough not to want to get to the other side of the road. He waved at a couple of farmers cutting hay and didn't care that they didn't notice him or ignored his friendly gesture. "This is so different from Toronto," he gloated.

He thought back to how he'd arrived here. Nora and he had met at Simon Fraser University in British Columbia where they were both majoring in English and working towards bachelor's degrees. This career choice had really prepared them for little except to teach school or to continue studying. Nora had found a job teaching at a secondary school in Vancouver and Henry decided to pursue his Master's degree. He also decided to ask Nora to marry him, she eventually accepted, and they took a tiny one bedroom apartment, all that they could afford on Nora's beginning salary and the few dollars that Henry made as a Teaching Assistant for a professor who taught a couple of under-graduate classes. This meant that Henry did most of the grading of the essays assigned by the teaching prof.

At the end of his second year as a Master's student, Henry had to submit a thesis. Because he loved Shakespeare, he wracked his brain for a topic dealing with The Bard that had not been done to death by four centuries of students faced with the same academic challenge. It finally struck him that he had never heard much about the dogs in Shakespeare's works. He proposed to his advisor the topic, *Dogs and Canine Imagery in Shakespeare's Lesser Plays*. His advisor promptly agreed to this learned quest, his focus at that time being elsewhere. He was in the process of carrying on a fling with two of his students, each of whom had found out about the other. And the prof's wife had just found out about the two girls. Henry and his dogs assumed a spot well down on his list of priorities.

Henry proceeded to generate eighty pages on this vital subject, the highlight being that Launce in *Two Gentlemen of Verona* achieved his modest success as a clown solely because of the presence of his mutt. Henry's advisor, hard pressed by a trio of viragoes, did not need the additional strain of a rejected candidate to deal with. He prevailed upon the evaluating board that would bring judgement to bear on Henry's opus to deal with the paper in the most lenient possible manner. And so it came to pass that eighty pages on Shakespeare's dogs were never read, nor ever would be read, except by the author who could now proudly append the letters M.A. after his name.

The dilemma of vocational preparation yet continued. The newly minted Master could now either join his wife, Nora, in the high school classroom, or he could carry on becoming more and more educated. Henry again chose the latter. They moved to Toronto, Nora once more found a teaching job, and, once more Henry was a Teaching Assistant, but now at the University of Toronto. And once again, Henry was saddled with the evaluation of papers assigned by a professor who declared herself too busy to do her own marking. But because Henry was now working towards a Ph.D., he was granted permission to conduct seminars of small groups of students, who wrote some of the essays he was grading. These students loved him. Henry did not cleave to the customary procedure of marking, returning and forgetting of undergraduate writing efforts. If a student bombed a piece of work, Henry would meet with the kid, show why the work was not up to scratch, and, most importantly, show how to do it properly. Then he would allow the author to re-write and re-submit.

As well as his course work and his T.A. duties, Henry once again had to find a topic for his doctoral dissertation. This time he struck gold. While researching the Bronte sisters for a course in 19th Century Literature he found that Anne Bronte had been a tutor with a family named Robinson. This in itself was of little interest. But deep in the darkest bowels of the U. of T. Library he stumbled upon a small tome that focussed on this same Robinson family. The book was very old, very dust covered, and very fragile. It had been published in Oxford before The Great War began. It might possibly never have been opened. Henry carried it in two hands back to his desk in the stacks, gently blew away some of the motes of ages, opened it and began to read. The Robinson family had been fond of Anne Bronte. But there had been a cousin, Moira Burwell, who had been smitten by the tutor. This Moira later was left stranded at the altar by a nasty man on the day of their wedding. Her grief was vast. To deal with it, she strove to emulate the woman she so admired and attempted to narrate the sad tale in semi-autobiographical fashion. Henry returned the ancient text to its place on the remote shelf, scanned the surrounding texts and found it, *A Heart So Cruelly Ripped* by M. R. Burwell.

Henry ran with his topic, *The Influence of Minor Tragediennes on the Tenor of Mid-Nineteenth Century Women's Literature*. His advisor was a woman, his evaluators were all women, and all of them were delighted to be associated with a man of such obvious sensitivity to the world of female authors. He soon had the letters Ph. D. to follow his M.A. His dissertation was read by few and interested even fewer. And so followed five years of toiling in the rock strewn fields of General Arts academe.

Henry smiled as he drove closer to the town. He could see the sunlight bouncing off the chop of the lake's water. He turned left at the water's edge and within three minutes was in the centre of the campus of Sir MacKenzie Bowell College. The buildings belied the weak reputation of the place. They were beautiful, six four-storey limestone structures topped with copper that had been shaped to resemble tiles of the sort often found in Italy and Portugal. The grounds were, if not expansive, at least spacious and were meticulously groomed. Because it was July no students were to be seen and few other pedestrians at all. He parked on the street outside the building identified as 'Arts and Humanities'.

He chuckled as he got out of his ten-years-old Chevy Impala, thinking of the origins of Bowell College's nickname. Rather condescending types at the Universities of Toronto, McGill and Queen's had taken to referring to his new place of employment as 'Colon U'.

On the fourth floor he found the door he wanted, labelled 'Dr. Jean Whitmarsh, Dean, Arts and Humanities'. He introduced himself to a secretary who invited him to take a seat and then used her intercom to announce his presence to the dean within.

The door opened a few seconds later and a woman of perhaps forty-five years of age greeted him, smiling broadly. "Dr. Miller, I am so glad to see you. I have been so looking forward to this meeting." She stood aside and waved Henry to a chair at the right side of the room. She was dressed in a blue skirt, black blouse covered with a light blue cardigan, and set off with a serious string of pearls. Her face was oval, her eyes were startlingly blue, and her hair was a tight mass of brownish-blonde curls. She never stopped smiling, a full 100 watt radiance. Henry regretted having worn only jeans and a golf shirt.

"Your office has a beautiful view of the lake. We must be looking straight south. Do you ever get tired of looking at it?"

"Actually, I spend most of my time looking away from it. I'm always at my desk working, you see. And it faces away from the outside exposure." The smile never faded.

The sun from the east was shining directly into his eyes and he had to squint somewhat to see his new boss.

"So, Dr. Miller - - -"

"Please, call me Henry."

"Very well, Henry. I must confess to some surprise when I discovered that you were a man."

"Yes. I always have been. Rather like being a man actually."

Through his squint, Henry thought he saw the smile falter, just for a second.

"Your doctoral dissertation was what originally led me to that conclusion. I had assumed that such a topic would have appealed to a woman. What triggered your interest in Moira Burwell?"

For an instant Henry was tempted to tell the truth: That he chose the old spinster because nobody had ever heard of her, nobody wanted to know anything about her, and that she paved the easiest road he could find to his Ph. D. He thought about his old drinking buddy, Ed Ehmann, who had actually done his dissertation on *The Coloration of Beer*, but he replied, "I have a strong and abiding interest in women's literature, of all eras. Women over the centuries have been so deeply wronged, and it is through their writings that we can begin to understand the harm done and begin to atone for it."

Despite the brightness of the sun, Henry saw the smile expand towards each ear. "How reassuring, Doctor, er - -, Henry. I think you'll fit in well with our faculty. We are a very progressive English Department and your views seem quite congruent."

Dr. Whitmarsh looked down briefly at some papers on her desk. "You'll find the pace of life here rather different from what you've been used to in Vancouver and Toronto."

"I sure hope so. I absolutely will not miss the two hour commute I've endured every day for the past few years. Took me under a half hour to get here today."

"So you have lodging?"

"Indeed we do. We've bought a century-old farm house just south of Whippletree."

"How quaint."

"We love it."

"Does your partner teach?"

"She did, but she's going to stay home with our two kids now."

The smile tightened. "How quaint."

Henry offered no more information and let the silence grow.

"Well, I suppose that we should discuss your teaching responsibilities. I'm afraid that, as you are the low man on the list, so to speak, you are getting the remnants of the remaining courses. And as we are an undergraduate institution only, you'll not be seeing any grad programs. Those are all to be found down the road at Queen's or U. of T. But I'm sure you'll not mind that." She beamed brightly.

"Not at all. And as a matter of fact, I prefer teaching to doing straight research."

"Do you, indeed." Dr. Whitmarsh glanced again at the papers on her desk. "You'll be instructing two classes of third-year Engineering students. It's a compulsory English course for them. And one class of fourth-year Women's Studies students. This too is a compulsory course"

"Great."

"You don't mind?"

"Not a whit. Where do I find the curriculum?"

"That poses a bit of a problem," the dean said. "We've not had great success with the engineers in our past experience. Some of the lecturers have found these students to be somewhat irreverent and in some cases bullying."

"Bullying?"

"Evidently they don't like being instructed by women and most of the English Faculty are female."

"And the Women's Studies course?"

"I feel that with your avid interest in women's literature, you can provide a most adequate range of meaningful writing for these senior girls."

"So in both cases, I can do my own thing?"

"Yes, I suppose that is what I'm saying." She paused to see if there would be a reaction to this news. Seeing none, she went on, "Now, why don't I give you a tour of our building and show you which room you'll be teaching in. It's in the basement. And you'll find your office quite conveniently located just down the hall from it. Near the custodians' office, actually."

II

Henry got into the Impala, started the engine, then placed his arms on the top of the steering wheel and rested his forehead on his arms. He began to giggle. "How bloody quaint to get the remnants to teach; how bloody quaint to be teaching in the basement; how bloody quaint to have no curriculum; how bloody quaint everything was behind that shit-eating smile. Oh God." He put the Chev into gear and did a fast three-point turn so as to retrace his route of the morning. "Welcome to quaint old Colon Fucking U," he sighed.

Nora was solicitous. "How did it go? Do you know what you're teaching? Did you like Jean?"

"Fine. No. And, no. But let's talk about it later, because the honeysucking machine is pulling into the driveway."

Percy Baxter got out of the behemoth he was driving. He resembled his truck in appearance, huge, dirty and smelly. "Got a bit of a problem, have you?" He strolled over to the exposed septic tank, gazed into it for a few seconds, then turned to Henry and Nora. "This is a hand-built tank, probably about fifty years old. I'll pump her out and we'll see if she's still functional. She might be. Some of these old tanks last forever."

Percy pulled on his oversized rubber work gloves, returned to his truck started up a gas engine at the rear of the machine and began to pull a five inch leather pipe to the septic tank. "Can I do anything to help you?" asked Henry.

"Yeah, go over and throw that switch beside the gas motor and that'll start the pump goin'."

Fifteen minutes later both chambers had been emptied. Nora had arrived with the long garden hose and Percy used it to spray down the sides of the walls and the retaining baffle wall as well. Then this residue, too, was sucked out. Percy examined the tank and turned to Nora and Henry. "Nothing wrong with this rig at all. She'll last for another fifty years. But you'll need a new cap of course. I can order it and set it on for you. It'll come in four equal slabs. But the question is, why were those two chambers so full? They should have been flowing into the weeping bed. I'll hook this pump onto the outflow pipe and we'll see what's doin'."

Five minutes after that Percy turned off the gas motor. "You've got a problem. I should have been getting all kinds of liquid out of the tile bed. But there's nothing there. The old farmers who built these things used red tile pipe for the weeping bed. But tile isn't like concrete or plastic. It doesn't last for half a century. If you start digging you'll find that the tiles have all rotted away. There's just nothing there. You'll need a new bed. I've got a bunch of calls yet to do today, but I'll be back tomorrow and we'll set up a plan."

Henry finished his first beer while kicking a big beach ball around the wood pile with the two girls. "Annie, go inside and ask Mommy to give you a beer for me. And don't drink it on the way back."

"Daddy, I'm only six. I can't drink beer yet."

"Well, I'll ask you again in two weeks and see if you're old enough then. But go and get it for me now, please."

Rachel was two years younger than her sister and skinny as a pencil. But she was a hell of a runner, and so Henry kicked the ball out into the field and grinned as she sped after it. He turned his eyes to the woodpile. This was the firewood for the winter a year and a half from now. Eight full cords, four-by-four-by-eight, 'bush cords' they were called. These logs, eight feet in length had to be cut into sixteen inch chunks so as to fit into the two stoves, split and stacked under cover so that the wood would be dry enough.

"Here's your beer, Daddy."

Henry made an elaborate pantomime of examining the contents of the bottle to ensure that each precious drop was present, then said, "Thanks, Annie. Now you and Rachel play by yourselves for a while."

Nora joined him carrying a mug of tea. "You worried?"

"Kind of. Remember I said we have about twenty grand left? Well, I think we're going to blow through it with no difficulty. We've got this new tile bed, the cistern has to be replaced, we'll have to order wood for this coming winter because we can't burn this stuff. It's too green, too wet. And then there are the goddamned eaves to be replaced. I remember when we first moved down here and we had all that cash left and I started babbling about what to put in first, a swimming pool or a tennis court. And you looked at me as if I were nuts. Well, you were right. As always, actually."

Nora gave him a brief hug. "Why don't we eat out here tonight. It's warm and there aren't any bugs. You do the chicken if you can get that grill started."

The barbeque started and Henry assigned the little girls the task of gathering some wild flowers. A number of flowery-looking weeds were slaughtered in this exercise, but a small bouquet adorned the old picnic table.

After dinner Henry and Nora sipped their wine and gazed south over Elmer's farm as it gradually slipped down to the river a half-mile away. Thirty Herefords grazed two fields over. Nora put her arm around Henry's waist. "All in all, though, this is pretty nice. We'll get all of this stuff done. And we'll make do with the money we have. You'll get paid soon enough. But do me a favour and stop boring me with your litany of work that you've got ahead of you. You've gone through the whole catalogue twice in the last few days."

"Sorry."

"Don't be sorry. But listen to me. We do have enough money. Barely. We can't afford to hire people for all of it, so yes, you'll have to work your bum off. Unless we go into debt, and neither one of us wants to do that. So let's prioritize your damn list. We all have to use the bathroom every day, so the septic system gets done first. We can squeak by this summer with the bit of water that old well gives us, but a new cistern gets done second. Then you do the eavestroughs. We can order wood for this winter any old time and you can cut up this pile here during the autumn. Simple."

Henry looked at Nora for a long moment, then leaned towards her and kissed her cheek. "Thanks."

"Now I'll give the girls their bath, and you can read them a couple of stories afterwards. Then maybe you can give me a better kiss than that feeble effort."

Much later as they lay in bed holding hands and letting their feet touch, Nora said, "Well, the good news seems to be that you can chart your own course at Bowell. You could have been saddled with some of that dreck that poses as literature on so many campuses. What do you think you'll give the engineers?"

"Shakespeare."

"You're kidding!"

"Nope. *Shakespeare's Clowns, Drunks and Warriors.*"

Nora snorted. "And the Women's Studies ladies?"

"Shakespeare."

"Henry!"

"I'm serious. *Shakespeare's Strongest Characters: Women.*"

"From what you've told me about Jean Whitmarsh, she'll go nuts."

"Probably, but she told me to organize the courses myself. And by the way, there's going to be a faculty and partners evening reception and barbeque at somebody's place out in the country at the end of next month. Try to look pretty for it."

Nora slapped his arm, and turned onto her side. "Turn out the light when you're ready."

"In some circles, I've heard, they have bedside lamps on bedside tables."

As he got back into bed Henry touched the small of her back lightly. "Je t'aime. Non, je t'adore."

"Je t'aime aussi."

As he snuggled under the covers, Henry started to laugh.

"What?" Nora mumbled.

"Percy the Pumper said, 'There's nothing there.' He could've been talking about Bowell, not just our tile bed."

• • •

The next morning, Professor Cynthia Kennedy ignored the dean's secretary, strode to the door of Jean Whitmarsh's office, rapped once and sailed in. The dean looked up, startled, hid her annoyance behind a flashing smile, and waved Cynthia to the sun-drenched chair which had been occupied by Henry Miller the previous morning. Cynthia ignored the suggestion, settled herself in the chair that looked west, crossed her legs and looked coldly at the Dean of Arts.

"So you've met him?"

"I did, Cynthia. He seemed very nice."

Cynthia snorted contemptuously. "Very nice, indeed. He shouldn't be here. And you should have backed me up when I fought against it."

Jean spread her arms, "What could I have done? We'd been warned about the imbalance of women to men on our faculty. As you well know, at first I thought he was a woman because his correspondence used initials and not his whole name, and we were not exactly inundated with applicants."

"Come off it, Jean. You could have stonewalled," Cynthia snarled. "Look how I fought against it in front of the Board of Regents. You could have backed me up; you could have said he was unqualified. But all you did was bow and scrape and say 'Anything you want, boss' to that bastard Charley Lee. Just pathetic."

Jean attempted to hold her ground. "Charley Lee happens to be the Chairman of the Board. And Miller's qualifications are perfect: a doctorate in female authors and sky-high teaching recommendations." She saw the look of contempt in the other woman's eyes and her resolve wavered. "He was perfect," she added weakly.

"He was a man," shot back Cynthia Kennedy.

"Cynthia, I acknowledge that you have been most badly used by the men in your life. I did not know your first husband, but I did know the second one and you were certainly well rid of him. However, I think that you are letting your private and personal problems bias your thinking about our programs. We can't be exclusively female, Cynthia," Jean whined. "Why are you so totally adamant against hiring just one man?"

Cynthia withered her with a look of scorn. "I've had enough of men to guarantee I'll never have anything to do with one again. But you just continue to pussyfoot around Charley Lee, and trail your little Marxist husband behind you, and pretend that everything is just fine. Well it isn't. And I intend to do something about it."

"What do you mean?"

"I'm not going to just sit back and let this Miller person come waltzing in here and do whatever he wants with the program that I established. I'm going to get rid of him."

"And how do you propose to do that?"

"You'll see, Jean; you'll see. But he'll never know what hit him. And it will not be gentle."

"Cynthia, that's quite enough," Jean began, but she was addressing an empty chair as Professor Kennedy was already heading out the office door, leaving it wide open.

• • •

Percy Baxter reappeared the next morning. "Now I'll tell you, Henry. You don't want to be dealing with the Department of Health when you're fixing this mess. They'll make you get permits and God knows what and hold you up for months. And you need to get this done right now. And besides they're a bunch of pricks. So what I'll do is I'll come over on Sunday when no inspectors are lurking about, and I'll excavate all those old runs and get rid of what's left of the tiles. And I'll dump a whack of three-quarter inch gravel for you and all the new plastic weeping tile you'll need. I'll bring my transit so we can get the flow angle right. That'll take care of all of Sunday. Then all you'll have to do is backfill all of the trenches. Can you do that? Because I can't run the risk of being seen doing it."

"Sure. I've got a shovel and I'll buy a wheel barrow."

By Wednesday morning only one run out of a total of six was left to be backfilled. Henry was sore and his hands were blistered but he felt a deep sense of satisfaction. Percy had come by the night before to hook the new pipe up to the tank, and presto a system that would last for a century had been installed. Shovelling dirt could be a mind-numbing activity. But an old relative had told him long ago that there's no such thing as unskilled labour. It was true. And as he learned the art of productive shovelling, Henry also learned how to use his legs to take the pressure off his back, and how to use leverage to move the stuff efficiently.

But mostly he passed the working time thinking about Shakespeare and the students he had not yet met. Filling these courses would not be a problem. If the engineers were at all similar to ones he had met as an undergrad they would have ultra-heavy course loads, filled with labs, lectures and a lot of field work. They would use their free time to drink as many beers as possible, would see a mandatory English course as an intrusion and an exercise in the unnecessary, and would show up to the Monday morning class terminally hung-over. More esoteric teaching would best be reserved for the Wednesday and Friday slots. Certain of Shakespeare's characters readily offered themselves for this unenthusiastic audience: Sir Toby Belch, of course, and Petruchio, and always Sir John Falstaff in all three of his plays, and Oh Lord, why not do *Titus Andronicus* as a comedy? Henry had never been able to see it as a serious drama; it was way too far over the top. And as for heroic warrior figures, you couldn't go wrong with Prince Hal, and why not show that version of *Henry IV, Part 1* where Hal's buddies wore crimson Mohawks. Those engineers would love that, and - - -. Henry became aware that he was being watched.

He looked up and sure enough a car had stopped out on the road. The driver was looking at him. Henry waved, but got no response. Instead the car slowly moved forward and turned left into the driveway. The driver stopped, turned off the vehicle and got out. "Good morning," he said.

"Good morning," Henry replied. "How are you and who are you?"

"I'm from the Department of Health."

"Oh. What are you doing out this way?"

"Elmer Knobber, your neighbour, is severing a lot and he needs approval for the siting of a septic system for the house that he wants to build. But more importantly, can I ask what it is that you're doing here?"

"Actually, I'm putting in a number of beds of asparagus."

"It doesn't look like it. Do you have a permit for this work?"

"Permit? I didn't know I needed a permit to do a bit of maintenance."

The inspector got back into his car and through the open window said, "We'll be back tomorrow."

Henry dropped his shovel and walked back to where Nora was hanging a wash on the line. He walked past her to the edge of the pile of logs, unzipped and had a pee. As he was finishing Elmer appeared out of his barn and started back to his bungalow. Henry watched him, considered for a second, and then strode a few paces so as to intercept his neighbour. "G'day, Elmer."

"G'day, Henry. I've been meaning to ask you what you're doin' out in your front yard."

"You couldn't guess?"

"Well, it isn't my concern, is it?"

"I think you've made it your concern."

"What are you saying?"

"For Christ's sake, Elmer. You called in the inspector when I was finishing off my goddam septic bed. Which didn't bloody well exist when we bought this place, by the way. And now I have the Department of Health all over me."

"I wouldn't know anything about that. And I don't like being cussed at."

Henry glared at the old man then turned and walked back to Nora. "What was all that about?"

They went back into the kitchen while Henry filled her in on the inspector's visit. "They'll be back tomorrow and we don't have a leg to stand on."

Nora smiled up at him. "When sorrows come, they come not in single spies, but in battalions."

"Yeah, but Claudius didn't have a septic problem, he just had Hamlet on his back."

Henry finished the last run, raked it smooth, dumped all the rocks and residue in the ditch that ran on the other side of the driveway and went in for lunch.

"So what's on for this afternoon, Job?"

Henry couldn't help laughing. "But Job was on top of the dung heap, he wasn't right in the bloody stuff. I'm finished out front for now, so I'm going to go and buy us a chainsaw. I might as well start whittling at that pile of logs."

"You may as well go and see that stone mason in the village and get the cistern process going, too."

The next morning they were still finishing coffee when a car appeared in the driveway. Henry strolled out, mug in hand, to see a different man from the day before staring intently at the neat mounds of earth piled in six rows and leading to a spot thirty feet in front of the house. Henry approached him, smiled, and asked, "Department of Health?"

The man didn't answer, merely looking at Henry coldly and nodded. "I understand you don't have a permit for this work." It wasn't a question.

"I didn't think I needed one for repair work."

"This is a lot more than repair work. And you needed a permit."

"Look, the original tank is in good repair and is still there. I just replaced the tiles."

The inspector gave him a look filled with scorn. "This is not just repair work and it's going to all come out."

"What are you talking about? I'm not taking this out."

"That's not all that's going to happen. This ground doesn't have enough proper soil to accommodate a tile bed. You have to cover this entire yard with new soil. I'd think at least four feet deep."

"Are you nuts! That'd come halfway up the front windows! And this soil has been adequate for waste absorption for fifty years. We don't need four more feet of dirt."

"And those maples will all have to come down."

"Those trees are as old as the house. They're 125 years old. They're not being cut down."

The man turned to look full into Henry's eyes. "I don't think you quite understand. We can make you do anything we want you to do."

Henry started towards him, his fists tight, but checked himself, and through clenched teeth managed to say, "I think now you'd better get into your car and get the hell off my property."

"I'll be back in two weeks. I expect the work to have begun or I'll institute legal proceedings against you."

After the girls had been put to bed, Nora and Henry sat on the porch listening to the crickets and watching the barn swallows and bats performing their nightly acrobatics.

"So, Don Quixote, you've got two major battles on the go. The English department at Bowell College that's going to go nuts when they find out that you're rejecting The Canon of the Sisterhood, and the Ministry of Health that's going to sue your sorry ass or else bury this house under a thousand truck loads of dirt."

"That sounds about right."

"Well I don't mind serving as your Sancho Panza, but exactly how many windmills are you planning to tilt at all at once?"

"Just the two, I guess." Down on the farm near the river the coyotes had made a kill and their choir erupted into an eerie chorus.

"Don Quixote, eh? How would you like to see my lance?"

• • •

At breakfast, Henry reminded Nora that he had a meeting with Jean Whitmarsh at 11:00 that morning. "But I'm starting to wonder again if we really dropped the ball by moving into this old barn."

"Oh for heaven's sake," his wife exclaimed. "Listen to those girls out there."

The sound of laughter and shrieks of excitement poured in through the screen door.

"And obviously, the air here is affecting you as well. You've performed nobly two nights in a row. Do you think that might be too often?"

He was worried nevertheless. Because of that old fart, Elmer, he'd been caught dead to rights. But cutting down trees that had been growing there since before Sir John A. Macdonald had first taken office? That was not just stupid, it verged on the criminal. And four feet of soil? Craziness. But what really pissed Henry off was the arrogance of the inspector. 'We can make you do anything we want you to do.' That truly riled.

He fumed as he drove south to Bowell College. But getting angry wouldn't solve anything. He needed help and his thoughts turned to his old buddy, Seamus MacPherson. They had been pals since grade five, and had gone all through high school and the undergrad years together. Seamus had gone on to study law at Osgoode Hall and was now a partner in one of Toronto's most prestigious firms. Major corporations sought his counsel in civil lawsuits and his successes in criminal cases were becoming legendary. In fact he had stopped doing murder trials. One night over a number of scotches, he had explained his decision to Henry. "I took these guys on assuming we'd lose, and then I could bring pressure to bear so that they'd be sent to Penetanguishene, to the psychiatric prison there. They'd at least be getting some kind of treatment up there. The problem was that I was getting the bastards off. The prosecution couldn't close the deal. And I just couldn't live with that kind of result, murderers back out on the street. So I don't do them anymore."

Should I call Seamus, Henry wondered. But over a septic tank? He decided to wait and see if the jerk did in fact come back in two weeks.

Dean Whitmarsh had told him where the parking lot was and Henry wheeled into the spot reserved for faculty.

III

Once again Henry found himself seated in the chair to the right of the dean's massive desk, the sun glaring into his eyes. Today, however, he and Dr. Whitmarsh were joined by another woman. "Dr. Miller, I am pleased to introduce you to our colleague, Dr. Cynthia Kennedy."

Henry rose to shake hands with one of the most beautiful women he could recall seeing. Above average in height, with long and shapely legs, a gorgeous figure and face, all crowned with an abundance of glowing brunette hair. But if her face was angelic, her manner was icily cold. She offered neither smile nor word as she accepted his outstretched hand. Rather she fixed him with an icy glare.

"Dr. Kennedy is the driving force behind the Women's Studies program here at Bowell. I've asked her to join us as she is keenly interested in what ideas you have formulated for the curriculum for the fourth year course."

"Great."

"Well what have you decided then?" asked the dean.

"For the engineers, Shakespeare."

A gasp of incredulity exploded from the beautiful Dr. Kennedy. "For those cretins? Don't be ludicrous. Those 'things' in Engineering couldn't understand anything more complex than a comic book or a *Harry Potter* novel."

Henry looked at her for a couple of seconds, then turned back to Jean Whitmarsh. "Correct me if I've misunderstood you, Dean, but you did direct me to organize the course of study I was prepared to teach, did you not?"

"Well yes, I did suggest that. But it strikes me that a course on Shakespeare for these fellows might be just a bit ambitious."

"I gather from what you told me last week that the track record for this compulsory course has not been marked by overwhelming success. And I do appreciate your referring to these students as 'fellows'."

"What do you mean?"

"The word is definitely preferable to 'cretins' and 'things'."

"How dare you say that!" snarled the lovely Professor Kennedy. "Don't you ever attempt to pass judgement on me."

"That won't be necessary, Dr. Kennedy. You've already done that."

Dr. Kennedy jumped to her feet, eyes blazing. "Dean Whitmarsh, I will not remain here to be insulted by this, this - - - MAN."

"Please, can we all just calm down," the dean pleaded. "Cynthia, we haven't even heard what Dr. Miller has planned for the Women's Studies course. So please do be seated again and let's deal with the core of this meeting. Dr. Miller what do you have in mind for the fourth year students?"

"Shakespeare."

"What!" shrieked Dr. Kennedy. "You're planning to force the propaganda of another dead white male author on these young women. Jean, I won't have it. I won't stand for it."

"If I might clarify one point," Henry interjected, and turned to face the furious Dr. Kennedy. "Shakespeare is indeed dead and white and male. But he's not just 'another' male author. With the possible and debatable exception of Sir Winston Churchill, he is the greatest Briton of the past 1000 years. And even man-haters should be exposed to him."

"Are you going to tell him or are you just going to sit there, Jean?"

"Tell me what?" asked Henry.

Before the dean could respond, Dr. Kennedy snapped, "The only reason you're here at all is that we were being wrongly accused of gender imbalance. If it weren't for your testicles you would not be sitting here."

"Cynthia, please. Remember yourself," pleaded the dean.

"Oh, I remember myself very well, thank you. And you had better remember that I sit as faculty representative on the College's Board of

Regents. And this entire sordid conversation is going to be brought to their attention."

She stormed from the room, the door slamming shut behind her.

After a few seconds of silence Henry asked the dean if she would mind if he moved to the chair vacated by the departed Cynthia Kennedy. Getting no reply he moved and immediately appreciated the absence of the sun's glare in his eyes. More silence ensued until Henry said, "I think that was a darned good beginning, don't you?" and he smiled at the dean.

Jean Whitmarsh did not smile back. "I found that interchange distressing in the extreme and I do not see any humour in it."

"You're right, of course, Dean. But may I ask if Dr. Kennedy is always - how shall I phrase this – so indignant?"

"She is a very strong woman with very strong beliefs and she is prepared to fight for those beliefs. But she was not the only one who was out of line this morning."

"I assume you mean that I, too, was off base. But why, Dean? I merely did what you had told me I was free to do. I selected the curriculum content that I am sure will be both educational and exciting for the students I'm assigned."

"Dr. Miller, did I not make myself clear at our previous meeting? This is a progressive and forward-thinking faculty. I gave you a perfect opportunity to select course content that would lend itself to the thinking of this Arts department. You have chosen not to do so. Rather you have reached back 400 years for material that has only tenuous relevance to today's young women."

"And men."

"I beg your pardon?"

"And men. I am also teaching men, Dean. But you just used the term 'progressive'. Are you suggesting that were I to teach in the same mode of literature that has been presented to the Women's Studies course for the past three years that I would somehow be progressive?"

"Our program for the past three years has been quite successful, Dr. Miller. I see no reason for there to be such a shift in focus as you are proposing."

"Dean, if I adhere to what the format has been for those three years, does that not make me a conservative. And sadly that term has become synonymous with reactionary, has it not? So, you see, there is an inherent confusion here."

"Dr. Miller, I am not going to let myself become embroiled in semantics with you. Are you prepared to alter the program you have suggested to make it more amenable to our goals?"

"Dean, I'm afraid that my answer must be 'No'."

"Then, Dr. Miller, your length of stay at Bowell may be rather brief."

"That may be so, Dr. Whitmarsh, that may be so. But you really should recall why you hired me in the first place. There is in fact a stark gender imbalance in your teaching faculty, and you were not exactly deluged with applicants. So my departure in 'unseemly haste' as Hamlet would say, could have the potential of causing you more headaches than if I were to be here quietly doing my job."

"Do you have any more questions of me today, Dr. Miller?" the dean asked dismissively.

"I do, actually. My perception is that an adherence to an ideology is more important than educating our students. Is that true?"

"Totally false. We are trying to mould our students into caring and socially responsible citizens."

"Interesting word 'mould'. It seems to imply a top-down process of formation rather than educating thoughtful citizens who can make their own decisions. But let's leave that. My second question may be somewhat impertinent. I was really taken aback by Dr. Kennedy's tone and manner this morning, especially given that you are her boss. Does she have something on you that entitles her to act in that way?"

"I do not appreciate the question, Dr. Miller. You are quite right. It is impertinent. Grossly so. I'll bid you good morning."

"Perhaps so, Dean. But the debate about appropriate curriculum and appropriate school goals is one I hope that we revisit. And so, I'll wish you a good morning as well."

Henry stood and made for the door. As he opened it, he turned back to see the dean's hands clenched as if in prayer, eyes staring into the unresponsive surface of her desk. For a second Henry felt a notion of sympathy for the woman. "Nevertheless, Nora and I are looking forward to seeing you and your partner at the faculty barbeque in a few weeks."

Jean's head didn't move, but he heard the faint words, "You mean my husband."

Outside, the day had continued to be glorious. The breeze off the lake took away the heat of a cloudless sky. The gardeners were weeding and pruning and the grounds reflected their efforts. The place was gorgeous. What a pity that it had such a poor reputation. Henry paused to chat with a couple of the groundskeepers and to tell them that their work and good taste were appreciated. Then he looked at the six limestone buildings. There were two student residences, the Applied Sciences building, the Science building which was home for the studies of Physics, Chemistry, Botany and Zoology, the Management Studies building, and of course, the Arts and Humanities building in the basement of which his classroom was located.

As he stood there admiring the patterns that the ivy made as it sought to gain footholds ever higher, a man appeared at his side. "Lovely structures, are they not? Now I look at you and think you're too young to have a child in attendance here, so I'll guess and suggest you might be a new member of our teaching fraternity. Would I be right in that speculation?"

"You would be indeed. I'm Henry Miller. I'll be teaching English Literature. For a while at least."

"Ezekiel Silverstein. Please call me Zeke."

The two men shook hands and Zeke said, "I teach History. But my office is over there in the Management Studies building. Come on and I'll give you a tour."

The building turned out to be a replica of Henry's and so the two soon found themselves sitting in Zeke's second floor office. His window faced east toward the featureless back wall of a factory some 400 metres away. "Nice view," observed Henry.

Zeke laughed. "You would be amazed at how few perks find their way to the door of this office. Certainly a glimpse of the lake never did."

He went to a closet in the corner, reached to an upper shelf and turned back holding two glasses and a bottle. "Writer's Tears," he said identifying the brand. "It's a little known but very fine Irish whiskey that I suspect you'll enjoy."

"It's a tad early for me," said Henry.

"Young fellow, it's after noon, and you'll need all the moral and spiritual sustenance you can get to deal with this place." He poured a couple of fingers into each of the glasses, handed one to Henry and asked, "Why are you here? Could you find no position elsewhere?"

Henry swirled the whiskey in his glass, smelled it, and took a sip. "That is superb!"

Zeke smiled at him but did not speak.

"The answer to your second question is that I could have gone elsewhere. I had offers."

Zeke took a sip but again remained silent.

"OK. I came here for two reasons. My wife and I found an old farm house north of here that we fell in love with. You know, the dream becomes reality kind of thing. And the price of housing in Toronto is totally ugly."

Zeke nodded.

"The other reason is that I really believe that the role of teaching undergraduate students is not accorded the prominence it merits. It's heresy, I know, but I think teaching is at least as important as research. Maybe more so. Bowell has no grad school, so its mandate should be to teach. And when I checked the record for papers published in the last five years by the faculty here, it was pretty evident that not a hell of a lot of research was going on."

Zeke finished his drink, poured himself another, and cocked a quizzical eye at his guest.

"Not for me thanks. I've got to drive that highway back home and a ton of work is waiting for me when I get there."

"So you're an idealist?"

"I'm not really a fan of –isms and the –ists who propagate the -isms if you see what I mean. So, no, I would not say that I'm an idealist. But listen, you're asking me some pretty probing questions. Why are you doing that?"

"I'm no Sherlock Holmes, Henry, but I am not without some deductive reasoning. I saw you come out of the Arts and Humanities building and there wasn't a good deal of joy in evidence on your face. Then you stopped on the sidewalk and stood there just staring at the other side of the road. I am not unfamiliar with the harridans who frequent those hallowed halls and as there are no students to get in the way of meaningful activity, I deduced you were at a meeting with Dean Whitmarsh and perhaps her compadre, the lovely Cynthia Kennedy."

"But you seem to be taking quite an interest in who I am."

"I saw what looked like a man. He seemed to be all fire from the waist down and to shine and glitter like brass from the waist up."

"What are you talking about?"

"The Book of the Prophet Ezekiel, my boy, Chapter 8, verse 2. I have much of it memorized for obvious reasons. As I was approaching you outside, the sun was at your back and its rays flowed around you."

"I'll have to think on that one, Zeke. But, tit for tat, why are you here? You're a man of, shall we say, mature years. And you've published some papers in some prestigious journals, but none lately. So what's your story?"

"You have done your homework, haven't you? But you didn't dig deeply enough. Had you done so, you would have discovered that those papers did not meet with critical acclaim from my peers. Have you noticed that there is a certain Jewish quality about my name? And I also happen to be a strong supporter of the State of Israel. Not a Zionist, exactly. I share your reservation about -isms and -ists. But Canadian academe is not a friendly milieu for a Jew who doesn't genuflect in front of current correct thinking. Gradually I became marginalized, even to the extent of being banished from the Arts building, and I wound up here to end my days. To 'measure out my life in coffee spoons'."

"Do you have a family here with you?"

"Of children have I none. And I lost my Leah four years ago."

A silence followed, broken when Zeke poured himself another small touch.

"Henry, you did say that you were to be here 'for a while at least'. Was that significant?"

"I'd just been informed that the only reason I'm here is because I have a pair of balls. And it was suggested that I not make myself too comfortable."

Zeke started to laugh just as he was sipping the Irish dew and he started to snort. He managed to sputter, "Get out of here, glittering boy. You've got work to do."

As Henry closed the door, the loud peals of laughter followed him down the corridor.

• • •

Nora demanded a blow-by-blow account of his meeting with the dean and Henry spared no details. At the end of his narration, Nora was once again convulsed with laughter. "You're the second person to laugh at my troubles."

"Who was the other one, Balls Boy?" She began to giggle all over again.

"A History professor named Ezekiel Silverstein."

"Well he's obviously got a sense of humour, so at least that's promising. What's he like?"

"I really liked him, but I think he's got a drinking problem." Henry was outlining his conversation with Zeke when Nora interrupted.

"Hold on there. You were radiating streams of glory? What does he see you as, the Messiah?"

"Don't be silly and stop butting into my story."

"To hell with your story. What does he look like?"

"OK. Picture Zero Mostel, you know, that old Broadway actor who played the leads in a slew of great comic plays. Except this guy isn't fat, and he's not bald and he's a lot taller than Mostel."

"Nice description so far, Saviour Boy. So he's like Zero except in appearance?"

"Yeah, exactly."

"Terrific. The stone mason is going to be here this afternoon some time. And by the way, I need a car or something. I can't be stuck out here with no transportation. What if one of the girls has an accident? And besides I could get bored out of my boobs here all by myself. So see to it, would you, O Great One"

Henry was cutting one of the eight-foot logs into sixteen-inch lengths with his new chainsaw when Walter Ruttan drove down the lane. He was a lean man, dressed in a red-checked workshirt and a pair of very worn jeans. His face was angular and deeply tanned, covered with a three-day stubble, and topped with an old camouflage baseball cap. "G'day," he said as Henry turned off the chainsaw. "Not hopin' to burn that this winter, I hope."

"Nope. Next year."

"At the earliest. Best to get two years ahead."

"I do need some for this winter coming, though."

"I can help you out with that. I know a guy who'll drop off seasoned hardwood, and even stack it for you. But you should also talk to him about logs. Some of those big bastards in this pile here are too damn big for that saw of yours. I'll tell him to come and see you. Now what's your cistern problem?"

Henry led Walter into the cellar through a low entrance door cut into the three-feet thick limestone foundation. They had to bend almost in half to get down the slope and when they arrived in the basement they still had to stoop. The joists supporting the main bearing beam and the floors above them were old trees, some with the bark still on. Most were eighteen to twenty inches in diameter. The old cistern stood in the corner.

Cisterns were central to a clever system of water supply employed by the self-reliant people who cleared these farm lands and built these powerful houses. The cistern, essentially, was a big storage tank designed to hold the rainwater that was funnelled to it from the roof some twenty-five or thirty feet above. It had to be strong to withstand the pressure exerted by 15,000 or more litres of water. Thus its walls had to be thick and solid. Then these walls had to be parged on the inside, with several coats, to ensure they were waterproof. An electric pump at the base of the wall sucked water through a hard plastic hose from the cistern and fed it into a series of pipes leading to the various destinations in the house above. The eavestroughing around the perimeter of the roof had to have a sufficient drop in each run to enable the rain to flow to one of three downspouts which then fed into the holding tank. If all of these component parts were in good working order, and if there was sufficient rain or melting snow, a plentiful supply of water resulted. The component parts in Henry's house were not in good working order.

Walter took a look, stepped back and said, "Yeah, we're gonna have to tear this old bastard right out and build a new one. It looks like no one's paid any attention to it in years."

"And the eaves are all shot, too. All the way around."

"Yup. Noticed them on the way in."

"Walter, what the hell do you think they did for water?"

"Well, some people take baths; some others are partial to showers; maybe the folks who used to live here just dusted. Do you want me to get some guys to tear this down and get it out of here."

"I'd love that, but I don't think we can afford it. Gotta do it myself. This place is just gobbling up our money. And my wife just told me she needs a vehicle."

"I can help you with that," said Walter. "But how is she with a stick shift? I know a guy who has a truck he needs to get rid of. Good truck, too. I'll tell him to come and see you."

"I'd appreciate that."

"Think you can do this?" asked Walter nodding at the old wreck of a cistern.

"I guess I'll have to."

"I'll be back in four days to lay the new concrete floor. Can you be ready for me?"

"I guess I'll have to be. Can I buy you a beer before you go?"

They leaned against the box of Walter's truck, beers in hand, and felt the sun warming their backs. "You were smart to buy this place, Henry. It'll take a hell of a lot of work to renovate it, but it'll be worth it. It has wonderful potential."

They each drew on their beer. Walter went on, "Here's a hint for you. Getting that old girl out of the cellar is going to be real tough, because you'll be bent over all the time, don't you see. So build a ramp out of these old pieces of plywood I've got in the truck here, and nail some thin pieces across so you'll have some purchase as you're coming out. Otherwise you'll just be spinnin' dirt."

IV

That afternoon, Henry drove into the village and bought a sledge hammer to go with the round-nosed shovel and construction-grade wheelbarrow he'd recently purchased. As instructed by Walter, he built the ramp, and then set to his task. It was the hardest physical work he had ever done. Breaking up the old stone walls was straight-forward, even though they, like the house's foundation, were three feet thick. And loading the stone and rubble into the wheelbarrow was not a problem. But being constantly stooped over caused Henry's back to be-gin to sing. He was an inch over six feet and lean, and the trip out of the basement bent double, pushing a couple of hundred pounds of material, revealed muscles in his back whose existence he had never suspected. Again, he dumped each load into the ditch on the west side of the drive-way and soon covered up the residue from the old weeping tile bed.

After dinner, Henry volunteered to read to the girls before they went to sleep. And it was here that Nora found him, on his back, sound asleep and snoring, a little girl also asleep on either side of him.

The pain in his muscles was worst on the third day. Henry had anticipated this from his days as a runner, recalling how the first week back on the track was a form of Purgatory. By the fourth day, and the day when he had to finish this job, the soreness had mitigated, the up-ramp loads seemed to be easier to handle and the pile of stone and old mortar grew small and then disappeared.

Walter showed up after dinner that evening followed by a man Henry did not recognize who was driving an old Ford pick-up.

"Did you get her done?" Walter asked.

"C'mon and see."

They left the other man in his truck while they reconnoitered the basement.

"Excellent," said Walter, examining the now empty space. "I've arranged to have the blocks, sand and cement and mortar bags dropped off early tomorrow. I'll pull my cement mixer over behind my truck. And speaking of trucks, this here is the fella I was telling you about. He wants to sell this blue rig because he and the wife are moving West. I've checked it over and it's in good running shape. And the price is right, too. I'd do it."

Nora came out and waved as the two men were driving out of the lane. She nodded at the blue Ford now sitting beside the wood pile. "Why is that still here? Wouldn't it start?"

"My Sweet Chuck, you are now looking at your new vehicle."

"Henry, that is so sweet of you. But you seem to have made a mistake. That lovely old Chevrolet Impala is my vehicle. You are now, apparently, the proud owner of an old blue Ford pick-up."

"Ah, yes. Precisely so, Sweet Chuck."

It was a fast learning curve for Henry the next morning as Walter explained the ratios of sand, aggregate, cement and water that were to be fed into the maw of the electric cement mixer. Wheeling the mixture into the cellar had one advantage over the preceding days' toil; this time gravity was working with him as he struggled down the wooden ramp, trying desperately not to let the handles of the wheelbarrow get out of his control and spill the whole mess over the earthen floor. Walter worked quickly, and Henry found that he had no time to take a breath between each load mixed, transported, dumped where Walter indicated, and returning to repeat the steps over and over and over. But by late afternoon, the floor had been laid four inches thick, smoothed, and now rested securely within the wooden restraining boards. At one time during the frenetic process, Walter had smiled at Henry and observed, "Good thing you don't smoke, isn't it."

"Now, Henry, we'll let that floor ripen for a couple of days before we start the walls. What you can do though, is haul all those ten-inch blocks down here so they're ready for me three mornings from now."

The blocks were moved, Walter showed Henry the correct ratios for the making of mortar, 'mud' he called it, and the process of wheeling this new fine mixture started over again. But at last it was done. "Now we'll let this unit mature for a few days, then I'll parge her a few times and you'll have yourself a cistern."

• • •

As they got ready for bed that night, Henry saw Nora staring at him in a way he'd not noticed before. "What?" he asked.

"I'm just looking at you, Henry. You've lost weight. My God, you look like one of those paintings of Christ by Goya. You're nothing but muscle, skin and eyebrows."

Henry eyed himself admiringly in the mirror. "I'm a bloody Greek god, I am."

"I believe Zeke would prefer you to be a bit more on the Hebraic side."

Henry laughed. "You know I've been doing a lot of thinking about those people at Bowell."

"When did you have time to do that?"

"A trick I learned when I was training for races. The worst drills of all for me were the goddam hill repeats. You'd find a steep hill and sprint up it, jog down, sprint back up, and repeat about twenty times. It was a killer. But I used to get through them by fantasizing about girls that I wanted to lay."

He stopped talking as Nora's pillow hit him on the head. "You're such a pig. What do your disgusting adolescent fantasies have to do with the college?"

"Well those wheelbarrow loads started to remind me of hill repeats. They were really tough, Nora."

"Go on."

"So I started to think about my conversations with Whitmarsh and Kennedy and Zeke. And I started to worry. But they took my mind off the cement."

"What did you decide?"

"I don't think I really needed to take on Kennedy right off the bat. I could've waited."

"You could have. But it was inevitable from the sound of it. And she comes off like a witch."

"Then I started worrying about Jean Whitmarsh. Was I too hard on her?"

"From what you've told me, I think you were. I think you bullied her. It takes a strong person to stand up to you when you get your game face on. Are you sure she's that strong?"

"Explain, please."

"Idiot. All your life you've been surrounded by strong women. Look at your mother; look at your sisters. If you'd tried to pull your macho male bullshit on them they'd have pounded you."

"Or kicked me in the pills."

"And some of the great influences in your life have been women. What was the name of that nun?"

"Mother Saint Francis. Best teacher I ever had, at any level. And absolutely the best professor."

'So you're used to dealing with strong women, women who had confidence and were a light year away from feeling they were some sort of victims."

"And don't forget yourself, O Sweetest of Chucks."

"I'm being serious here, Henry. Not all women have this kind of make-up, this genuine independence. And the reality is that most men take advantage of that. Gloria Steinem wasn't just some bra-burning crackpot. She spoke a lot of truth. And men don't like to hear it sometimes."

"So was I taking advantage of Dean Jean?"

"You were. You know that you have teaching options. You chose Bowell because it was convenient and you weren't interested at this time in doing research, and you also pressured them into giving you tenure after one year if you've been a good boy. But if they were to fire your butt, you know there's going to be another teaching spot just an hour down Highway 401."

"All right, all right. So now that you're in this incisive and analytical mode, tell me what you think of Zeke."

"Ah, the man of mystery. I don't have a clue. He could be a terrific source for you, a kind of mentor even. Or he could just be another drunk. Now give my pillow back to me and come to bed. I feel like massaging your Goya-like bod."

• • •

Henry damned near killed himself getting the old eavestroughing off. He had brought a thirty-six foot extension ladder with them when they moved their possessions in the two U-Haul trucks. And he needed the entire length to get high enough to get sufficient leverage to pry off the rotten mess. But sharp pieces of metal stuck out everywhere and by the time the entire 140 feet were finally on the ground he had blood oozing from a half-dozen sites.

Annie stared at him wide-eyed. "Daddy, you're bleeding. Do you want me to get you a beer?"

Just at that moment Walter drove down the lane. "I was going to leave the cement mixer here until the parging was finished, but I need it at another site. What the hell have you done to your arms?"

"Ah, I usually wind up bleeding somewhere or other, Walter."

"You going to try to put the new pieces up yourself?"

"That was the original plan, but I'm starting to have a few doubts."

"Good. Because I can help you with that."

"Let me just get some paper towelling for these cuts and I'll be right with you."

Henry returned with some damp towels, a few bandaids and two beers. The two men sat on the end of the Ford's tailgate and swung their legs, taking leisurely swigs from the bottles.

"I don't want to step over the line here, Henry," said Walter, "but I do have a few years on you and I've been doing this kind of work for as long as you've been alive. First off, though, I know that you're one hell of a worker. You're really tough in your mind as well as the other kind of toughness. That job you did with the cistern was about as mean as it gets. However, I guess carrying squares of shingles up to the roof of a three-story building is right up there as well. And you did a hell of a good job. But don't think that you have to do everything. This friggin' eavestrough is an example. There are guys who can do the job perfectly in one day. It'd take you a week or so and you still wouldn't have the slope right so that the water would run where it was supposed to.

"Puts me in mind of when I tried to make my own wine a few years ago. It never did get any better than weasel piss, and I finally realized that there were people out there who made wine for a living, made it very well, and were prepared to sell it to me at a reasonable price. I got the hell out of the wine-making business right promptly. Put my time to better use."

"Can you recommend someone?"

"Not really. Just look in the yellow pages. They're all pro's. You're going to have your hands more than full with carving up all these logs and then splitting and storing it all. And have you thought yet about the inside of the house? I'll wager there isn't a scrap of insulation in the entire building, knowing that cheap old bastard Elmer Knobber as I do. I'm guessing, of course, but I'll wager that you'll have to gradually gut every single room, put in insulation and vapour barrier, and then hang drywall. You and Nora really took on a job when you bought this place."

The two took a long and reflective pull on their beers. "Yet I'll tell you this, Henry; it was absolutely the right decision. This place will be a gem when you're done. But let me say again: Don't hesitate to get help from people who know what they're doing. Like plumbing and electrical."

"I know what you're going to say next, Walter. 'I can help you with that.'"

Walter laughed. "Yup, I guess I can. My cousin, Gerald, is a damn good electrician and won't screw you in the cost. And there's an Englishman, lives north of here, does plumbing and does it all out of his truck. I use him myself if it's a tricky job."

"Don't tell me. You'll have him call me."

Walter laughed again. "I've babbled on too much. But I do hate to see something that could be beautiful fall into ruin. Look at that old barn behind us. It'd be two or three years older than the house. The barn always got built first. I've been inside that barn. The bearing beams in there are huge, some of them twenty inches square and forty feet long, and the adze marks are still in them running down the sides and - - -."

Walter was interrupted by a car approaching them down the driveway. "Who's this then?"

"Oh, shit. I was hoping he wouldn't be back. He's the inspector from the Department of Health."

"I noticed your new tile bed. Who did it?"

"Percy Baxter."

"Then it was done to code; done right. Did you have a permit?"

"Nope."

"Oh, dear. These boys tend to get right cranky about that sort of thing."

Henry got down from the tailgate and approached the inspector who was now out of his car. "Good afternoon."

His greeting went ignored. "Have you made arrangements to have this dug up and the required topsoil brought in?"

"I have not. The whole idea is illogical. The system has been repaired and is in perfect condition. I see no need to do any further alterations. And I won't be doing any."

"Then I'll institute formal legal proceedings to force you to comply. As I told you before, we can make you do whatever we want you to do."

"I guess you'll do what you have to do," Henry said. Nora approached her husband and placed her hand on his back.

The inspector's tires spat out gravel as he reversed back down the lane.

"I'll just hook my cement mixer on to my truck and leave you folks alone now. You've got enough to worry about without me here. But I'll be back in two days to put the first parge coat on, and then a coat each of the next two days. So tell those seamless eavestroughers they've got to be here in five days or you'll get somebody else."

Walter paused before he left and leaned out of the window of the cab. "What the hell are you going to do about that asshole?"

"Walter, I had a beer today with a very wise man who counselled me to not hesitate to seek help from a pro when I was out of my depth. I do believe I'll do just that."

Walter smiled, nodded at Nora, said, "Good luck," and pulled down the lane.

Nora turned to Henry, smiling, "Don't call Seamus at work. He may just have a couple of items on his plate of greater significance than our septic system. Call him at home tonight."

Henry and Seamus had been friends for almost thirty years. And their exploits were legendary, at least in their own minds. Their high school education at a private Catholic boys' school run by the Christian Brothers had not resulted in a noticeable increase in knowledge or maturity. Henry had graduated believing that an engineer drove a train. Seamus allowed that the brothers were neither Christian nor brotherly. They both arrived at university with no identifiable idea of why they were there. They sought out what they had been told were the easiest gut courses to be found, signed up for them, and then promptly sought out the locations of the nearest billiard parlor and tavern. They were underage, of course. In fact they were over a year younger than the incoming freshman cohort's average age. But in rapid order they found phony identification that showed them to be twenty-one years of age and possessed, therefore, of the right to get stinko whenever the mood struck. It struck often.

Realizing that the first year was going to end calamitously, they sought to find a summer job that would provide a substantial distance between them and their parents when the results came out in June. Ironically, a family connection allowed them to be hired on with the surface crew at a uranium mine on the north shore of Lake Athabasca, safely secure some 2,000 miles from righteous parental wrath. Here they worked hard and well at the tasks assigned, but at night raised hell, persecuting other student workers and occasionally persons better left unannoyed. They pulled in their horns after a meeting with the Mountie in charge of security. He had called them into his office, invited them to take a chair, poured coffee for all three, then said, "If you two little pricks ever touch my jeep again I'll hoof your asses up between your shoulder blades. What do you take in your coffee?"

Repeating first year resulted in a modest improvement in their scholarship. They went to some classes, read a few books, and were content with the mediocre grades they were receiving. They still set records for immaturity. In the fall they went to see Seamus's brother at the University of Western Ontario and proceeded to promptly get themselves arrested by attempting to carry a case of beer into an afternoon tea dance. Unfortunately they carried it between two ranks of city police who, not seeing the humour of the situation, commandeered the beer and escorted Henry and Seamus to the city limits with orders never to return.

Slowly, however, they began to grow up. After second year Seamus took himself off to law school and flourished. Henry began to see merit in the literature he was reading, and then fell in love with it. Their paths followed different directions, but they succeeded wonderfully. They also remained close chums.

"Henry!" shouted Seamus that night. "How's the farmer doing down there in God's country? How's Nora? Tell her I yearn for her."

"We're all well and you keep your disgusting hands off my bride."

"What's happening, old buddy? You usually have a reason to call."

Henry recounted the saga of the septic tank and weeping bed.

"So you're literally and figuratively in shit," said Seamus.

"I am. Can you do anything to get this dick-head off my case?"

"Henry, you haven't provided me with an iron-clad argument for the defence. You're dead meat."

"C'mon, Seamus. Something?"

"I'll try to scare them a bit for you, Henry. But you'll have to come up with something. So I'll send them a letter, and you've got to find a solution. However I really get steamed with that line, 'We can make you do anything we want.' Now tell me how the new college is going."

Henry entertained Seamus with tales of academe and added a few embellishments of a salacious nature until Nora let a bellow out and told him to cease being such a male chauvinistic oinker.

"So," said Seamus, "you've got a dean with a ramrod up her bum, a screaming leftie who hates your manly self, and an Old Testament prophet who sees you streaming clouds of glory."

"That's Wordsworth not the Bible. But, yeah, they're the ones I've met so far."

"If I may, a word of caution, old pal. Be careful of the beautiful screamer. We're starting to see more and more complaints filed with these so-called Human Rights Tribunals. And it's getting scary. Some moron can hear what he perceives to be an insult, lay a charge, and he's off scot-free as far as any costs are concerned. The prosecution, for what the moron says was a hate crime, is supplied by the Tribunal. But the defendant is on the hook for 100% of his defence costs. It's disgusting, but it's going on across the country. And it's not so different from that prick who tried to scare you about your septic tank. So watch that damned mouth of yours."

A week later, Henry received a phone call from a Dr. Charles Baker who identified himself as the Associate Director of the local Department of Health. He had received a letter from Mr. Seamus MacPherson who had requested that all action concerning the septic system in question be put in abeyance until he had completed a most complex murder trial just now getting underway. "We'll certainly accede to his wishes, Mr. Miller."

Lying bastard hasn't done a murder in six years, thought Henry. "I see," he said aloud, "that is certainly good news."

"And I wanted to assure you, sir, that any impression you may have had that you were being persecuted was not based on policy from this office."

"You know, Nora," said Henry after he'd hung up, "That's the first time any one of them has called me by name. And this guy actually called me 'Sir'."

"Well, 'Sir', to celebrate the return of civility, and to also celebrate the end of six days of sponge baths, why don't we test the new water system in our shower? That is if you can get your mind off all this new-found respect."

V

Henry had to go into Bowell College to arrange for the campus book store to stock sufficient copies of the Shakespeare anthology he was going to use that autumn. His students would require only the one text and its cost was modest, under fourteen dollars. "That's less than two pints of Guinness," he thought. Nora had given him some stern marching orders. He was to clean up the mess that she maintained he had created with Dean Whitmarsh. When he protested that, really, he had done nothing wrong, she assured him that that mattered not one iota. That he was to fix it anyway. She herself was taking the girls off to the local library where a children's summer program had been instituted.

Once again, he relished the pastoral drive into the college. The rural quality of the trip, however, in the newly purchased truck was not enhanced by the unceasing bouncing of a vehicle sadly in need of shock absorbers. As he pulled the Ford into the faculty parking lot, he was still fumbling in his mind for an approach that would mollify Dean Jean. Should he rely on his Oscar Wildean wit to restore some sense of bonhomie? Should he just pretend that nothing was amiss? Perhaps a straightforward manly apology? He decided that the manly approach had triggered this situation and might best be reserved for another occasion. He still had not decided as the secretary told him to go ahead and rap on the dean's office door.

Once again, the door opened promptly and the wide smile, the flashing teeth and the cold eyes of the dean appeared. The teeth and smile disappeared instantly. The eyes remained unchanged. "Oh, Dr. Miller," she said in flat voice. An awkward pause ensued, then she added, "Come in."

Henry sat in the same chair that ensured he had to squint to see Jean's face. "I had to come in to see about ordering the anthology. So I thought I'd pop by."

"The anthology. So you're going ahead with your proposed course work?"

"I am. But I also wanted to see you. I feel uncomfortable about how our last meeting concluded."

"Do you indeed. I think you made your position quite clear, Doctor. You suggested you won't be here long and that our methods don't quite measure up to your standards."

"Dean, that is exactly the impression I don't want you to have. I feel a commitment to being a part of Bowell College. But I also feel a commitment to students being exposed to the best that our culture has given us. And I'm afraid I agree with the stodgy old view that there is a canon of recognized great works that we should be presenting to these young people."

"Do you indeed. How quaint. I, on the other hand, Dr. Miller, am afraid that we see our program as rather more modern and more progressive than this stodginess that you seem to admire so."

"Well, so be it, Dean. I hope we can disagree in a spirit of academic respect and remain open to dissenting views." As there was no response to this, Henry went on, "Look, Dean, it's almost noon. Could I invite you to lunch at the bistro in town? A bite to eat out on the terrace overlooking the lake, a glass of saucy white to wash it down? What do you say?"

"I'm afraid, Dr. Miller, that I have a great deal of work that requires my immediate attention. Another time, perhaps." Her eyes were flat.

"Then I'll bid you good day and see myself out."

Once outside, Henry wondered what terrific stratagem Nora could suggest next. His eye happened to fall on the Management Studies building and he decided to see if maybe Zeke would deign to have a sandwich and a pint with him.

"Henry, dear boy! I was sitting here wondering what the hell I was going to do to fill the empty afternoon hours, and here you are in your accustomed role of regenerator of hopes and restorer of dreams Where shall we feast? What elixirs shall we quaff? You look subdued, my dear boy. Have you been crushed by the malignant spirits of those viragoes who worship in the cathedral of 'What's Fashionable Now'?"

A server seated them at a table under a huge umbrella that provided a shield from the scorching sun, but faced directly towards the huge lake. A breeze wafted over them bringing only the sound of waves and gulls. The bistro's patio was located at the back of the restaurant so that even the sound of light traffic was gone.

"Ah, Olive, my favourite waitress. You never forget my preference for this most royal of tables."

She laughed. "What can I get you today, Professor Silverstein?"

"Nectar, my sweet Olive. But first, may I present my young colleague and new friend, Professor Miller."

"Olive, I'm quite happy being called Henry and you'd better get the Professor something to drink before he becomes desiccated."

"Sweet Olive, as Henry and I strolled here from our campus, I find the exercise has rendered me peckish. Are you serving your splendid Hunter's Pie today?"

"We are, Prof, and with it?"

"Guinness, of course."

Henry ordered a toasted BLT and a Sleeman's lager, and as they began to eat Zeke asked Henry for details about the farmhouse, the "dream that became a reality" as he recalled Henry describing it.

It took two Sleemans for Henry to work through all the details, from the swim in the sewage to the cowed tone of the call from the Department of Health. And during this Zeke spoke not a word. After the tale was finished they shared a comfortable silence, watching a half-dozen sparrows busying themselves with the work of cleaning up the floor of wayward crumbs.

Finally, Zeke turned to Henry. "I am curious, Henry. What do these limestone foundation walls of your house rest upon?"

"Bedrock."

"'He is like a man who, in building his house, dug deep and laid the foundations on rock.'"

"That doesn't sound like it's from the Book of Ezekiel."

"Luke, Chapter 6, verse 48."

"You can quote from both ends of the Bible."

"I call myself a progressive Jew. And I like to be informed about where you goys are coming from. Tell me Henry, you are married?"

"I sure am. As Zorba the Greek said, 'Wife, children, house, the full catastrophe.'"

Zeke called Olive to the table and they ordered two coffees. "And, Olive, do bring me a thimbleful of the Irish Tears you thoughtfully keep on hand for emergencies."

Again they sat quietly, neither one in any hurry to break the silence. The coffees arrived, they stirred in sugar and cream, Zeke took an appreciative sip of his Irish whiskey, and then as his eyes focused far out over the lake he said, "I would give my all to share in such a catastrophe."

"You said your wife died a few years ago?"

"Leah. Yes, it was four years last month."

"Can you tell me about her?"

Zeke stirred his coffee idly, then took a sip. "She would not have fit into the culture in your new place of employment. She liked men, saw their faults, forgave them, yet was acutely aware of her own shortcomings. She saw and understood the human condition. She was well-versed in current works by women writers, but preferred the classics and those works that are bound to become classics."

Zeke paused to watch a pair of squabbling sparrows, then started to chuckle. "She, too, was an author, but not one destined to be read by scholars in distant times. She did have a readership, though, and many of those readers evidently were women."

"Go on. What sort of writing did she do?"

"Novels. A series actually, featuring a gorgeous woman who had served with the Canadian Armed Forces in Afghanistan, a Captain in rank. When she returned to civilian life, this woman found that she'd seen too much, experienced too much, over there, and could not fit in to civilian life. So she travelled around Canada and adventure found her. And there were always bad guys. And she always wound up by killing them. Of course, they deserved what they got. Anyway a surprising number of female fans spread the word, sales of the books zoomed, and Leah made quite a bit of money. Unusual in Canada for a writer."

"And you didn't have kids?"

Zeke took a sip of the Writer's Tears, gazed out at the water, and held up a finger in a silent request to Henry for silence. Henry took note of the moistness in the older man's eyes and wordlessly signalled to Olive for a coffee refill. He busied himself with sugar and cream, sipped, and waited.

At last Zeke said, "Yes. We did have children. Two of them were lost through miscarriage, both times late in Leah's pregnancies. And when a child was born, a little girl, she was frail and she died within hours. We stopped trying. There had been too much pain." He sighed and turned to Henry with a smile. "But do tell me about your family."

Henry went on at length, rhapsodizing about the wonders of Nora, her brains, her sense of humour, her good looks, her ability to keep him in line when he needed to be checked, and her skills as a mother.

"And your children?"

"Two girls. Annie is the older. She's six."

"And the younger?"

"Rachel. She's four."

He went no further. Zeke had turned to him, his eyes widened, a look almost of shock on his face. "In Genesis, Rachel was the younger sister of Leah."

"Are you alright, Zeke?"

"I'm just taken aback. Forgive me Henry."

"Zeke, would you like to meet them?"

Zeke merely nodded.

"Olive, do you have a phone I could use? Mine's back in my office."

"End of the bar. Hit nine to get an outside line."

Henry dialed home and while it rang he looked back at Zeke on the patio and saw him take out his handkerchief and dab at his eyes. Nora answered.

"Hello, Sweet Chuck. I'm bringing someone home for dinner. Is that okay with you? And do you want me to pick something up at the store?"

"Naw, that's not necessary, L'il Abner, I'll just make a pass through the barnyard and wring a chicken's neck." She heard Henry laugh, then she asked, "Who are you bringing?"

"Zeke Silverstein. And he doesn't have a car so I guess we'll be putting him up overnight."

"Great. A real flesh and blood prophet in our guest room. Sounds cool."

The two men separated outside the restaurant after Zeke had arranged to have Henry pick him up in an hour at his home, which was not much more than a stone's throw from the campus. "And Zeke, don't forget to pack a toothbrush and pyjamas. I don't want to see a naked Jewish patriarch prowling about my hall in the middle of the night."

VI

Zeke asked Henry to pull in at a local greengrocer's. When he emerged, he was carrying a large paper package of flowers and two small boxes. "And now we're off," said Zeke as he scrambled up and into the worn seat of the Ford.

The girls were waiting on the side porch as the truck turned into the driveway. Henry grabbed Zeke's overnight bag and Zeke, arms filled with his purchases, approached the two children. They were dressed in denim overalls, tee-shirts and running shoes. And they stared bug-eyed as this tall, thin and old, man came up to them. "Let me guess your names," he said. "Let's see. You are Jeremy and you are Michael."

The girls giggled and Rachel squealed, "Those aren't our names!"

"Well, don't tell me; let me think about it and I'm sure I'll get them in a little while. In the meantime, I brought a small gift for each of you." He handed each girl a box and they raced inside to show their mother.

"So this is the spread," said Henry. "That barn back there isn't ours, but we have these four acres," and he waved his hand to show the extent of their land.

"Henry, this house is wonderful. It really is. It is imposing, it looks very solid and even as it stands, it is quite beautiful. You mentioned that a lot of work remains to be done. What do you have in mind?"

"New roof, new shutters, new front porch, replace that old summer kitchen that you see hooked on to the back of the house."

"Good heavens that's a lot! And inside?"

"Come on in and meet Nora and I'll give you a tour."

Inside, Zeke presented Nora with the bouquet of flowers. After she had thanked him, she asked, "Can the girls open theirs now?" The small corsages that were inside the boxes turned the girls speechless. Nora pinned them on a strap of their overalls and their eyes never left the tiny roses.

"You might take a lesson here, Miller. You know, as in how to act like a gentleman with ladies." She turned back to Zeke, "I hope that you don't mind, but we'll be eating a bit early because the girls go to bed shortly after seven o'clock. So grab a beer, Captain Debonair here can give you the royal tour, and then we'll be all set for dinner."

Once the plates had been served, Zeke looked intensely at the girls and then said, "I believe that I have solved the mystery of your names. You are Annie, and I suspect that your name is - - -." He paused, gazed at the ceiling for a few seconds, and then, "Rachel."

"How did you know?"

"Oh, I have special powers."

"What's your name?" asked Rachel.

"Ezekiel."

"That's a strange name," said Annie. "How did you get it?"

"My mother and father gave it to me a very long time ago."

"Annie, Ezekiel was a prophet in the Bible," Nora explained.

"Do you know what a prophet is, Annie?" asked Zeke.

"Like Merlin in *King Arthur*," she answered.

Zeke looked at the child for a long moment, then smiled, nodded his head and said, "Very like; very like."

With the kids safely tucked into bed, they returned to the dining room table to have coffee. "I don't have any Writer's Tears, Zeke, but I do have some cheap scotch."

"You know, I haven't been out socially in several years. You can have no idea how pleasant this is for me and how much I appreciate it."

Nora spoke. "I don't understand. Do you not see even your colleagues?"

"I'm rather afraid that it is a case of their not seeing me. You see, as I mentioned to Henry when first we met, my views are not congruent with the accepted manner of thinking about things at Bowell. To be specific, I have spoken out about the right of Israel to exist, in peace, with a peaceful Palestinian neighbour. To speak such words is not the done thing on our campus. And my views as to what constitutes the study of history are seen as reactionary and misguided."

"So you're shunned?"

"I suppose I am. And you will understand how grateful I am to the string of coincidences that resulted in my sitting at this table with two such gracious people. Except that I don't believe in coincidences."

"Why not?" asked Nora.

"Carl Jung suggested that they do not exist. The older I get, the more I find that I agree with him about so many things."

"Like what?"

"Well, for example, he posited that at different stages in our lives we pattern ourselves on a mythic model and that these change as we age and our circumstances, and bodies and minds, too, also change."

"Let me freshen your glass, Zeke," said Henry. Then, "So what myth do you currently see yourself in? You're older, you're a widower, and you're being shunned. Is there a mythical figure that you fit into?"

"Yes. The Wandering Jew."

"Oh, Zeke that's awful," said Nora.

"Don't despair for me as yet. I mentioned coincidence, in which I do not believe. I was brought to this house to be taught, and I was taught by a child."

They stared at him questioningly.

"Annie. She paired me with Merlin. And like me, Merlin was old, alone, (save for Arthur), and under suspicion. I'd never seen the resemblance before, and it certainly makes me think."

"Zeke," said Nora, "you mentioned the coincidences, which of course don't exist – except that I suspect they do – that brought you here. What are they?"

"Seeing the disconsolate and shell-shocked Henry standing outside the Arts building was the first."

"With the sun radiating around him?" laughed Nora.

"Just so, Nora, just so. Because, and I'll tell you two this, I was about to go to my office and type out my letter of resignation. A second was this entire house business you're now immersed in. The process that you are undertaking here is precisely what needs to be done at that 'whited sepulchre' of a college. And for me the clincher was your daughter's name, Rachel. My wife was not named after Jacob's first wife. No, her parents named her after Shylock's dead wife in *The Merchant of Venice*. But when Henry mentioned the name of my beloved Leah's biblical sister, Rachel, I knew that he was special."

Outside far down on the farm, the coyotes began to wail. They took their coffees outside to the west porch and watched as the sun was slowly consumed by the horizon. The coyotes had made a kill and were now squabbling over portions. It was the warm and welcoming time of evening when the swallows from Elmer Knobber's barn were in an ecstasy of aerial dynamics, their sharp calls competing with the sound of their wings as they wheeled and banked and gloried in their freedom. As the dusk progressed the birds were joined by hundreds of mosquito-hunting bats whose inner radar allowed them to compete, almost, with the barn swallows in flying skill.

"Another scotch, Zeke?"

"Thank you, no. This is perfect and I don't care to have another thing."

Nora asked, "What are these reactionary views that you hold about history that are in such conflict with the orthodoxy at Bowell?"

"Well, things like the dates of events. And wars. It's not seen as sufficiently progressive to examine wars and their origins and effects and so on. But I'll say no more. You'll meet my colleagues in the history department at the annual pre-orientation barbeque. You can chat with them and form your own opinions. You may even agree with them and disagree with me. But isn't that what is supposed to go on at a university? Debate? The clash of competing ideas, civilly presented and heard with open minds? I may even attend the affair this year, that is, if you two are planning to be there."

"Oh, Henry has already informed me that I'm to be radiant for the do. That is, as radiant as a mere woman can be without the sun's rays streaming from around her."

The two men laughed and Zeke said, "From what I've heard you'll enjoy it. And now, as I am an old man and need my sleep, I'll bid you two a fond good evening, and ascend to sleep the rest of the just." He gave Nora a kiss on the cheek, shook Henry's hand and went back inside.

They could hear him climbing the stairs, running water in the bathroom, and gently closing his bedroom's door.

"What do you think, Nora?"

"I like him. I like him very much, in fact. I think he is a very sad man, and a lonely one, but not one with a drinking problem. He really had bugger all tonight. That Jungian stuff fascinates me, though. He really jumped on the Merlin myth. Remember, he said Merlin was alone except for Arthur. Does that mean you'll be patterning yourself as a King Arthur?"

"Naw. Remember that when Merlin was teaching the young Prince Arthur, the kid was known as 'The Wart'. Maybe that's my role."

"Let's watch the moon clear Elmer's barn and then go to bed, too. I'm tired."

• • •

The following weeks were busy ones. Wood for the coming winter was ordered, delivered and stored in the old stable that formed one end of the summer kitchen structure. Henry finished chainsawing the eight bush cords into firewood lengths and was now splitting these into pieces that would fit into the old Findlay Oval cookstove in the kitchen and the smaller but more efficient Vermont Castings stove that heated from its place in the family room. It was hard labour, and as with all such tasks it required a specific set of skills. Henry learned how to read the grain of a round as it stood upright on the chopping block. He learned where the maul's blade had to land so that the piece would split into manageable sizes. He learned that oak split cleanly and evenly with a blow to the middle of the block, but that elm could not be dealt with in this fashion. It had to be split by following a circular path around the perimeter of the block. Maple often had the origin of a branch buried deep in the block and this could foil the harshest of maul strokes. The knot had to be isolated.

Nora had taken on the task of stripping the wood that framed the interior of the house's many windows. To her dismay, she discovered that a house that was 150 years of age had accumulated an impressive number of coats of paint, varnish and some substances that did not lend themselves to easy identification. But she persevered and finally, having completed the exposure of the wood around the first window, was delighted to discover pure walnut trim. The work, like Henry's, was hard and especially tedious. She wore out scores of rubber work gloves, every piece of scrap fabric in the house, a dozen paint brushes, and gallons of wood stripping liquid. By the end of three weeks she had exposed the beauty of only six windows. Ten remained buried behind their shield of accreted paints and oils.

One night at dinner, Nora said to Henry, "We're in danger of becoming house-aholics. We need a break, and for sure, Annie and Rachel could do with some fun time with their parents."

Annie said, "Can you take us swimming?"

Her parents laughed. "We had better do something before they figure they're orphans," said Henry. "Do we still have that little hibachi we had from when we were first married? Let's go swimming tomorrow. We'll take the hibachi and we'll have a barbeque beside the lake. Would you like that Annie? Rachel?"

"Speaking of," said Nora, "when is that Bowell barbeque? Good Lord, it's this Friday. I'd almost forgotten."

VII

Henry and Nora drove cross-country, following a map sent to them by George Harper, their host for the evening. As they entered the grounds, Nora sucked in her breath. The view was magnificent. A tall cedar hedge provided privacy from traffic on the road, and as the drive approached the house it passed beds of perennial shrubs on either side. The lawns were extensive and interrupted occasionally by mature maples and oaks. The house itself was two storeys and built entirely of limestone. Six windows, equally spaced were divided in the centre of the building by a huge wooden door with brightly polished brass fixtures. Three dormers jutted from the roof.

A man wearing a patch over his right eye, waved them to a parking space and came over to open Nora's door. "Welcome, welcome," he said, holding out his left hand. "You must be the Millers and you don't want to shake my right hand. I still have difficulty gauging the force I'm exerting. I'm George Harper." His right arm moved with a noticeable stiffness and ended in an artificial hand. "Let me give you a tour before the crowd shows up. I've arranged for a couple of buses to chauffeur most of the hordes and they'll be here presently."

George led them to another manicured lawn behind the house where an entire pig was slowly rotating over a white-hot bed of coals. This roasting had begun before dawn that morning, and was being attended by a man who, they were told, taught in George's department.

"And what department would that be?" enquired Nora.

"I'm the Dean of Engineering," he said. "Now let me show you my darling, my draft beer set-up." A tub, from what had once been an old-fashioned washing machine, held a keg of beer which was surrounded by crushed ice. An extension cord ran from this to an electrical plug on the wall of the house and the old machine emitted a low whirring. George drew a pair of mugs of icy draft for them, and continued.

"I got the Regents smashed one night and almost had them agreeing to let me use the spit and the keg cooler as the basis for an Engineering 101 course. Why not? They combine electricity, refrigeration, machine tooling, and hydraulics. See that round unit where the long spit is anchored? That's the screw from an old locomotive and that screw turned coal into the fire to generate steam. Almost had those Regents, I did." His laughter at the memory was interrupted as the first bus pulled in the driveway. "Listen, I want to talk to you two later, so don't disappear on me." And he made his way to his newly arrived guests.

"Well, I'm off to work the crowd, Lover Boy. Try not to hamper my style." Henry laughed to himself as he watched Nora sail into the midst of the strangers, her hand outstretched. The second bus pulled in and he saw Jean Whitmarsh, Cynthia Kennedy and Zeke among thirty or so others climb down from the vehicle.

"Ah, dear boy, so glad to see you," Zeke said smiling.

"Why the buses, Zeke?"

"Human nature, Henry. Those who profess at tertiary levels of education, such as ours, tend to take full advantage of free spirits when readily available. And George Harper always has lots of free spirits. So, as the evening proceeds – and it was George himself who told me this, as I have not attended in several years – things can get quite lively."

"Zeke, let me get you a draft. Mine seems to have evaporated."

"I'll sample George's rather acceptable wine bar if you don't mind. I see that Nora has zeroed in on Ms. Kennedy."

Nora had indeed done so by looking for the most beautiful woman in the throng. She approached Cynthia and said, "Hi, I'm Nora."

Cynthia looked her up and down, spied the wedding ring on Nora's left hand, and asked, "Is your wife here?"

"No, I'm afraid that I'm just a prosaic old straight. But my husband is here if you'd like to meet him."

"Where?"

Nora pointed to where Zeke and George were talking to a woman.

"That prick!" said Cynthia.

"Oh, you've already met him, have you?" Nora smiled. "It certainly is true."

"What? You agree your husband is a prick?"

"Not at all, certainly. I thought you were commenting on his wonderful endowment." Nora watched Cynthia turn abruptly away and smiled to herself. She saw her husband pull a third draft for himself and thought, "I'd better cut myself off, because he sure won't be driving home."

Zeke and Henry filled their plates with succulent roast pork, potato salad and an ear of corn, filled a glass with a splendid burgundy, found seats at a picnic table and proceeded to tuck into the grub. They were joined by the woman whom Nora had seen them chatting with. Her name was Megan Fiorini.

"Do you prefer Megan or Meg?" asked Henry.

"I'm fine with either," she replied around a mouthful of food.

"What's your connection with this outfit?"

"I was George's first hire. He arrived three years ago and I've been here for two. I'm in charge of the Materials Engineering program."

"Isn't it a bit unorthodox to have a woman boss for an Engineering section?"

Zeke smiled at Henry's question and said, "If I may, let me explain. George is ex-military, my boy. He finds and attempts to procure the best people available, and gender, age, religion or any other irrelevant factor be damned. Megan, here, was the CEO of a small but thriving manufacturing company and George harassed her until she finally agreed to join the college."

"I just couldn't resist being in an environment that was 95% male. The freshmen and faculty are not calculated to drive me mad with desire, but those senior Engineering students! Oh, my!"

Henry's eyes widened and he took a long slurp of wine.

Megan laughed. "Don't worry, darling. I look but never touch. That's against the code."

"Any trouble with your students because you're a woman?"

"Never. I know my stuff, I'm smarter than most of them and I make them laugh on occasion. That's really what most students respect."

"Zeke, you mentioned that George was in the military. What's that about?"

"It's a fascinating story, dear boy. Let me recharge our goblets and I'll fill you in." Their glasses refilled, he began. "George was a career officer in the Canadian Armed Forces, Royal Military College in Kingston, all the hoops and courses and postings that follow, and he did surpassingly well. He was also, finally, in combat. In Iraq. Very few of our countrymen are aware of this, and certainly most of the people you see here gobbling up the free munchies and booze would have a seizure were they to know, but a select group of our warriors fought with our American brothers-in-arms in that venture. He also did two tours of duty in Afghanistan. In fact at one point, he was seconded briefly to Joint Task Force Two. That's our Special Forces Unit," he added looking at Megan. "Quite secret."

"Was that when he was wounded?" she asked.

"No, it was after that. He was a lieutenant-colonel, but he evidently led from the front, as they say. That's one of the reasons that his troops loved him. And one day his vehicle ran over an IED. His driver and gunner were killed and he was badly hurt, but survived."

"Were you aware of this, Megan?" asked Henry.

She shook her head and Zeke went on, "How he came to be here at Bowell is another tale, but one that you should ask him yourself."

A roar of laughter erupted from near the barbeque spit and they looked to see their host regaling a delighted audience. They also saw Cynthia Kennedy approaching their table.

"Ezekiel, I'm surprised to seeing you partaking of forbidden flesh."

"My dear," he responded, "I am satisfied that the creature slowly turning on that spit is, happily, a veal calf. Leviticus would approve of my consuming it."

"Well I think that it's disgusting for anyone with half a brain to be filling himself with meat. I should think that at an institution of higher learning, such as ours, that it would be intellectually repugnant to not embrace vegetarianism."

"Dr. Kennedy," said Megan, "I'm very happy to be embracing this splendid slice of beast, whatever it is. So you can challenge me intellectually, if you wish. But be warned, it would be like your challenging D'Artagnan, and you're armed with a pickle."

Cynthia Kennedy's eyes blazed with anger, and once again she turned on her heel and stormed away.

"That lady," observed Zeke, "will not be happy until all the earth follows precisely in her footsteps."

"If we did, we'd sure be the final generation, wouldn't we?" laughed Megan.

"There's my dean," said Henry, "I'd better go and make nice."

The sound level had risen considerably since the Bowell College faculty had discovered the wine, beer and food, and more importantly, remembered that it was free. The beautifully coiffed grounds were covered by knots of animatedly chatting academics, and each of the seven long picnic tables was filled with happily munching merrymakers. Henry slipped between several groups of people he did not know, saw Nora in discussion with a woman he did not recognize, and finally approached Dean Whitmarsh.

"Good evening, Dean, I'm glad to see you."

"Oh, Dr. Miller." The teeth flashed; the eyes did not. "This is my husband, Leonard Twilley." The two men shook hands. "Is your wife here?"

Henry pointed to Nora and the unknown woman. "Perhaps I'll go and introduce myself," she said and was gone.

"I'm afraid your wife is still a little miffed at me from our last couple of meetings."

"And rightly so, from what she's told me," sniffed Leonard Twilley.

"Think you so. Well let's just leave it. Do you teach as well?"

"I'm in the history department."

"Excellent. What courses do you teach? What's your specialty?"

"American history. I try to reveal to my students the inestimable damage that's been done to the world by the Yankee juggernaut."

"Do you also reveal to them the many benefits the Americans have contributed to the world?"

"That would be the shortest lecture that I've ever delivered."

Henry looked at Leonard thoughtfully and decided to take a different tack. "Tell me, how do you find the students at the College? Have they been adequately prepared? Are they competent academically?"

"Oh absolutely not. It's as if they received no meaningful instruction before they come to us. They can't write well. They make egregious grammar mistakes. I'm not sure they can even read to a minimal level of sophistication."

"Interesting. What do you have them reading in your course?"

"*A People's History of the United States* by Howard Zinn."

"I've read it. Don't you think he does a lot of cherry-picking to support his rather extreme socialist views?"

"I really don't think that socialism can ever be described as extreme. And as for what you term cherry-picking, the facts are the facts."

"Rarely, I've found, is that so," said Henry. "Using that criterion, I can build a conclusive case that Abraham Lincoln was a homosexual. He did, after all, sleep in the same bed with other men. That's a fact. Of course, it's also a fact that those sleeping arrangements were standard in those days simply because there weren't a hell of a lot of beds available. And Zinn was most honest when he admitted that he was not a historian, but a polemicist who wanted to present what he saw as history from an exclusively Marxist point of view."

"Do you have difficulty with that?"

"Given that Marxism has failed as a system of fruitful governance wherever it has been attempted, I do indeed have a lot of difficulty with that."

Leonard stared at Henry and his mouth twitched as if to speak, but no words came out. Finally, he said, "If you'll excuse me, I think I'll get another glass of wine."

"Go for it, Leonard. It's free after all."

Henry watched him go and his gaze fell on a scene near the still glowing coals. A red-headed woman was in what appeared to be heated debate with the man he had earlier seen tending the spit. It appeared that the free booze had not succeeded in spreading amiability to all the guests as these two seemed to be closer to blows than to hugs. His thoughts were interrupted as Nora tugged gently on his arm and said, "My chivalrous prince, may I introduce one of your colleagues from the English-teaching fraternity, Linda O'Connor."

Henry had to look down to meet Linda's radiant smile. She stood barely five feet in height, had eyes that were as warm as her smile, and sported a bob of light brown hair.

"Henry, I'm so glad to meet you. Your fame, as they say, has preceded you, and I for one am delighted that you're here."

"Not a universally held view, I'm afraid, Linda."

"Oh dear, no. Horror and trepidation are scurrying about our sacred halls. A reactionary, a barbarian reactionary, is about to violate our most precious dogmas. The Hun is going to teach Shakespeare. We must prepare our defences."

"I can assure you, he's a pussy cat, Linda," laughed Nora.

"Well, I want you to know, Henry, that I'm in your corner. But very quietly, I'm embarrassed to say. I've got a houseful of mouths to feed, and frankly, I need this job."

"What do you teach?"

"What I teach is not what I'd like to be teaching. For example, I've got one course called 'Literature in the Vietnam Era'. Dear God, the best it has to offer is *Who's Afraid of Virginia Wolff*? And the best that can be said for that crap is that it resulted in an entertaining movie which showed in public what Richard Burton and Elizabeth Taylor were actually doing in private. And the pressure is on from the dean to push an anti-American, anti-imperialistic slant while I'm doing it."

"Ah," said Nora, "the creeping stench of neo-, semi-, para-, crypto-imperialism."

"That's just about it," chuckled Linda.

"I was asking the dean's husband a minute ago about the academic quality of the kids here at Bowell."

"And you heard a whole bunch of bitching and whining?"

"I sure did."

"Lots of them have problems with effective writing and with the notion of error-free prose. But this is nothing new. I offer an early morning remedial class once a week for anyone who's interested. I get up to thirty kids every time."

"I do believe that what you're doing is called 'teaching'," said Nora.

Their chat was terminated abruptly by a loud scream from the spit area.

"You fucking fascist! How dare you bring your militaristic, murderous propaganda onto our campus." The red-haired woman, whom Henry had noticed earlier, was threatening the guardian of the spit with a long-handled fork on the end of which hung a dripping piece of the pig.

Zeke approached and observed, "And so the Games begin."

The obscenity, delivered at full voice, succeeded in hushing the crowd into a taut silence. Very quickly, however, George Harper appeared on the battlefield and his words could clearly be heard by the attentive onlookers.

"Now, Felicity, you are quite correct in calling him militaristic, but he really is not a murderous chap." He slipped his left arm around the outraged Felicity, and Henry could see that George's grip was such that the enraged woman's feet made only the slightest contact with the ground as she was gently ushered away from the source of friction. "And I am most surprised, Felicity, that a scholar of your erudition would categorize the man as a 'fucking' anything. Surely a less offensive adjective could be employed. May I suggest 'copulative' as a replacement term?" And with that the pair disappeared into the limestone house.

"It's always fun, don't you agree," suggested Linda, "when the members of the peace-at-any-price crowd resort to violence and obscene insults. I believe I'll nominate her for the Presidency of the University Women's Club. Anyhow, I haven't eaten yet, and George's wife, Miriam, always has some terrific vegetarian and tofu goodies available in the kitchen. So I'm off."

"You don't eat meat?" asked an incredulous Henry.

"Nope. Don't proselytize either."

"She's a keeper," said Nora. "But, Zeke, who the hell is that Felicity woman?"

"Henry will get to know her well. She's a prominent member of the English Literature faculty. Felicity Barth-Drill is her full moniker. And she's a card-carrying member of the Peacenik faction. She certainly has her hands full, what with her teaching and an Air Force base situated just ten miles down the road. She is very much involved in protesting Canada's involvement in any activity that might require the firing of a gun. If you can believe it, she has even led protests outside the restraining fence when the bodies of dead Armed Forces men and women are coming back from Afghanistan."

Henry and Nora looked at Zeke.

"But let's do give her credit. Tonight she has brought the first awarding of a laurel crown for outrageous behaviour to the English department. Be proud, Henry."

"Not so fast, Zeke," said Nora. "Look yonder."

Three naked figures emerged from around the far end of the house, galloping and whooping toward the duck pond at the far end of the lawn. It was a full hundred metres away and this gave time for the assembled multitude, who had only just recovered from the Felicity drama, to observe them carefully and make what were in some cases rather unkind comments about body measurements and deviations from classic norms.

"Definitely two men and a woman," observed Henry.

"Indeed," said Zeke. "The Mathematics department has some feisty younger faculty members who do not adhere rigidly to the more elegant protocols of conduct. And there goes Miriam with towels to assist the drying process and perhaps to alleviate the further corruption of our innocent eyes. But, I'm afraid, Henry, that the floral arrangement bestowed on the fair Felicity must endure a brief residency atop her brows. The laurel clearly must be given to these brave young mathematicians."

The frolics continued with no further mayhem. At ten o'clock the big buses were seen pulling into the long driveway and a few took this as a signal to finish their drinks, visit the portable washrooms that had been strategically placed behind a row of miniature fruit trees, and get back onto their ride home.

But a larger contingent seemed resolute in their intention to stay until the last drop of the second keg had been drained. To these George announced that as his final service of the evening he would display a gesture of friendship he'd witnessed in the deepest hills of Afghanistan.

"And I do suggest that those of more tender sensitivities might find their seats in the bus at this time." He waited dramatically for a few timid souls to depart, and then approaching what was left of the pig's carcass he plucked an eyeball from the porcine skull, held it aloft on the long fork, asked if there were any takers, and seeing none, popped it into his mouth, chewed briefly and happily, swallowed and said, "And so I bid you all a fond evening."

He approached Henry and murmured, "Except for you two and Zeke. I'll see you inside."

VIII

When they strolled into the central drawing room of George's house, his wife was addressing the small blaze in the huge fireplace that formed most of the west wall of the room.

"I'm Miriam and we don't really need this fire," she said. "But I agree with my husband that it looks so lovely, and it may get a bit chillier outside."

She waved Nora and Henry to two over-stuffed leather chairs. "Let me give you a tour. The beer is in the fridge in the kitchen and the booze is on that old antique thing in the corner. And you can wander anywhere you like in the building." She laughed. "And that's my tour."

"You're a fine hostess, my love," said George on entering, with Zeke and another man in tow. "Nora, what can I get you?"

"I'm driving, but I'd love a soda and lime, if you have it."

"And Zeke," said George, "I've got your drop of the Writer's Tears here. But Henry, for yourself? Some of the Irish? Or a snifter of some brandy that I'm sure even old Winston Churchill himself would have praised."

Henry glanced at Nora. "Take advantage of the offer, O Sybaritic One," she said. "It's the only one you'll be getting tonight."

The man who had arrived with George and Zeke laughed merrily. He approached Nora and said, "I apologize for the bad manners of our host in not introducing us. I'm Charley Lee."

Nora took his hand and was surprised at the strength of his grip. She looked into his eyes that were such a dark brown as to seem almost black. "Naturally enough," she thought, given that he was clearly of Chinese descent. His entire face was involved in his smile.

"Charley, that one over there hoovering down the 100-year-old cognac is my husband, Henry."

"I've heard of him from Zeke," he said, nodding to Henry. "I'm really pleased to meet you both."

"Miriam, your house is absolutely gorgeous," observed Nora. "How old is it? Was it like this when you bought it? And when did you buy it?"

Miriam chuckled. "So many questions! The original house is 162 years old. And I say 'original' because after we bought it, we had to gut it right down to studs, joists and rafters. It was an incredible mess. We bought it almost twenty-five years ago and had to do most of the work ourselves because we couldn't afford to hire people. You do actually get used to living in plaster dust and seeing every wall the colour of the pink insulation."

"I suspect that you're describing what's in store for Henry and me."

"Well, in so much of life, the process, even though it may be inconvenient and difficult, is a source of pleasure and growing. Oh, dear. That does sound pompous, doesn't it?"

"Pompous, but true, my love," said George. "Things got a bit easier about ten years ago, though. I found myself with a bit of extra cash from serving a year with an American armoured battalion in Iraq. I don't advertise that, however. It does upset our knee-jerk anti-Yank friends so."

"And the grounds?" asked Henry. "They're in superb shape, I noticed."

"Have you noticed the grounds at the College, Henry?"

"Yeah, they're beautiful, too."

"There's a good reason for that. I hire the same three guys to do our landscaping and grass cutting and such. So they'll come here on weekends or after their shift at Bowell is over. They do a great job and I pay them accordingly. It's a win-win. And every summer we have them and their families here for a barbeque and their kids can swim in the duck pond."

"That's really lovely."

"I guess so. But it's also a bit shrewd, because it lets me get to know them better. And I feel that it is an important part of my job as a dean to know the foundation of an institution. I learned that as a very young second-lieutenant. If you don't know the cooks, the truck drivers, the soldiers who run the motor pool, then your troops at the pointed end of the spear are not going to be as well served as they should be, must be.

"The same at Bowell. I make it a point to get there early every day and have coffee with the maintenance staff before their shift begins. They maintain the lecture rooms so we can teach in the damn things. They're essential. If we don't take care of them, then the entire operation is running at a much lower level than it should be."

"A beautiful segue, George," commented Zeke, "because you see, Henry, that leads into why we are sitting here at this moment sipping these marvellous restoratives, which, it must be noted, are in need of restoration themselves, George."

Charley Lee laughed again, waved to George to keep his seat, and got to the business of refreshing glasses himself.

"I don't know about Henry, but while I'm happy to be here, I'm not sure why I am," said Nora.

Miriam spoke up. "Let me try to explain, Nora. I became close with Leah Silverstein many years ago. We met initially at the synagogue, and that meeting developed over several years into a strong friendship. Our husbands had never met at that time because, while George is not a Jew and Zeke is, there is as much religious impulse in the two of them as would fit into the backside of a gnat."

"Miriam, Miriam, I do protest," exclaimed Zeke. "George and I, while not conventionally devout, are intensely religious."

Miriam snorted derisively and continued. "Anyway, Nora, eventually Leah invited us for dinner and these two really hit it off."

"Let me pick it up from there, dear," said George.

Henry noted that Charley Lee sat motionless except for an occasional pull on his scotch. But a happy smile never seemed to leave his handsome face. "Good listener," thought Henry.

"I'll make this brief for you two. I was a full colonel, had no desire to get a star and become a brigadier, had had enough of combat, and decided to get my doctorate at RMC. I did, too. Ph.D. in Mechanical Engineering. But what the hell was I going to do with it? It was about that time that Ezekiel, here, started to badger me about Bowell College. I thought teaching might be interesting, and as an adjunct professor I'd still have lots of time to smash things up around here. So I was hired, and truth be known, it was not a hard fought campaign to land the position. I believe I was the only applicant. So I taught a class or two every year for five years. Finished off the house, as well. I was as happy as a pig in poop for about a month. Then the boredom set in. What's to be next? And that is when I met our quiet bartender, the inscrutable Charley Lee."

Charley picked up on his cue, put his tumbler on the table beside him, pressed the tips of his fingers together and studied them for a few seconds; then he looked at Nora and finally settled his gaze on Henry.

"A number of years ago I was invited to serve on the Board of Regents for Sir MacKenzie Bowell College. Essentially it's an honorary position and its responsibilities are not onerous. I accepted because I am a business man and a profile of public service is conducive to the generation of good will. I suspect the fact that I am a Canadian of Chinese heritage had something to do with my appointment as well. We must always appear to be tolerant and inclusive, mustn't we? Before too much time had passed, the natural progression and rotation of leadership positions on the Board resulted in my becoming the Chairman of this Board. For me, however, such a role is not a mere sinecure. In my life and in my business interests I strive for excellence."

Charley stopped, took a sip of his scotch, and observed to George, "The world is a better place because of the presence of the Highland Park single malt."

Charley looked at Nora and Henry before he continued, "While at a conference of University Boards of Regents from around the province, I first came to hear the pejorative phrase 'Colon U' being used in reference to our College. I did some investigation and in very short order I realized the depth of the scorn and contempt in which we were held. Initially, I was hurt. And then I became angry. And when I am stirred by anger I do not let the emotion eat at me. Rather, I act."

"What did you do?" asked Nora.

"Like George, I believe in establishing a strong foundation. For me the foundation was the student body. I started eating lunch at the school cafeteria. I visited the pubs where the students hung out. And I asked the same questions: 'What do you think of the calibre of the teachers? Who do you think are the really fine teachers? Are you getting value for your tuition?'And after a winnowing process a handful of names came to the fore and two of them were George Harper and Ezekiel Silverstein. And the two strongest faculties were Math and Science, and Engineering, and the School of Management got some positive reviews as well. I met with George, was highly impressed, and asked him if he would be interested in taking over the position of Dean of Engineering. I pulled a few strings, made a few calls, and it came to pass. Now over to you, George. Give us an update of your School of Applied Science."

"Wait a minute. Time out," said Nora. "What do you mean that you pulled a few strings?"

"My business interests are many and varied. I am not without some influence in places that can effect change."

George laughed. "Essentially, Charley asked me if I could administer and improve the Engineering school. And I told him that in contrast to leading a battalion in combat, dealing with a small school was a fairly simple operation. My predecessor wanted to retire, that was facilitated, and I became dean three years ago and started to cut out dead wood. I shuffled people out of courses they had become too comfortable in, brought in a bunch of adjuncts and made some good hires. You met one tonight, Megan Fiorini. She's great. We're starting to make waves. A couple of the big universities recruited several of our kids last year for their graduate studies programs. We'll be okay. And so will the school of Math and Science."

"Charley, you mentioned that Zeke's name came up in your interviews. What's happening there?" asked Henry.

"Nothing. Zeke is too old to be of use to me."

Charley had to stop talking as Zeke erupted in peals of laughter. He finally said, "I'm being facetious. Kind of. Perhaps. Maybe. The real reason is that you cannot overestimate the level of anti-Semitism that exists on modern Canadian campuses. Of course, it's always hidden under the premise that being opposed to Israeli policies is certainly not being anti-Jewish. So, Zeke, fine teacher that he is, cannot be the spearhead for dealing with the flab that exists in the history department and in the Arts faculty in general."

"Do you want to have what took place in Engineering take place in the Arts faculty?"

"Impossible. The situations are very much different. But, look, I'm sweltering in here with that fire going, and these folks have all heard my proposals repeatedly, and they're going to get bored and become disruptive. So let's us go outside for a walk and I'll let you know my thinking. You, too, Nora."

"Thanks, Charley, but I'm fine here. And Henry will fill me in later. Be warned, though, Charley, he tells me everything. He can't keep a secret."

The night was warm and bug free. Henry noticed six men packing up garbage and litter from the grounds in large green bags, disassembling the beer keg fridge, collecting leftover food, cutting up the remnants of the roasted pig and placing these pieces into a super-sized cooler, and arranging a fine mesh screen over the coals in the fire pit to prevent any wayward sparks from escaping. Charley explained in response to Henry's question that this clean-up crew was composed of teachers from the Management and Engineering departments. "And all the extra meat and corn and salads will go to the Food Bank program in town tomorrow."

The two men strolled toward the duck pond. A gibbous moon hanging in a cloudless sky lit their way and they sat on a bench at the water's edge.

"Henry, be assured that I'm not some Machiavelli or Svengali orchestrating a palace coup. As I mentioned, however, I want the people with whom I'm associated to be striving for excellence. I put no stock in complacency. The College is moving forward on several fronts, but the Arts Faculty is treading water."

Henry took a sip of the marvellous brandy that puddled at the bottom of the snifter he had brought with him from the house.

"You want a school that reflects your personal way of thinking, don't you?"

"Absolutely, I do not! I hate Marxism, but it should be taught at Bowell. In fact I feel it must be taught. I strongly disagree with the interpretation of feminism that is being promulgated at the College, but at the same time I strongly endorse the Women's Studies program. For far too long women have been denied the role they must play as leaders of a civilized society. And it may be shocking to you, I know, but I see you and George as feminists. Look at the women you've married. What is missing in the Arts program is the presence of an alternate point of view. For example, where is a course that debunks Marxism. If our students are to strive to reach excellence, we must provide the mechanisms so that they can exercise their ability to think, to distinguish, to make meaningful comparisons rather than merely reciting from the 'Current Canon of Nowness'."

"Charley, it's cast on a stone tablet that university professors must have freedom to teach their own points of view. Let me give you an example. I had a conversation with Dean Whitmarsh's husband earlier tonight. A guy by the name of Leonard Twilley. You can't just tell someone like Leonard Twilley that he has to be more even-handed in his teaching of history. He has academic freedom even though I think he's very much wrong."

"I agree. What can be done, however, is to assure that a course is in place that exposes the failings of his beloved Marxism and to base these failings on empirical evidence. Obviously the current Dean of Arts won't take such a stance. And that's a problem."

"And another problem is that you cannot just fire people with whom you happen to disagree. A little item called 'tenure' gets in the way of that."

"True. And tenure is indispensable in guaranteeing academic freedom. But the attainment of tenure could be made a much more stringent process in the future."

"Charley, you're not looking to orchestrate a situation where I suddenly become dean, are you?"

Charley shook his head. "Certainly not. For one thing you're too young; for another, you should be in a classroom teaching. That is where you can effect meaningful change. And it won't happen all of sudden. It will come in incremental steps. But outstanding teachers are the key to the change. And I know that you are a fine teacher. Zeke has mentioned your conversations and that prompted me to look into your teaching record. Those kids at U of T loved you. That means a lot."

"Well, thank you, kind sir."

"I also am impressed by what you're planning to teach in this coming semester. A couple of people have filled me in."

"Okay, Zeke would be one. Who's the - - -? Wait a minute. Cynthia Kennedy has already been at you about me?"

Charley laughed heartily. "Weeks ago. Called me up and raved about old, dead white men corrupting the morals of her young sisterhood. Or something like that. She wanted me to call a special meeting of the board and have your contract terminated. I told her in quite unvarnished terms that as someone who was very much alive, decidedly male, and distinctly yellow in hue, that she could go straight to hell. I also told her that I could not think of a more germane course for young women about to go into real life, than a consideration of the valid premise of the strength and intelligence of old Billie Shakespeare's women. She hung up on me."

They sat for a few minutes without speaking, watching the moon settle lower into the darkness over the western horizon and listening to the lapping of the tiny waves on the pond. Occasionally, one of the ducks stirred in the bulrushes, but otherwise all was still.

"I guess we should wander back. We've got a sitter and it's a lot later than Nora and I anticipated staying."

"How long a trip to your place?"

"Only twenty minutes. No problem."

As they approached the house, Charley placed his hand on Henry's arm and halted him. "Inevitably you'll be involved in friction as the school year gets going. Rely on your teaching skills. And do not worry about the politics that are going to come at you. I want to really emphasize that. I'll have your back."

Nora looked over at her husband in the Impala's passenger seat. "All right, tell me all. What did you and Charley talk about?"

"He's got this idea that my being a good teacher is going to be a catalyst for change in what he says is a school that's just treading water. And he also said that I'm not to worry about Dr. Kennedy and her ilk. That he'll cover me."

Nora focused on the dark road unfolding before her and said nothing.

Henry turned to her. "I gather you were talking to Jean Whitmarsh. What did you think of her?"

"She reminded me of some of the guidance counsellors at my schools in Vancouver and Toronto."

"How so?"

"When she smiled, which she did a great deal, she showed a lot of teeth. But her eyes were as cold as a snake's."

IX

Henry was awakened when Nora pushed his shoulder and demanded that he face the other side of the bed. His breath, she suggested, resembled that of a dog's that had been snacking from the cat's litter box. Then he heard Annie and Rachel downstairs, and feeling some sentiments of guilt, decided to do the noble husband thing and go down to feed them breakfast. Nora snuggled deeper into the covers as he closed their bedroom door.

He got the girls some granola and milk, fruit and juice, and then made coffee for Nora and himself. He was sitting on the south-east porch facing the warming sun when he heard a vehicle on the drive. Henry strolled around the house and found Walter Ruttan studying the pile of split wood that was ever so slowly growing to a respectable size.

"You're doing a good job here, Henry. But look at the pile you've still got to split. You really should be using a hydraulic wood splitter. It'll let you do the job in about one-tenth the time. I can help you with getting one if you're interested."

Henry allowed that he was indeed interested, learned that Walter had such a machine, and could deliver it that evening. "Built her myself, Henry. She'll make short work of those pieces of elm and maple. They're bastards to split by hand."

The real reason he was visiting, Walter explained, was that he was worried about how cold the house would be in the coming winter. "I see that you've got this season's wood delivered and stored inside your summer kitchen. That's good. But, as I mentioned to you before, I doubt there's a scrap of insulation in those walls. And you'll have to do something about that."

The two men went inside, Henry poured a coffee for Walter, helped himself to a refill, and then poured another mug for Nora who had just come downstairs, wearing her dressing gown. Walter suggested that the girls' bedroom be the place to begin the process of insulation.

"Grab your framing hammer and a wrecking bar, Henry, and I'll show what's involved."

The three proceeded upstairs to a room cluttered with stuffed animals and children's books. Walter stated that it was a good room to begin, because being on the south-west corner of the house, it faced the prevailing winter winds. He looked at Nora for permission, then made a small one-foot square hole on an outside wall. The plaster fell apart easily underneath several layers of wallpaper of indeterminate pattern and exposed the narrow strips of lath inside to which it had been attached. Walter broke these apart and waved Nora and Henry to approach for a closer look. They could see the rough surface of a stud and then four inches of empty space leading to the exterior wooden plank sheathing beyond which, they assumed, would be the red brick veneer.

Henry picked up one of the larger pieces of plaster and pulled on some coarse threads that were interwoven throughout it. "What the hell are these?" he asked Walter.

"I can tell you," Nora interjected. "Do you remember that tour of London I went on in my senior year? Well one day they took us to see the site of the new Globe Theatre they were building. And they were using the same materials and tools that would have been used in Shakespeare's time to make it as authentic as possible. That's one reason that it took so long. But the inside of the walls was exactly like this. And those threads are horse hair. They used it to bind the plaster so that it wouldn't just fall off the lath. And the lath looked exactly like those pieces, too."

Walter looked at her admiringly. "Never knew that," he said. "Means that the method of building didn't change for a hell of a long time. And if you look at that lath and that stud inside the wall you'll notice how rough they are. Lumber 150 years ago wasn't milled smooth the way it is today. So that stud is a real two-by-four, not like today's which are about a half inch shy of that. And these old buggers are really rough to the touch, too."

Walter went on to show Henry how to remove the entire six-foot high window from the wall, thus opening up a space through which the old interior wall could be shovelled into a receptacle. He suggested that a rented steel waste disposal bin would be an option, but that given that there were four rooms plus a bathroom to be gutted, such a bin would not lend itself to being easily shifted.

"I'll just use my truck, I guess," said Henry.

"When do you start teaching?"

"Two weeks from now."

"You'll need to start this soon, then. I'll come over after dinner tonight and we'll get the splitter going and see if we can make a dent in those rounds that need to be split."

They did. Walter stayed until after nine o'clock when it became too dark to continue. The pile had been reduced by over a half.

"Why is he so generous with us?" asked Nora as they lay in bed that night.

"He really believes in restoring beautiful old buildings. And he wants us to succeed, I guess. I sure appreciate him. He told me to start on the gutting tomorrow and he'd come over next weekend and help finish splitting the wood."

● ● ●

The girls and their mother cleared the bedroom of toys, clothes and books. Henry moved their beds and dresser into an empty room, went to the main electrical switch box and disconnected the one room from all power, and then started the business of extracting the window from the wall. Each window on this floor was a full six feet in height, and once removed, as heavy as a dead minister. Henry moved the truck so that it backed in at a right angle to the house and was just below the edge of the steel roof that covered the porch. When he went downstairs to get some heavy gauge, six millimeter, plastic sheeting to seal the door into the main hallway upstairs, Nora was just getting the girls ready for another trip to the library in Whippletree.

"Please make sure you get a tight seal," she said.

"I will. I'll staple this plastic over the doorway and then I'll cover the edges with duct tape. Should work."

"A small philosophical question, Henry. Once it's sealed, how in the name of God do you plan to get out?"

"Ah, well played, Sweet Chuck. I shall this very second go and get our ladder and lean it up against the porch roof."

Nora smiled wryly, shook her head, shooshed the girls and their books into the car and disappeared down the drive.

Tearing down the plaster and lath from the two exterior walls went quickly and easily. At one point, though, Henry had to go to find a mask to cover his mouth and nose, and a pair of goggles to protect his eyes. The dust was thick and plentiful. He returned by climbing the ladder and brought a snow shovel as well. He then moved on and repeated the process on the interior walls. The mess was huge, and he started to shovel it out the open window space where it landed on the steel roof and slid directly into the waiting box of his truck. Works as smooth as baby poop, he thought smugly to himself.

The truck was able to accommodate most of the rubble and when it was full, Henry climbed down the ladder, pounded his pants and shirt vigorously in an attempt to rid them of at least some of the fine plaster dust, left his mask and goggles on the porch, started the truck and headed for the dump some five miles away. Before he reached the end of the drive he realized he had no means of getting rid of his load, backed up, retrieved his snow shovel from the partially gutted room, and finally set out.

He was back in just over an hour, positioned the truck into a receptive mode once again, grabbed his mask, goggles and shovel, ascended the ladder and climbed back into the bedroom. He was almost finished hurling out the last remnants of the walls when Nora returned.

"How's it going?" she called up.

Henry leaned against the window frame and replied, "Really well. I've taken one load up to the dump already. So it's going well."

"Wear a hat next time. You'll plug up our new septic system when you shower with all that powder in your hair."

"Daddy, you look like a ghost!" exclaimed Rachel and started to giggle.

"I think you look like a raccoon," observed Annie, and both girls broke into laughter at the apparition presented to them by their father.

"What's next?" asked Nora.

"I'll finish the bit of the walls that's left on the floor and then start on the ceiling."

"Do you have to do the ceiling, too? We can blow insulation in on top of it. You're making extra work for yourself, aren't you?"

"I might as well do the whole shooting match while I'm at it."

"I think you're nuts, but go ahead. I'm going to get the kids a snack and some juice and then we'll come out and watch the show."

Henry finished shovelling the remaining rubble from the floor and into the truck and then inspected the ceiling. On this storey the ceilings were nine feet high. With his arms extended and holding his sledge hammer at the very end of the handle, Henry could only just bring enough force to bear to start the plaster falling in sizeable chunks. He found working over his head difficult and soon his neck started to ache as much as his arms. He took a break and started to shovel up the mess he'd brought down. This also cleared up the area where he was standing so that he wasn't tripping on all the rubble on the floor.

Nora appeared carrying three aluminum lawn chairs and she and the girls sat on the driveway, sipped their drinks and prepared to be entertained.

"What stage are you at now?"

"I've got a lot of the plaster down, but the lath is giving me trouble. I'll have to pull it down with the four foot wrecking bar that Walter loaned me."

He returned to action and succeeded in pulling down a few individual strips. "This is really tough," he shouted through the window.

He gave another heave on the wrecking bar and suddenly an entire section of the ceiling crashed down upon him. Henry felt something on his head, and it hurt. He put his hand up to investigate and felt something furry that was moving. He let out a scream and made for the open window, his hands flailing at the top of his head.

"Mommy, why is Daddy wearing a squirrel on his head?" asked Rachel.

Nora heard her husband scream again, saw him successfully dislodge the rodent and sent it flying down the steel roof and into the truck. The squirrel jumped out of the truck onto the lawn, and raced up the nearest tree from which it proceeded to hurl a non-stop barrage of insults at the two-legged creature that had violated its home.

"There are more of the goddam things," shouted Henry. And soon he had managed to chase another four squirrels out of the window.

After Nora had cleaned the plaster dust and blood from Henry's head, she sprayed the squirrel scratches with Bactine, told Henry to shush when he started to whine, and then asked him, "Did you have any idea that we were infested up there?"

"None." Henry paused, then added, "But the eavestrough guys did say that there was a hole in the facer board. I just never thought about it."

"I guess you'd better nail a board across it and get the window back in before it gets dark and those rats with furry tails get back in. And I bought a bottle of plonk at the booze store in the village for dinner. Thought you might need a bit of a reward."

The table in the kitchen, Henry noticed as he sat down for dinner, was covered in a fine dusting of plaster dust. How, he wondered, can this be? That room is completely sealed. He dragged a finger across the table and it left a clear trail.

"There's dust over everything," said Nora.

"I don't understand. It's as if it came right through the walls. Maybe it acts like neutrinos. I'll get a shop vacuum tomorrow morning."

• • •

When Walter arrived on Saturday morning, Henry was able to report that the girls' bedroom had been gutted, that the dust had finally succumbed to the ministrations of the expensive shop vac he'd bought, that batts of pink insulation had been fitted between all the studs and the ceiling joists, and that everything had been covered with six mil plastic vapour barrier.

"All that's left to do is to screw on the drywall."

"Ever done drywall before?"

"No."

"I see. Let's get this pile of wood split and then we can discuss it."

They worked straight through, except for a twenty minute break for soup and sandwiches that Nora had prepared for them. And by three o'clock they were done.

"Get this stacked in that stable section of your summer kitchen, and in fifteen months, while it won't be perfect, it'll be adequately dried to burn."

"Many, many thanks, Walter."

"You're welcome. But the bad news is that now you have to order another eight bush cords for the winter after that. And now let's talk about drywalling. Which you say you've never done."

"True."

"It's very heavy, it's very awkward and it's almost impossible for one man to do it at all well. Henry you've run out of time. Remember when I advised you to get pro's for your eavestroughing? I'm going to repeat what I said then. Get some professionals in. They'll do it better and they'll do it faster, too. And also, they know how to tape the seams. You don't."

"Walter, I just don't have the money right now."

"Then wait until you do, and then do it right. And if you have to save on costs, you could do the gutting. It's a dirty job, but it doesn't take too many brains." He looked at Henry and smiled broadly.

Nora approached. "Walter, would you do us the honour of joining us for dinner tonight."

"Why thankee, ma'am, that's right neighbourly of you. But my wife and I are having company in ourselves. I could do with a beer though. Enjoy this last week of summer, Henry. Don't even think about attempting to gut the next room. Get this wood stacked and enjoy your family. You've worked hard enough. And from what you've told me, this fall is not going to be any picnic either, is it?"

X

Nora had asked him that morning if he felt nervous about his first day and Henry had assured her that he did not. But he had lied. He did feel the familiar butterfly sensation; he always did on the first morning of a new term of teaching. This time, however, it was more intense than usual. This time he was heading into a situation that was not at all happy to see him. This time he was facing two classes that trailed a record of snarliness, in the case of the engineers, and a class of presumably gender-conscious young women who would not be overjoyed to be instructed by a lapdog of the patriarchy.

It was still early when he arrived at Bowell College. Henry unlocked his office door, retrieved some white cardboard pieces that were about six-by-eight inches in size and which had been creased in the middle so that they could stand by themselves on a desk. Then he walked to the next office, introduced himself to the two building caretakers, and enquired if his lecture room had been opened.

"We'll go check," they responded. "Anything you need taken down there?"

"Just these name cards and I've got them."

One of the men unlocked the door, gave an extra key to Henry, wished him luck, and Henry was alone.

It was a beautifully designed room, shaped to promote dialogue. At the front was a long whiteboard about twenty feet in length. Ample space for the lecturer separated this board from a similarly long desk. Sixty student desks, three deep, arranged in a sharp horseshoe, faced it. The ends of this parabola came to within three feet of the long desk.

There was a space in the centre of the horseshoe, but it was only about ten feet across. Students were almost forced to look at each other by this seating arrangement.

Henry had been told to expect about fifty engineers in each class, and he set about placing fifty of the white cardboard name cards making sure that one appeared at each of the front row desks. Then he waited.

At twenty-five after eight they began to arrive. Henry was wearing his battle dress of sport coat, blue shirt and dark blue tie, grey slacks and black loafers. He leaned back against the whiteboard, his hands in his pockets and studied them as they milled around and finally found a desk to their liking. He was pleased to see that the front row had no empty spaces. He stayed where he was until the room was quiet. Then he wrote his name on the white board, 'Dr. Henry Miller'.

"I'm Henry Miller," he said. "But you now have the advantage of me. So if you would, please print your name in letters large enough that I can read them from here on those little white cardboard things. Then prop them up." He waited a few seconds. "If you find yourself at a desk that presents a problem to you, if, for example, you hate the person next to you, please move now to a seat that suits you. And be sure, because that seat is where you'll be sitting for the duration of this course." Nobody moved.

"Okay," Henry said. Then he slipped out of his jacket, laid it on the long instructor's desk, loosened his tie, rolled his sleeves up not quite to his elbows, walked around the long desk, through the narrow channel between it and the first row, moved to the centre of the long desk, and facing the class, placed his hands behind him on the edge of the desk and hoisted himself quickly to a sitting position, and sat there, his feet swinging slowly in front of him.

"There are a number of items of business I want to discuss with you this morning. They can wait. You know nothing about me, and we're going to be spending a substantial amount of time together over the next three-and-a-half months. And this is a course you need to be successful in. As you know it's compulsory. You have a right to be aware of the kind of person you'll be dealing with. So fire away. Ask me anything about anything. I ask only that you raise your hand so that I can acknowledge you by your name."

He waited in the ensuing silence, his legs swinging slightly. A hand went up. "Jason?"

"How did you wind up teaching this course?"

"Nobody else would take it."

"Did you want it?"

"I was late getting here and so I was given no choice. Having said that, had the opportunity been given, I would have chosen it. I admire and respect engineers."

Another hand. "Adnan."

A young man, with the olive skin tone of the sub-continent, said, "We were kind of hoping for that beautiful professor, Dr. Kennedy. What happened to her?"

"Nothing. I suppose she wasn't hoping for you, Adnan."

Laughter rippled across the room and Adnan smiled widely.

Another hand. "Matt?"

Matt was wearing a tee shirt and it revealed two muscular arms filled with colourful tattoos. He had close-cropped hair and a smirk played about his mouth. "You said we could ask you anything." Henry nodded. "Okay, the word is that most of the profs in this building are gay. Are you?"

The room went deathly still. Henry kept his poker face, his feet kept swinging.

"Nope. I'm straight. I was born that way. Your sexual preference is constitutional. So I had no choice. Same as you, whatever your preference is, Matt." Some scattered chuckles were heard. "I would have preferred to have been born a woman, but apparently, I wasn't smart enough."

The room broke into laughter again, the tension gone. Matt did not join in.

"I notice," Henry said, "speaking of women, that there are six women in this class. Do any of you have a question?"

A tall girl with long auburn hair and wearing glasses, put her hand up.

"Stephanie?"

"Do you have any bias against women in Engineering?"

"None."

"Would you elaborate, because the six of us have all experienced it at one time or another."

'I would. An observation first, and then an anecdote. Can women succeed in Engineering? Should they even be there? I'll answer that in three words: 'Professor Megan Fiorini'." He was pleased to see nods of agreement from a number of students. "And my anecdote is this. My sister chose Engineering out of secondary school. One of her Math teachers told her she might just as well tear up her application. She did struggle in years one and two, primarily because she was a party animal. But she did well in third year, was elected president of her class, and then graduated top of her class in fourth year. And I would also add that any male who harbours a prejudice against women in general is a certifiable moron. Does that clarify my position, Stephanie?"

She and the other five beamed at Henry. He did notice, however, a number of interesting facial reactions among his men students.

"Again, having said that, let me emphasize that individual women can be as vile and loathsome on occasion as individual men can be. They need not take a back seat in that category either."

A girl named Deborah asked, "Are you married?" and was subjected to a chorus of good-natured boos and cat calls.

"Deborah, I am. I am madly in love with my wife, we have two little girls, and we're in the middle of renovating a very old farmhouse in which we may all freeze to death this winter."

He paused and then said, "If that's all then - - -"

A young man in the back row interrupted him. "Professor Miller, there is one more question. I've been waiting for someone to ask it, but no one has. So here it is: Why Shakespeare?"

Scattered applause met this query, and Henry waited until the silence was total.

"Eric, thank you very much. I had decided that I was going to have to ask that one myself. It's central to everything we'll be doing and you need to be very clear why we're doing it. So let's go."

Henry hefted himself off the high platform and stood in the middle of the space created by the arc of the students' desks. Here, he was no more than a few feet from anyone in the class.

"I doubt that there is anyone other than me in this room who gives a damn about William Shakespeare. That is going to change. By Christmas I want you to have fallen in love with him, or at least some of his characters." He paused to allow the skeptical chuckles to cease. "Shakespeare is not easy. Some of his language is out of date. Do not let this faze you. Some of the language, the idioms, that I grew up with, you would not understand. And they're only fifteen years old, not 400 years old. Also, he writes in verse. What's that about? Three reasons: It was the convention of the time for writers of dramas. Secondly, it was for audience pleasure. Human beings do not like an absence of challenge. We intentionally make things difficult. For example, why don't we make the hole in golf a lot bigger? Why not get rid of base lines in tennis? Let's expand the goal in hockey to twice the current size. Why don't they make the cryptic crossword puzzle in the paper easier? Because we enjoy the challenge. You might want to ask your-self the same question about why you enrolled in Engineering. It's sure no cakewalk."

Henry paused, put his hands into his pockets, and seemed to be studying the pattern of the tiles on the floor. There was some murmur-ing as the students commented to each other on his last few sentences. Then he looked up and went on.

"And, thirdly, and most importantly, verse enables poetry, and poetry is far more packed with meaning than is prose. 'You are the wind beneath my wings,' says a lot more than "I look to you for support". There are literally hundreds of words, phrases and lines that you have read, heard, and even used, that were created by Shakespeare. His plays usually run between two-and-a-half and three hours. He could say a great deal more about human beings by using poetry than by using prose."

Eric put his hand up again. "That's all well and good. That's why his stuff is the way it is. But you still haven't explained why we should be studying him."

Henry looked at Eric thoughtfully. "What kind of Engineering do you want to practice?"

"Architectural."

Henry nodded. "Excellent. You ask good questions, Eric. The answer to Eric's question has a couple of key components. One is the concept of foundation. Think back to what you learned in your first year. Consider that without that material you could not be studying at the level you're currently in. Shakespeare was, essentially, the first important writer to use what we consider to be modern English. You couldn't sit down with a copy of Chaucer's *Canterbury Tales* and start in reading. It's Middle English and very much different from what we speak. Shakespeare's language isn't. He is the foundation from which all our literature springs. And, Eric, you'll be familiar with the architectural need for a foundation. I'm going to go further. Every story that you have ever read or heard or seen in a film has its origins in a Shakespearean tale."

Matt put up his hand. "Question."

"Go ahead, Matt."

"Are you saying that Shakespeare's behind the movie *Evil Dead*?"

"That's the one with torture, blood everywhere, body parts strewing the landscape?"

"That's the one."

"Actually, Matt, you'll be studying the direct ancestor of that movie. And all the other slasher films as well. It's called *Titus Andronicus*. I suspect you'll like it."

Henry walked back to the high desk, turned and again hoisted himself up to a sitting position.

"Let me finish this up. I want you to be well educated, not just jugglers of numbers and algorithms. I want you to be leaders of society. I want you to have a strong foundation. And in saying all of this, I guess I'm saying that I hold a conservative view of education. Now I have good news and bad news for you. The good news is that I have met with a number of your faculty members including Dean Harper. I know where they want this School of Applied Science to go. The bad news for you is that their views and mine are congruent. That's a term from Euclidian geometry that I thought you might like. The further bad news is that Dean Harper and I are, and I'll use a simile here, like two quantum particles that are physically very far apart and yet are inextricably linked. He wants you to study Shakespeare."

Stephanie spoke up. "You know quantum mechanics?"

"Anyone who says she knows quantum mechanics, Stephanie, doesn't know quantum mechanics."

He swung down, walked to the white board, and wrote the name of the Shakespearean anthology on the board, and turned back to them. "You got the name of this by email a few days ago. They've got copies of it in the book store waiting for you. It's cheap and it's the only text you'll need. And you'll notice that I'm not flogging my own book. Somebody named Willie wrote this one. I'll see you on Wednesday. And remember where you were sitting because, being a reactionary Neanderthal, I take attendance."

Henry shrugged into his jacket and watched them leave. He was close enough to hear Adnan say, "He's pretty good", Matt respond, "He's a prick", and Deborah tell Matt to shut up, that he was being a jerk. Then he set about the task of placing the class's names on the master seating plan that he'd prepared the night before.

Henry returned to his office, but remembering that he would not see his second class of engineers until four o'clock that afternoon, decided to pay a visit to Zeke. On his way out the front door of the building, he met Cynthia Kennedy.

Her opening words, "How did they react to finding out they're studying Shakespeare?" were not oozing with friendliness.

"And a very good morning to you, too, Dr. Kennedy. It went well, thank you. As a matter of fact they were asking for you."

"What do you mean?"

"Well, certainly at least one of the lads has been smitten by your unquestioned beauty and had been hoping to see you three times a week. He was underwhelmed at my being the replacement for his visual desires. But the rest were most enthusiastic about their upcoming explorations of the Bard."

"You won't be laughing in a few weeks. They're going to eat you up." And she stalked into the Arts building.

Henry and Zeke strolled to the bistro for a mid-morning coffee served by the attentive Olive. "You seem to have been apportioned the fuzzy side of the lollypop when it comes to the timetabling of your classes, Henry. The first lecture slot on Monday mornings and the last one on Friday afternoon strikes me as a bit harsh. You haven't alienated anybody in the Faculty of Arts, have you, my boy?"

"Certainly not, Ezekiel. I'm glad to be of service to my colleagues who have assured me that the high quality of their teaching requires that they have at least Monday mornings and Friday afternoons, and preferably both days in their entirety, free to polish and hone their lectures to the highest possible standard of excellence."

They sipped their coffees, gazed at the lake and took pleasure in the warmth of the golden September sun.

"The good news, though," added Henry, "is that someone at least tried to show consideration to those Engineering kids. And pretty creatively, too."

Zeke cocked an enquiring eye at him.

"Yeah, they set up the English classes so that one group gets the three early classes and the other one gets the late ones. And then each week that rotates. Equalizes the pain a bit for them."

"You're not pissed off?"

"For everything its season."

"Ecclesiastes, Chapter 3," said Zeke and smiled.

Henry's afternoon class followed the same pattern as that of the morning, and he returned home in his truck mostly content with the initial meetings with these two groups.

X I

"Well, you're not being carried home on your shield, so you must have triumphed. Tell me all, my faithful bread-winner."

"I only heard one guy refer to me as a prick. So total mutiny was avoided."

"How did he find out so quickly?"

Henry put both arms around Nora and nuzzled her neck. "You're a cruel and heartless woman, Sweet Chuck. Where are the girls?"

"Upstairs in their bedroom. Annie's reading to Rachel from a book she got at school today." Henry pulled a beer from the fridge as he listened. "And she's informed me that she doesn't want me to drive her tomorrow. She wants to go on the bus with a new friend she met today."

"What did you and Rachel do today?"

"Went to the library again. They've got a neat section with little books and toys for tots like Rachel. And I did some research on your college's namesake. Sir MacKenzie Bowell hisself."

"About whom I know bugger all."

"You and ninety-nine percent of all Canadians, I'd guess. Let me blow away the fog of your ignorance. He was an immigrant from England, was self-taught, became the owner of *The Belleville Intelligencer* in the early 1850's, and served on the local school board. Let me see, what other nuggets have I for you?"

"So far it's pretty boring," said Henry and pulled on his beer.

"How's this then? He was the Grand Master of the Orange Lodge in all of British North America."

"Hey, I wonder if there are any 'mackerel snappers' teaching in the English department?"

"Just hold on there, sailor. Let me check my notes." Nora read over a scribbled piece of note paper. "Yeah, here. He was elected as MP for Hastings North in 1867, and served for the next twenty-five years. He was in Sir John A's cabinet for much of that time. Finally wound up in the Senate as government leader in 1892. Then in December of 1894 the incumbent Prime Minister died and the Governor General asked old Mackenzie to form the next government as PM. He did, too, and then in January he was knighted. And that's how you get Sir Mackenzie Bowell."

"How long did he last as Prime Minister?"

"Just seventeen months. It seems that our Mac was a vain old cuss. Got folks pissed off. He tried to imitate Sir John A. But he was not smart enough and didn't have anywhere near the political savvy to pull it off. Didn't have any people skills apparently. So there was a political rebellion, he got the hook, and was replaced by Tupper. Bowell went back to the Senate. And he was not happy about it, at all."

"That is not a particularly stellar record. He did get to be PM, though."

"Yes, he did, Henry. But two things really popped out at me. He may have been an ardent Orangeman, but he fought for the rights of Catholics in Manitoba when they were getting the shaft out there. When he died in 1917 'The Globe' acknowledged in its obituary that he had succeeded in making the Orange Order less hostile to Catholics. They also said that while he was not a skilled politician, he was a capable administrator and an honest man. There are worse things to be called when you die."

"And, Nora, my sweet, what was the second thing that popped out at you?"

"Your colleague, Felicity Barth-Drill, would not be happy to hear this, being the raving peacenik that she is, but Bowell was hugely involved in the local militia and actually organized the Belleville Volunteer Militia Rifle Company in 1857. Wound up as a colonel, he did."

"He's a hard one to figure out, isn't he?"

"He is, and that's because he was a human being. It's all nuance, Henry. There ain't no black and white."

"Are the girls still upstairs? I'm going to play tag with them."

"They went out the front door while I was haranguing you about the great man."

At that moment Annie appeared at the screen door of the kitchen. In her two hands she was holding a snake, while Rachel at her side was trying to place one of her little paws on the creature. Nora let out a gasp and headed for the stairs and a safe refuge in her bedroom.

"Daddy, what kind of snake is this and why did Mommy scoot upstairs?"

"It's called a garter snake and your Mom is not too keen on reptiles. But it's pretty, isn't it."

"I want to hold it. It's my turn," said Rachel.

"OK, Rachel, but do not squeeze it. Just hold it gently and then let's place it back in the grass. That's where it lives and it'll be happier there."

With the snake safely ensconced back in the field Henry turned in time to see his wife peering out of their bedroom window. He and the girls held their hands out to show Nora that no creeping creature still lurked there and he went back inside.

"Well, my sweet, I don't believe the Sisterhood would be impressed by your lack of courage in the face of Nature, red in tooth and claw."

"Don't you Sisterhood me or you'll be cut off for a month. And do not let those girls bring any more snakes near me."

That night as they prepared for bed, Henry asked, "What did you mean when you were talking about Senator Bowell and you said it was all nuance?"

"I was talking about your class tomorrow, actually. I can tell you're psyched up about it and maybe even a bit nervous. But remember that those young women are human beings, subject to all of our frailties and probably not too many of them are monsters. Nuances, Henry. Ain't no blacks and whites."

XII

Once more, Henry leaned against the whiteboard and watched as the students entered the lecture room. They were noticeably quieter than the engineers had been. As before, he had placed the white folded name cards on fifty of the sixty desks, and made sure that one appeared on each of the front row seats. As he watched, several of the students conspicuously took a card from the front row and returned to find a seat in the third and last ring of desks.

Henry repeated the procedure he'd followed the day before. His name went on the board, his jacket came off, his tie was loosened and his sleeves received the two rolls up towards his elbow. He went to the front of the long desk, placed his hands backwards on the surface and hoisted himself to a sitting position atop of it.

"You now have my name. I need yours. Would you please write it on the folded cardboard in front of you and be sure you're comfortable in the seat you've chosen because that's where you'll be sitting each time we meet."

He let his eyes pan across the name cards and noticed that the women who had chosen to sit in the back row had written the honorific 'Ms.' and what was presumably their last name. Unlike the remainder of the group, they'd used no first names.

"Because we'll be seeing each other three times a week until Christmas, you have a right to know something about me. So please go ahead. Ask away. All I ask is that you raise your hand first so that I can acknowledge you by your name."

A hand appeared in the back row. "Yes, Ms. Leduc."

"I don't think there's any need for questions. I've heard all about you."

Henry kept a poker face, replied, "Indeed," and let his feet continue to swing.

"You've been talking to your squeeze again, have you, Pamela?" a girl named Suzanne asked.

Henry quickly interjected. "Suzanne, before you speak, please raise your hand so that I can recognize you." But he noticed that Ms. Leduc's eyes were blazing with fury.

Another hand from the back row was raised.

"Ms. Reevely?"

"I'd like to know why we have a man teaching this course, first of all. And secondly, why the hell are we going to be subjected to Shakespeare, who, when all is said and done, is just another dead, white European male. Surely even you are familiar with some of the great feminist women of colour who deserve to have their works studied."

Henry observed that about half the class broke into applause at these comments. He also observed that about half did not.

"I'll attempt to deal with your questions and comments in order, Ms. Reevely. I'm confident that if I miss anything you'll pounce quickly." A couple of chuckles were heard.

"I'm teaching this course because it was assigned to me. I accepted it because I need the money. More importantly, I would have sought to teach this class anyway because of my attitude towards women. Let me explain. All my life I have been surrounded by extraordinary women. My mother, my sisters, my wife and my two daughters are, each one of them, possessed of three attributes. Each is strong, powerful at times. Each is possessed of preternatural intelligence. None of them has time for fools. And thirdly, and this may really irk some of you, each is drop-dead beautiful. There. I said it and I stand by it."

Ms. Leduc's hand waved wildly. "You're just another chauvinistic pig seeing only a woman's physical beauty as having any value."

"Ms. Leduc, if you'd been carefully listening, you would have noticed that I never said anything about physical beauty. Beauty comes in many forms, Ms. Leduc. I would imagine that you're not oblivious to the charms of one of those forms, the human body."

"Oh, you're not oblivious at all, are you Pamela?"

"Suzanne, hand please," said Henry. But he thought to himself, I may just have to buy that girl a sody-pop in appreciation.

"So, to get back to Ms. Reevely's question, I was delighted to have this class assigned to me. My doctoral dissertation dealt with female writers. And as I said in a class yesterday with some third-year engineers, any man who is biased against women in general is, I believe, a certifiable moron."

General applause greeted this statement.

"Second question: Why Shakespeare? Simple. He was the greatest and most important feminist writer of all time. Period. By Christmas you will have met and, I hope, loved some of the strongest, funniest and most intelligent women to be found in Western civilization."

Another hand waved from the back row.

"Go ahead, Ms. Lawton."

"You just completely identified yourself. You referred to Western civilization. That's all you white males can get your heads around. You probably support capitalism, colonialism and imperialism, too. I'm sick and tired of being subjected to what Sandra was talking about, dead, white, male Europeans. They're gone, they have no importance, and they sure have nothing to say to me."

Henry gazed at her for a long moment, his legs swinging, his poker face unreadable. Then, in a flat voice, "Who's Sandra?"

"Her for God's sake," fumed Ms. Lawton, pointing at her back row sister, Ms. Reevely.

"Ah," said Henry mildly. "We seem to be a bit repetitive here in our outrage against the poor deceased Europeans possessed of both 'X' and 'Y' chromosomes. But we have succeeded in widening the discussion to include not only Literature but Economics and Political Science. So let me begin with your points in sequence, Ms. Lawton.

"I do endorse capitalism. I assume that you're not a fan of monarchical dictatorship, feudalism, or a theological oligarchy. Therefore, let me explain why I do not endorse Marxism. I believe that in its very essence it offends the individual person, the individual citizen, intellectually, morally, physically and spiritually. That, of course, is my opinion, arrived at after much study and judgement. But it is ultimately an opinion and consequently a fit subject for debate. And I know that my opinion is not embraced by some of the Bowell faculty here in the Arts department. The most telling argument against Marxism, however, is that wherever a society has been governed under its canons, that society has failed. Every single one of them.

"Colonialism. Much wrong was perpetrated under the banner of colonialism. But much good accrued as well. Let me cite two examples, if I may. Zimbabwe was educated under capitalism in the ways of governance, economics and agriculture. When the whites ceded political power to the black majority, Rhodesia, as it then was, continued to flourish. Zimbabwe, as it became, was the garden of Africa. Then came the dictatorship of Mugabe. Need I really say more? You could write a most defensible Master's thesis arguing the benefits of colonialism to pre-Mugabe Zimbabwe.

"And secondly, let me refer to India. Did the British rule with arrogance, wilfulness, and on occasion, abject cruelty. Yes, indeed. As did the previous rulers for the preceding several millennia. Could India be the powerful, possibly world-leading, nation that it is without the infra-structure, language, and legal system given to them by the Brits? Doubtful. Here's another defensible Master's thesis for you: Was Churchill right in initially wanting to restrict Indian political autonomy to the municipal levels only? I do not know the answer. I doubt there is a correct answer.

"But, therein lies my point, ladies. Almost nothing in life is black or white. Everything is nuanced. And that is what the core of our study of Shakespeare will focus on. Now what have I forgotten?"

"Imperialism," snarled a voice from the back row. "And do not call us ladies."

"Ah, indeed. I shall attempt to refrain from that sobriquet in the future. But to your third point: I'm accused of being a closet imperialist. I didn't know that I looked Japanese. German, perhaps."

At this point Henry leaned back on his hands, maintained his stolid expression, and kept his feet slowly swinging. The outrage was fierce, immediate and palpable. He could hear a number of voices identifying his racism, others swearing that action would be taken, and that he was not going to get away with this. Henry watched the scene with interest and noted that about half of the class were merely sitting placidly at their desks. Some wore a facial expression of boredom or ennui. It was as if there were two separate cohorts of student in one class. Gradually, "The Outraged" noticed that their prof was just sitting watching them with an almost disinterested look. The furor died down and Henry saw a hand from, for the first time, the front row.

She was tiny, had jet black hair and matching dark eyes. "Ikuko. Have I pronounced your name correctly?"

"Yes."

"You wish to say something?"

"I do. You may have noticed from my first name and my facial features that I might possibly not be Caucasian."

"I had suspected something like that. And what is your last name?"

"Kawasaki. The final piece of evidence that will reveal that I am of Japanese descent."

The room became very still and quiet. Henry nodded at her to continue.

Ikuko stood up to do so. She looked directly at Henry but her words could be heard clearly throughout the lecture hall.

"Obviously, a number of my classmates were upset at your combining the words 'Japanese' and 'imperialist'. I am not. I have read deeply in my mother nation's history, perhaps the only person here to have done so. The history of Japan in the first half of the 20th century, and particularly from 1920 to 1945, is a tale of outright expansionism and imperialism. You can add slavery if you wish to be scrupulously accurate. You, Professor Miller, have said nothing untoward about Japan. I suggest that those upset by your words read some history and learn the facts."

She sat down and Henry waited to see if there would be a response. None was heard. Finally, he sat upright, slipped lightly to the floor, and returned to the whiteboard. As he had done with the engineers, he wrote the title of the Shakespearean anthology on the board, made the same lame comments about its reasonable cost and the fact that he had not written it, and then told them to leave their name cards at their chosen seat because he intended to take attendance and he also wanted to memorize their names.

A final hand went up. It was Suzanne again.

"This is the same book you're using with the engineers. Why?"

"Suzanne, it is. The basics of great art do not change. And interestingly, the engineers were quite open-minded about it. Surprised, but open. Perhaps that's because of their immersion in science and that they have learned not to bring pre-conceived ideas to a new experience. Now, before you go, please come up here and get the sealed envelope I have for each of you. Open it back in your residence or apartment or whatever, read it carefully, and come prepared to discuss it tomorrow."

He leaned against the board and watched them exit. He heard one girl state that he was just what she had been told to expect. Another asked in a loud voice how one went about getting out of this crap course. And another announced that 'this matter' was not going to be dropped.

As he gathered up his sport coat he noticed that one student remained sitting at her desk at the far end of the second row. She looked a few years older than the others, and wore a colourful blouse. Her skin was very black. She was looking at him intently.

"Hi, Naomi, is there something further I can do for you today?"

She smiled warmly at him. "Not today, but soon, maybe," and then she rose and came forward to get her envelope. "Would you mind if I read it here, right now?"

"Go ahead. I'll wait and see if you want to ask me about it."

She returned to her desk, opened the envelope and read.

"And dart not scornful glances from those eyes,
To wound thy lord, thy king, thy governor:
It blots thy beauty as frosts do bite the meads,
Confounds thy fame as whirlwinds shake fair buds,
And in no sense is meet or amiable.
A woman moved is like a fountain troubled,

Muddy, ill-seeming, thick, bereft of beauty;
And while it is so, none so dry or thirsty
Will deign to sip or touch one drop of it.
Thy husband is thy lord, thy life, thy keeper,
Thy head, thy sovereign; one that cares for thee,
And for thy maintenance commits his body
To painful labour both by sea and land,
To watch the night in storms, the day in cold,
Whilst thou liest warm at home, secure and safe;
And craves no other tribute at thy hands
But love, fair looks and true obedience;
Too little payment for so great a debt.
Such duty as the subject owes the prince
Even such a woman oweth to her husband;
And when she is froward, peevish, sullen, sour,
And not obedient to his honest will,
What is she but a foul contending rebel,
And graceless traitor to her loving lord?
I am ashamed that women are so simple
To offer war where they should kneel for peace;
Or seek for rule, supremacy and sway,
When they are bound to serve, love and obey."
The Taming of the Shrew, V, ii, 137 – 164

Naomi finished reading, carefully folded the sheet of paper, and replaced it in the envelope. She stood up, swung her purse over her left shoulder, again smiled broadly at Henry, and said, "Well, Dr. Miller, you're either a crazy man or a brave one. I sure hope it's the second."

XIII

Back in his cubbyhole of an office, Henry was hunched over his laptop when one of the custodians poked his head into the open doorway. "Everything all right, Dr. Miller? Your lecture room OK?"

"Good morning, Paulo. Everything is dandy. How are you this fine morning? And I'm very comfortable with you calling me Henry."

"OK, Henry it is. Is the hook-up for your computer working properly?"

"It is. But I have a question. Do you have any idea of how I can block internet access in that lecture room while I'm teaching?"

"So that the kids can't be texting and watching porn and stuff while you're giving them the good word?"

"Exactly."

"I'll take care of that and when you're in there tomorrow you'll find a little toggle switch under the big desk on the side away from the kids. Flick it to the left and they'll be forced to listen to you. I'll wire it up this afternoon."

There's somebody else I'll have to buy a sody-pop for, thought Henry, and turned back to his email. He found a message from Zeke inviting him to join an august few in the board room of the Engineering building for lunch with the dean. He was pondering the reason for this when a lovelier head than Paulo's appeared in his doorway.

"Linda O'Connor, as I live and breath. What brings you into the bowels of the catacombs?"

"Oh I wouldn't advise you to use that word here at Bowell, Henry. Actually, I wanted to see your reactions to the three classes now that you've met them all. And I wondered what your lunch plans were."

"Apparently the Women's Studies group had been forewarned about me. At least some of them had. It sure doesn't seem like a homogeneous group. But the engineers are just fine."

"Keep your eyes open. Lunch?"

"I'm invited to Dean Harper's inner sanctum for a nosh today. Why?"

"Me, too. I just wanted to see if you were on the short list. I had hoped you would be and in my undiplomatic way I was probing. If you like, I'll meet you here at 12:30 and we can go over together."

• • •

Fourteen people selected their soup and sandwiches from a sideboard in George Harper's meeting room, took their seats and were addressed by the Dean of Engineering. "Thank you for attending on short notice. I'm turning the agenda over to Charley Lee immediately."

Charley sat at George's right hand at the head of the long mahogany table. He took a sip of soup, appeared to savour it, then put his spoon down and looked at his audience.

"I've had copies of an important speech reproduced for you. You can read it later in its entirety. It was delivered by a renowned Classics professor at Yale University, Donald Kagan, an acclaimed scholar, now 80 years old, on the occasion of his retirement. In his address he describes American universities as having," and Charley turned to the text, "'a kind of cultural void, an ignorance of the past, a sense of rootlessness and aimlessness.' He condemned faculty for not having 'an informed understanding of the traditions and institutions of our Western civilization and of our country and an appreciation of their special qualities and values'."

Charley continued by explaining how the old professor had called for a 'common core of studies' to convey the history, literature and philosophy of Western culture to students. Professor Kagan had summarized his ideas of what should be taught by quoting Matthew Arnold's words, "The best which has been thought and said."

"Now can you guess the response that this address received? And please keep in mind that we are talking about Yale University, rightly acclaimed for most of its history as one of the finest institutions of learning on the planet."

Linda O'Connor spoke up, "It should have got the old standing 'O'."

"It did, Linda. From the students. The faculty that was present, for the most part, sat on their hands. The great bulk of the faculty boycotted the old professor's farewell speech."

Silence hung over the table. No one was eating.

Henry asked, "Is it not Yale that has the week-long sex seminars?"

"It is, Henry. And the most popularly attended unit of that program is the one dedicated to – and please excuse me here – blow-jobs. It's apparently a must-attend for students and faculty both."

"At Yale?" asked Zeke incredulously.

"At Yale, Doctor Silverstein. And lest we feel smugly Canadian, the University of Toronto has something similar conducted under the auspices of the Sexual Education program.

"I'm going to stop talking now so that we can actually eat our lunch. But would you please discuss the implications of this speech and its reception as they pertain to Sir Mackenzie Bowell College. I would very much like to hear your opinions after we've dined."

• • •

When Henry arrived home much later in the afternoon, Nora was in the process of getting Annie and Rachel their suppers. She took one look at her husband's face, brimming with excitement as he plucked a beer from the fridge and said, "Tell me all."

Henry planted a kiss on the tops of his girls' heads as they sat at the kitchen table, gave Nora a quick squeeze, sat down and thought for a moment, and then began. He reviewed the Women's Studies class in detail. He worked through his defence of dead European men, the accusations of chauvinism, of being a capitalist, a colonialist and a closet imperialist. He did his best to paraphrase Ikuko Kawaski's little speech."

"She wasn't pissed off at you?"

"Apparently not." However, Henry explained, her words had been prompted by the accusations of racism that had flown about the lecture room, that Ikuko had not been interrupted, but that apparently Henry's racist comments would indeed be acted upon.

"Your first class with the ladies seems to have been going swimmingly, Henry. How did you cap that? Let's see: So far you'd been accused of five different crimes against political correctness and that's not counting teaching arch-conservative literary works. Please, do continue."

When she heard that Henry had assigned Kate's description of the proper role for a woman, Nora bent over the sink and began to howl with laughter. "My God, did they storm the ramparts? Did you escape in one piece?"

"I gave it to them in a sealed envelope and told them to read it tonight when they were alone."

"Shrewd!"

"One woman stayed behind and asked if she could read it there in the room. She seemed older. I think she may be from Africa. Her name is Naomi."

"What did she say after she'd read it?"

"Said I was either nuts or brave. But she did smile at me."

"That's quite a day, O Beloved of Mine."

"Hell, that's only one part. Charley Lee called a special lunch meeting and I was invited. It was fascinating."

"OK, hang on a second. Annie, there's some frozen yogurt in the freezer for dessert. Give a little bit to yourself and your sister in these bowls, then the two of you can do the dishes. Let Rachel wash and you dry. And I said, 'a little bit' of yogurt. Daddy and I will be out on the porch."

Nora poured herself a glass of wine, got Henry another beer, and joined him on the porch facing the setting sun. "All right, tell me about this meeting."

Again, Henry paused, gathered his thoughts, and then recounted the gist of Professor Kagan's evaluation of American universities. Then, as best he could, he tried to summarize the conversations that had ensued.

"It's not just American universities, Nora. Ours are just as bad. In spades! It's not just me that's being pressured. And it's not just Zeke being shunned for being pro-Israel. One guy in the Math department, one of the streakers at the barbeque actually, had recently watched that old war movie 'Midway'. He said to a couple of his colleagues something about the fact that if that battle had not occurred and the Americans had not won, that we might all be speaking Japanese."

Nora looked at him and waited.

"'What's wrong with speaking Japanese?' was the response. And when he tried to explain about Japanese war aims in those days, they told him he was a racist and walked away."

Henry went on to catalogue some of the topics that were forbidden, that the conventional thinking in the faculty lounges of Bowell College had declared to be incorrect. Any recognition of American goodness or beneficence was not tolerated. That men were not universally malevolent towards women was not tolerated. That Israel was a thriving and decent democracy in a sea of incompetent dictatorships was not to be spoken. That meritorious literature existed before post-modernism, that Stalin was a barbarous murderer, that Mao was a butcher, that Marxism was a colossal failure, that unionism might have to be curtailed, none of these topics was to be allowed let alone deemed to be worthy of discussion.

"My God, Nora, some of these people at lunch won't even acknowledge that they read *The National Post*. If you do not get your news from *The Toronto Star* and the CBC, then you must hold fascist views. And apparently, one never acknowledges that one voted for the Conservatives. The faculty lounges are total dictatorships of left-wing thinking. And if you deviate, or express a contrary opinion, you'll be made to pay. Professor Kagan was right on the money and it's really very scary."

Some of Elmer Knobber's mixed breed steers and heifers strolled into view in the adjacent field. "How good are Elmer's fences?" asked Nora. "I've never seen him working on them."

"Neither have I. I see they've started excavating the basement for that new house on the lot he just severed," said Henry. "I should stroll over and see how they're doing the septic system."

They watched the falling sun and listened to the chatter and giggles from the two dishwashers inside.

"Hungry, yet, Henry?"

"Not just yet. First let me tell you about what came after these conversations. Neither Charley Lee nor George Harper said a word during all of this. But when the talk died down, Charley asked what had most struck us about the response that Kagan's speech had received. Most of us teed off on the faculty for treating him so abysmally, but Charley disagreed. "The students gave him a standing ovation,' he said. 'That is what is really important here.' Then he asked us what the implication of that was for us at Bowell."

"Let me interrupt you, Henry. This is reminding me of that school I taught at in Toronto, the one where the history department didn't teach war because war is not nice. And whenever I talked to my kids in English class about the Canadians in both World Wars, they always asked why no one had ever told them about this stuff."

"Charley would agree with you. Your high school kids and those undergrads at Yale are similar. They want to be to be taught meaningful stuff. They're sick and tired of options like gender studies, psychoanalysis and Marxism. So Charley told us not to back off. To take on the orthodoxy that's stifling our teaching. To present positions that are not congruent with the current politically correct morass of 'Nowness'. He really wants to rebuild Bowell College into something fine."

"And how does he feel about the situation you're in? Where you're bucking almost the entire department?"

"The guy was aware of it. Told me not to back off. That he would give me his support when the situation became really sticky."

They watched a heifer poke her head through the wire fence to get at some grass that evidently was juicier than the identical grass on her side of the fence. The fence looked ready to fall over.

"Henry, this whole situation at the College reminds me of this house. There's a strong foundation, but a whole bunch of tearing down has to be done before it becomes beautiful. And you have indeed fallen into a big pool of shit."

"Woman speaks truth."

"What's your plan for the lads tomorrow? The famous bullying engineers."

"And there are girls in there too, Nora. There are a dozen of them all together. Same play, *The Taming of the Shrew*. Except with these kids I'll start at the beginning, not with Kate's speech at the end."

XIV

Henry placed a scale model of the original Globe Theatre on the long desk and leaned back against the whiteboard waiting for his engineers to arrive. From that vantage point he could see the new toggle switch that Paulo had installed. He took a step forward, flicked it to the left, and resumed his casual stance against the whiteboard.

They strolled in punctually and looked with mild curiosity at the model. Eric actually came up to the front and gave it a close inspection. "Cool design," he said and retired to his seat.

Henry straightened up but stayed behind the long desk and began to speak. He explained that, although Shakespeare may have been the greatest genius to use the English language, he was first of all an actor, producer and businessman. Money had to be made in order for the company to survive. Bums had to be put into the seats. That was where compelling plays and writing came in. And the Globe Theatre was the centre of the action. He explained where the sets and costumes were stored, the thrust stage and the open roof design. He pointed out the trap door which accommodated sudden appearances and exits, as well as the occasional ghost. He indicated the four tiers of seats arranged in a horseshoe around the open space in the middle called 'the pit'.

"Let's talk ticket prices at this point. The cheapest were here in the pit. There were no seats; you stood. Now most of you are familiar with the cost of Leafs tickets. Which are the most expensive?"

Most of the hands went up. Henry nodded at Adnan. "The rails. You need to take out a mortgage to buy a pair of those."

"True enough," smiled Henry. "The cheapest tickets at the Globe logically were those for the pit. They cost a penny. A not insignificant amount in 1600. And the most expensive?"

Most of the engineers decided on the first row of the first tier.

"Not bad thinking, but 100% wrong. I'll tell you why."

Henry dove into a graphic description of hygienic practices in Shakespeare's time. He told how the lower classes bathed perhaps once a year, how the tin tub was filled once only and bathers used it in a pre-scribed sequence, the father, then the mother, then adult live-in rela-tions, then children in order of birth, then servants in the sequence of their stature in the household. "You can only try to imagine the state of the bathwater at the end of all this splashing."

Various gagging sounds resonated around the lecture hall. "Need I discuss dental practices or attempt to convey to you the quality of people's breath?"

"Please do not," said Stephanie. Smiles and laughter greeted these words.

"So imagine if you will, this pit jammed with folks who could afford only a penny. The working class, the lower class. They were called 'the penny stinkers'. And it was jammed. The Globe was essentially the only game in town. If you wanted entertainment, you went to a play. Can you imagine the perfume wafting up from this shoulder-to-shoulder crowd if it had been eleven months since any of them had bathed? So I ask you again: Where are the costliest seats?"

There was a hesitation before Eric put his hand up. "Last row, fourth tier."

"Bingo, Eric. Your thinking?"

"Those seats are the farthest from the stench that would be rising out of the pit."

"Question," said Matt, tattooed arms folded across his chest. "Given the smell, how did people reproduce?"

Henry joined in the laughter, then walked around the desk and into the open space between the rows.

"So let's begin. We're going to start with one of the most famous plays in English, *The Taming of the Shrew*. Can you tell me what a shrew is? Deborah?"

"It's a small mole-like animal that's very fierce. It also describes a woman who's a witch only it's not spelled that way."

"Very diplomatic and dead on, Deborah. This play is a comedy and it is often attacked for being an anti-woman diatribe. I was at The Shakespeare Festival in Stratford, Ontario, a few years ago and even there, where they should know better, the program notes railed against the so-called attacks against women. Well, I'm going to show you that Shakespeare had no intention of insulting women or elevating men."

Henry went on to talk about one of the great threads that flowed throughout the Bard's plays, the dissonance between appearance and reality. He also explained that most productions of the play ignored the introductory two scenes that preceded the play-within-a-play that formed the body of the familiar comedy.

"Has anyone here ever played a trick on a friend while he was drunk?"

For several minutes the room resonated with tales of eyebrows being shaved, of drunks being stripped down to the underwear and abandoned, and obscene messages written with indelible ink on coma-tose chums.

"This play begins that way. A lord is on his way home and finds a tinker in a ditch, dead drunk. A tinker was a guy who fixed pots and kettles. He decides to play a trick on him and has his servants take the drunk to the castle, put him to bed in the best chamber after dressing him in fine clothes and putting rings on his fingers, and have music ready to play when the drunk wakes up. The tinker, whose name is Sly, (remember appearance versus reality, people), is then persuaded that he is a nobleman who has been insane for seven years. To celebrate his return to sanity a play is going to be presented for his amusement. Let's read these two scenes together."

The reading went well until near the end of the second scene when Sly is told that the servant who is disguised as a beautiful woman is really his lady who, as she says, has for seven years been "abandon'd from your bed." Henry's class broke up in laughter for several moments when Sly said, "Servants, leave me and her alone. Madam, undress you and come now to bed."

Henry heaved himself up to a seat on the desk, grinned at his engineers, and thought, I believe they're ready for a little Shakespeare.

XV

"Daddy, we were watching the big digging machine today," announced Rachel as Henry stepped out of his truck that evening.

"What did you see, Rachel?"

"Two very big holes in the ground. And lots of dirt."

Nora and Annie joined them and Nora explained that they had been on a snooping mission to check out the construction being done for the new house to be built on Elmer Knobber's most recent severance. "It's going to be a big house, but the septic system seems to be tiny in contrast to ours. No weeping bed going out all over the place. Just a small web of pipes less than half the size of a tennis court. The man on the back-hoe said the new designs require just that and a pipe from the septic tank. He said they cover it up with special sand and there's a little hill and that's it. They cover that with topsoil, spread grass seed and you never touch it again."

"Could we run a pipe under the driveway and put it over in the field?"

"I asked him exactly that and he said it would be no trouble whatsoever."

"I better call Seamus tonight."

They walked back to the house each holding one of the girls' hands.

"Henry, I forgot. How did the engineers react today?"

"It was what teaching should be on a perfect day, Nora. They loved it. So did I. We laughed a lot and I think they learned a lot. But I can't see tomorrow being a repeat of today. I may get my head handed to me."

Later that night Henry called his ace legalist friend, Seamus MacPherson, and described the new method that Nora had observed.

Seamus laughed and said, "Make a deal, Henry. We have no case."

"You've been such a huge help, Seamus. I suppose you'll want half my salary plus my first-born for your most modest efforts. What did you do? Send one letter?"

"I'm coming down in October to see you guys. Let's play golf and we'll flip to see who buys the beer. But if those morons in the Department of Health give you any problem at all, let me know."

• • •

At 7:30 the next morning, Henry, traveller mug in hand, strolled into the maintenance staff's office. "Thought I'd join you for coffee," he said to Paulo.

"Henry, come in, come in. This is Tony, the other half of our crack custodial team."

The two men shook hands and Henry sat with them at the bridge table that served as the furniture for this little room. "Paulo, thanks for the toggle switch under my desk."

"Did it work?"

"I have no idea. I don't think anyone was trying to get on the internet."

"Tell me, Henry, what was going on in there? I don't hear a lot of laughter coming out of rooms in this building. But there sure was yesterday morning. And afternoon, too, coming out of your room. In fact, I saw Dean Whitmarsh and Dr. Kennedy down here yesterday afternoon while you were teaching."

"Is that so? Interesting. But to your question, Paulo. I feel really strongly that teaching requires passion; but it also requires fun. If one of those is missing, so is some of the learning. So we were doing Shakespeare and he is a very funny guy at times."

Tony spoke up. "I asked the two women if I could help them and the dean said that they were just doing an inspection tour of the building.

But I've never seen either one of them in the basement before. I'd say they were snooping. On you." Tony looked directly at Henry.

"Could well be, Tony. I don't think you'll be hearing a heck of a lot of laughter today, though." Henry looked at the clock on the wall. "I'd better get down there. My women's class will be arriving soon."

Henry placed the model of the Globe Theatre on the desk, flicked the toggle switch that prevented any internet access in the room, leaned back against the whiteboard and waited. The students filed in and he noticed a couple of empty seats. He waited for a couple of minutes and then checked his seating plan. "Does anyone know where Ms. Leduc and Ms. Reevely are?"

In the back row Ms. Lawton raised her hand. "I don't believe that you'll be seeing them in here again. But I'm pretty sure that you'll be seeing them at some point in the future."

This announcement was greeted with knowing smirks and murmurs from several desks. Henry looked intently at Ms. Lawton for a few seconds before replying, "Your comment is noted. And I thank you for it, Ms. Lawton.

"Before we get to Kate's speech that I gave you last day, I'd like to give you some background about the physical theatre, describe some of the more interesting facets of life 400 years ago in London, and explain some of the problems that Shakespeare faced as an entrepreneur and playwright."

Henry began by referring to the model of the Globe, and then he walked into the open area in the middle of the tiers of desks. He went into graphic detail about Elizabethan hygiene and was pleased, relieved in fact, to see the level of interest and reaction that these details aroused in the class. Like the engineers, the young women assumed that the best seats in the theatre were in the first row of the first tier. He went into more detail than he had the previous day in linking the problems of assuring a full house of theatre-goers to a play that would appeal across a wide intellectual range. But he consciously omitted any reference to the two-scene introduction to *Shrew*. Finally, he addressed the theme of appearance versus reality.

"I'm going to suggest to you that this dichotomy of what seems to be real, as opposed to what is actually real, is a constant in most, if not all, of his plays. I have the advantage of you, I suspect, in that I've read all of his plays and studied most of them in some depth. And it seems to me that all of his central male characters, with two exceptions, cannot make this basic distinction. Consider, people, an issue that rightly irritates most of you: The inability of men to see past a woman's appearance to what lies beneath."

At this point Henry knew he had hit the center of the target. Applause and shouts of "Right on!" echoed around the hall. He let it die down. Ikuko Kawasaki raised her hand.

"Who are the two exceptions?"

"Hamlet and Falstaff. Falstaff appears in *Henry IV, Parts 1 and 2*. And unless you pressure me, we won't be studying those plays."

"Why not?" asked Suzanne.

"Because this course, as I currently see it, is based on the premise that Shakespeare's strongest characters are his women. And much of their strength stems from their ability to see what is true, what is real."

The room was very quiet. Henry waited for more questions, saw none, hiked himself up on the long desk, and said, "Let's consider Kate's speech then."

Ms Lawton immediately waved her hand. "It is disgusting! It's a recipe for the total subjugation of women to men. I can't believe that you gave this to us to read. But I do have one question: Do you believe the crap that's in this speech?"

Henry let the silence develop. At last he said, "I do."

"That's it. I'm out of here," fumed Ms. Lawton. But before she exited she fired another salvo. "This is nothing more than an endorsement of institutionalized rape. And you believe in it. You'll be hearing from me, too."

Henry watched her leave, heard the slam of the door, then turned back to the class. "Further comments? Suzanne."

"I'm not going to go ballistic over it, but it does strike me as being really male chauvinistic. And I can't really figure out how you can say some things that are almost feminist and then say you agree with this speech. It doesn't compute."

"Thanks for your comment. Any more? Laura? We haven't heard from you."

Laura's face reflected her puzzlement. "Does this have anything to do with the appearance-reality idea you were talking about?"

"It does. Naomi?"

Naomi stood up from her second row, end seat, and took a couple of steps into the open area. She looked at her classmates, then said, "This is my fourth year in this program. I've rarely spoken up because I am really shy, but also because I'm older than you girls and my background experiences are so different from yours. At least I hope they are." Naomi explained that she was at Bowell College because it was the only university that would accept her. She came from another country, another continent, and her academic background was not strong. She had enrolled in 'Women's Studies' because she wanted to make some sense of her life as a teenager and young woman before she had immigrated to Canada. "When I heard Ms. Lawton talk about this Shakespearean speech as an example of institutionalized rape I was taken back a few years. I can tell you that I know what institutionalized rape is."

Naomi went on to describe the gang rape of her eighty-one year old grandmother, her six-year-old sister, and herself. She talked of the pain and horror of undergoing genital mutilation. This, she explained, was done by women, but at the behest of men. "I've heard a lot of negative things about men in our classes over the last three years or so, and sadly, some of them are true. But not all of them are true. I can assure you that I really know about reality. And this speech in no way is an endorsement of rape. It's something else and I don't know what that is. Maybe we should stop being so quick to accuse Dr. Miller of being a pig and listen to what the man actually has to say."

Henry looked down at his shoes, closed his eyes, and shook his head slowly from side to side. At last he looked over at the woman who had now resumed her seat and said, "Thank you for sharing, Naomi. I'll say only this. I do endorse what Kate says in this speech. But it is an endorsement based on the asking of a monumentally important follow-up question. And at this point in the journey we're on, I won't tell what I think that question is; I do want you to think about it, however. And to think really hard.

"We can do with some humour now. This has been a tough discussion and as Shakespeare would say, it's time for some comic relief." And with that they went into the encounter with the drunken Sly, the gulling of him into believing he was the lord of the castle, his frustrated attempt to bed his 'wife', and the presentation of the entertainment for his pleasure.

"So you see, none of what follows is real. Nothing in this play is what it seems to be. Read the play over the weekend; it'll take you only a couple of hours. Don't get hung up on minor points that confuse you. Just boogie on through it and when we meet next week we'll discuss two things: Who is stronger: Petruchio or Kate? And secondly, does Petruchio buy into Kate's final speech? And please do not forget to give some thought to what I referred to as the follow-up question to Kate's speech."

XVI

Later that morning when Ezekiel walked into the tiny basement office, Henry was on the phone and in full rant mode.

"So you were going to make me cut down trees that are over a century old? You were going to make us ruin the appearance of that beautiful house that is even older than the trees? You were never going to tell us that we had options that did not involve all that destruction?"

Zeke listened carefully, but try as he did he could not hear the response to these charges. Then he understood.

"You're being awfully quiet. Do you have nothing to say to this?"

This apparently generated a response, because Henry snarled back, "What do you mean I should talk to the Chief Medical Officer? I just talked to him. It was he who gave me the green light to put in the alternate system. It was he who said I should talk to you and try to resolve what he termed 'this unfortunate unpleasantness'. So I'm talking to you and I'm telling you that you are a bully. And like all bullies, you're chicken shit when someone stands up to you. All I had to do was to flash a lawyer of consequence at you and you all folded your tents and crept away. I've got one piece of advice for you: Don't ever again tell someone, 'We can make you do whatever we want you to do.'"

Henry slapped his phone closed and smiled at Zeke who was leaning against the filing cabinet, "What a prick!"

"My boy, you must be quite famished after the expense of that much emotion. Come with me to The Bistro. On Thursdays they specialize in tapas and at lunch time they charge about half of what they do in the evening for the same food."

"Zeke, I brought my lunch. It's down in the custodians' fridge."

"And it will keep there very nicely until tomorrow. Come along. We'll celebrate having survived almost all of the opening week and it's my treat."

On the way to The Bistro they noticed that although the sun shone brightly, the breeze was cool. They stopped partway to watch a huge v-formation of Canadian geese, their non-stop honking announcing their passing. "It may be invigorating, but it is a sad time of year none-theless," mused Zeke.

"I thought I might see you on tapas day, Dr. Silverstein. Inside or out?" asked Olive.

"Inside please, my dear. It's quite chilly outside, and I also like to be nearer the food when it's served buffet style as you do with these wonderful little Spanish goodies. And could you bring a bottle of that rather fine Spanish cooking wine that you keep for me on these pleasant Thursdays."

Olive laughed and went to get the wine.

"So how has the week gone for you, Henry? Any major battles? Any significant triumphs?"

"It really has gone well, Zeke. But there are a few things that are bothering me and that I'd like to ask you about."

"By all means. But you'll have to wait a minute. Here's Olive with liquid sustenance."

Zeke swirled a small sample, took a sip and held it in his mouth appreciatively and then nodded his approval of the vintage to Olive. "And Olive, your Thursdays are becoming famous. The table next to us is the only one still unoccupied."

"We're swamped, Doctor. But you're right. We're doing great business. Help yourselves at the tapas buffet."

Fresh arrivals caught Zeke's attention and he said, "Why, Henry, here are some of your colleagues."

Henry turned so that he could see the entrance and caught the eye of Jean Whitmarsh. She was accompanied by Cynthia Kennedy, and to his surprise, two of the students absent from that morning's class, Ms. Leduc and Ms. Reevely. Their eyes turned to the empty table and Henry waved. There was a half-hearted wave from Jean, but when Olive approached, Cynthia asked her if there were tables available outside.

"Well, Henry, evidently the threat of frostbite is preferable to dining in close proximity to you. What have you done to cause such strong sentiment among these fragile flowers of academe?"

"That's one of the questions that I wanted to put to you? What's behind such malevolence? It cannot be simply that I'm a man."

"And your other queries?"

"Those two students with Jean and Dr. Kennedy were pretty clear, right out of the chute, that they'd heard all about me. And that's before they'd even seen me. What's going on with that? And another student made a pretty snarky comment back to the one girl that she'd been talking to her squeeze, or something like that. And there have been some pretty blatant threats that I'd be hearing about some of the things that were said in class. All in all, the two classes went well. Maybe even really well. Except for this small cadre of young women who seem to have been prepared to get me. And those two with Jean were not in class this morning, but another one said that I'd certainly be hearing from them."

Zeke put his glass down, commented on the complexity of Henry's confusion, and suggested that they get some food before he responded. He had been right. It was very good indeed.

"Henry, you are correct. It is not simply that you are a man, although that unfortunate configuration of chromosomes does not help. More than that, you are a threat. Jean sees you as a threat because she is weak and she knows that she is. But she does not want to lose her position as dean. It's very important to her, and my suspicion is that she has few elements in her life that cause her any sense of pride. Her husband, Leonard Twilley, is a silly little Marxist professor of history in a silly little department of which, sadly, I am also a part."

"I'm not after her deanship, for heaven's sake."

"It is not you of whom I speak in that regard. No, your threat is more insidious. You're teaching some core texts. You are teaching from the great canon of Western literature. And after only two lectures you have aroused interest and debate among your students. I know this because a very wise Portuguese friend named Paulo told me. And this is a threat because if students were to develop a taste for, and then a hunger for, curriculum of substance, the current fluff that is plucked from the bosom of the God of 'Nowness', from whatever fad is currently the most politically correct, would be cast aside and Jean's tenure as dean would be revealed as one dedicated to placating the promulgators of trivialities. Oh, dear me, Henry, could I possibly sound more pompous?"

"Probably not, Zeke. But that's fine. Let's plow ahead. But first, I want more of those tapas. They're wonderful. So is this wine, by the by."

With their plates replenished, Henry returned to the gist of Zeke's thesis. "If I'm not after Jean's job, then who is?"

"The nubile Dr. Kennedy. She would love to have the position and power to establish her societal view on the entire Arts program. And it's not solely her views on feminism that she would institute. She is a committed Marxist, a fervent anti-American, a devout despiser of Israel. She's never read of a mid-east dictator or terrorist whose actions she could not rationalize. For her, Naomi Klein is a goddess and Herbert Marcuse is a god. Your coming in and bringing your reactionary, outdated, and male-written texts has the potential of creating a rather large ripple in the placid pond of her leftist ideology. She is using Jean Whitmarsh now because Jean is her 'useful idiot', to quote Uncle Joe Stalin. But she is furious with the arrival of a real teacher with balls, in every sense of the word, on the scene."

"It's hard to imagine that Petruchio and Kate could cause so much of a problem."

"Oh, there are further layers of the onion to be peeled. Have you not noticed that Bowell College is lacking a president?"

"I had not, actually."

"We used to have one, an odd old duck who taught mathematics at one time. But he had a certain courtliness about him that lent itself to the role. He died, however, two years ago and the position has not been filled. Our Dr. Kennedy would not be content to gain the dean's desk; she'd like the whole enchilada. Her ambition is very large indeed."

"Why has a president not been appointed, Zeke?"

"Charley Lee knows she wants it, knows she has supporters, as well as some who fear her, and he refuses to allow such a scenario to come to pass. So it's in limbo."

The two men paused to enjoy their food and savour the wine. Finally Zeke broke the silence. "Henry, remember when Charley Lee committed to having your back when the going got tough?" Henry nodded. "Well, it's going to get tough soon. You have made some comments in class that, taken out of context, can be perceived to be insulting to specific groups who are extremely prone to take offence at the mildest whiff of political incorrectness. You have not, my dear boy, cleaved to the rigid constraints of acceptable left-thinking orthodoxy. You must pay." And Zeke smiled beatifically at his young colleague.

"Now I'm worried."

"I can well imagine that you are concerned, my young iconoclast. But do not be overly so. Charley Lee is a man of quite boundless resources. And he is committed to this college and to you. So are some others, among them one George Harper."

"Nora and I were thinking of having him and Miriam out to our place for dinner, to thank them for that staff barbeque."

"Go ahead and ask them. I'll actually be at their place on Saturday night. Miriam and I have taken to attending synagogue together."

"Deal. I'll ask them for Sunday dinner, you can come over with them, and then you can stay with us overnight and I'll drive you in with me in my manly truck on Monday. Annie and Rachel have been bugging me about when that magician Zeke was going to come back for a visit."

XVII

"Apparently I've got a problem, Nora."

"Oh, you've got more than one problem, Lover Boy. Let me just fill you in. First of all, Elmer Knobber, the wonder neighbour, wants you to help him bring in some bales of hay on Saturday. He said there should be only about 300 of them."

"Three hundred! Why doesn't he hire somebody to help him?"

"You're psychic. I put that very question to Percy Baxter this morning. He feels very badly about the mess we're in with the Department of Health and our septic system. And he thinks he has a solution. Anyway, about dear old Elmer: Percy told me that no one in the community will have any time for him. They've all been stung by him in financial dealings of one sort or another. So he can't even get a hired hand for one day. That means that you're it."

"Damn it, Nora. Did you commit me to it?"

"I did. A little exercise and fresh air will do you a world of good after all of your intellectual exertions."

"Go on," said Henry glumly. "What did Percy the Pumper have to say?"

"Big doin's, I can assure you, Henry. Percy had been talking to Walter Ruttan who filled him in about our problems with that nice inspector from the Department of Health. Percy feels badly because instead of doing the pipe under the driveway to one of those new-fangled little hills, he was trying to save us some money. So he suggests that we leave the new system in the ground. It won't be going anywhere and it sure won't rot. But he's prepared to run the new pipe under the drive, lay the new plastic bed over there and cover it all up with the new sand, and he'll do it for material costs only. No labour."

"Oh God, more money. I guess it's a good deal, though. And we actually have no choice. Do you have more glad tidings for me, Nora?"

"The last one, Henry, but definitely the most important one, concerns the health and well-being of your spouse and children. This house is bloody well freezing! Did you happen to notice the outside temperature this morning? It was six degrees! And it was almost that cold upstairs. The girls' room is fine because you insulated it. But the rest of this place is going to resemble a meat locker this winter."

"We can start using the two wood stoves. Surely that'll help. And we have electric baseboard heaters. We can crank them on."

"Do you have any idea how much our power bill will be if we try to heat this place with electricity and no insulation? Henry, we have to get the damn thing insulated. There's no way around it."

Nora looked at her husband, slumped in a kitchen chair, feet thrust out in front of him, head drooping. She went to him and leaned on him from behind, her arms resting on his shoulders. She kissed his neck, passed her fingers through his hair, said, "I'll get you a beer."

She twisted off the cap. "Henry, I'm sorry to hit you with all of this crap as soon as you walk in the door. But we'll get it done. We'll figure out a way."

Nora handed him the beer and sat on his lap. "And I never even asked you about your problem. What's happened?"

"I think I'm going to have to appear before the College's Human Rights Board. I'm not sure, but I suspect it could happen."

He put his arms around her and sitting together on the chair he filled her in on the events of the week and his luncheon with Ezekiel. "And by the way, Zeke and the Harpers are coming for dinner on Sunday and Zeke is staying overnight."

Nora seemed to stiffen and she moved his arms and slipped off his lap. "What's the matter?" he said.

"Let me get this straight. These three men, Charley Lee, George Harper and Zeke, are all sure that you're going to be getting into some sort of trouble. But you're not to worry because they'll have your back. And you may be pulled in front of that ridiculous Court for the Defence of the Very Thin-Skinned. Have you read about those crazy proceedings? Whoever lays the charge has his legal fees covered. But the accused is responsible for his entire defence. It's absolutely nuts. And these guys are saying not to worry. This might be a most interesting dinner on Sunday."

On Friday, Henry worked the engineers through the rest of *The Shrew* and told them that on Monday there would be a simple writing assignment to be done in class and that they should bring their laptops. He wished them a happy weekend and felt a pang of envy as he watched the afternoon class bubbling out of the hall, smiling and bantering. I don't imagine too many of them will be tossing bales tomorrow, he thought.

By four o'clock on Saturday Henry and Elmer had cleared the fields of the hay. "Elmer, why in this day and age are you still dealing with these oblong bales when you could have the hay gathered into those big round ones? I've heard that one of those round ones holds as much hay as twelve of these little buggers."

"Do you have any idea what they'd charge me for that kind of baling? I'd never waste my money that way."

"You saved a bunch of money today."

"What do you mean?"

"The hired hand comes pretty cheap."

Elmer looked at Henry but did not respond.

• • •

The Sunday afternoon socializing began smoothly. Nora took Miriam under her wing and showed her the grounds, the features of the exterior of the house that made it a unique dwelling, and the panoramic view down over Elmer's fields and finally to the river half a mile away. The three men tagged along behind, but when they returned to the kitchen, George asked for a tour of the upstairs. He appeared fascinated by the old plaster and the lath behind it. With his left hand he fingered some strands of the horse hair that were used as binding. "This is history.

This method goes back hundreds of years, not just to when this place was built."

"We know all about that. And we also know that it all has to come out. We are really concerned about freezing this winter."

George Harper looked at him closely with his one eye but said nothing.

Once they were seated at the dining room table, the roast beef served, the wine glasses charged, the appropriate toast 'a la cuisiniere' made, Nora could no longer restrain herself. She looked at George and Zeke, took a sip of claret, then began.

"You may not like what I have to say. But I am worried about what is happening to Henry. And I have one key question for the two of you. 'Is Henry being set up to serve your own political interests?'"

Zeke began to reply, "My dear Nora, ---" but he was cut off by George.

"The simple and most honest answer to your question is 'Yes'. We are using him because he is the only professor in the entire Faculty of Arts who has enough principle and teaching skill to pull off the change that is so desperately required to save that branch of Bowell College."

"But how can you know that? He's been teaching for a week. You've barely met him. What do you know of his principles."

"Short answer? Linda O'Connor, a superb teacher in her own right, apprised us of the stink that arose when they found out they had to hire a man. When we found out that the man was your husband, Charley Lee approached some of his contacts at the U. of T. and researched what kind of job Henry had been doing there. It turns out that he walks on water. We needed to get acting on our reclamation plan, you two were on site, and now you're a key to what is going to happen."

"This is the Scopes Monkey Trial all over again, isn't it?"

"Well, Nora, the stakes are not quite as high. We are not waging a battle of science versus fundamentalism, but we are fighting a very important battle for the soul of our university. And if we win, we may influence some of the larger and more prestigious universities across Canada. Obviously, I've been in battles before." George laughed and tapped his knife on his artificial hand, "And while this fight is not one with mortal danger, it is extremely important, nevertheless."

Henry broke in. "Will I be hauled in front of the school's Human Rights Board?"

"We hope so."

"Then what the hell is in it for Henry? And me?" asked Nora. She glared into George Harper's single eye, her food untouched.

"For you I have a deal."

George laid his cutlery down, ignored the others at the table and spoke directly to Nora. He talked to her about tactics and strategy and the difference between the two, and the interrelatedness of them as well. He talked of the future of Sir MacKenzie Bowell College as a light of excellence in the Canadian academic field focussing on teaching and the undergraduate experience. He talked of a future when slowly, incrementally, a graduate component was added to the school in the areas of Business, Engineering and Arts. And he talked of the need for a campus-wide commitment to the principle of diversity, diversity of genders, demographics, and most importantly, a diversity of opinions.

"And it is here, Nora, that our battle must be fought. We are facing an opposition that will not tolerate divergent views. This opposition must be converted or defeated."

"You sound like a jihadist, George," she said.

"No. I sound like a soldier. And that is what I am. A soldier fights for those who cannot. I read that somewhere and it's a good definition."

"You still have not answered my concerns about my husband. And what is the deal you mentioned?"

"Nora, I had a young lieutenant under my command one time when I was in Afghanistan. The platoon he led had been through terrible combat. They had taken casualties including two deaths. They were due to be pulled out. And I had to order him to take them into battle one more time to secure a position for us that was essential. I still dream about his face as he looked at me and nodded and turned back to his guys to tell them that they were going into hell one more time. They took the ground that was needed. But I brought in so much firepower, artillery and aircraft, that they suffered no casualties. Not even minor wounds.

"Henry is not being asked to do what that young lieutenant and his men did. But he is the tactical weapon that we must use to force a larger issue. He is essential. And, Nora, I give you my word as an officer that he will have all the firepower he could ever want in support of him."

Miriam, Zeke and Henry had been slowly eating during this exchange, but now they stopped and all turned their attention to Nora wondering how she would react to George's words.

Nora picked up her knife and fork and sliced a small piece of beef. She put it into her mouth and chewed it slowly. Then she took a long sip of claret. She gazed intently over the rim of the glass into George's eye. He had not moved since he had finished speaking.

"That's your deal for Henry. Okay. But more importantly, what's in it for me?"

The tension broke and they all laughed. George took a swallow from his glass.

"I will take care that you and Rachel and Annie do not freeze this winter." George took a healthy mouthful of roast and began to explain. The Engineering faculty was in a constant search for hands-on practical projects for their students. Evidently Nora's house was an ideal opportunity. It was old, unique and in need of creative destruction.

"Just like Bowell," observed Zeke.

"Quite so," replied George and continued. The first-year engineering students needed to be able to see into the guts and skeleton of a house, they needed a lesson in architectural history, and they needed to see how precision in deconstruction could open the possibility for renovation or, hopefully, restoration.

"Nora, can you and the girls move out of this place for a week, say in the second half of October?"

"Of course they can," replied Miriam, "because they can move in with me. Whether or not you are there as well is of no relevance to us girls." She smiled sweetly at her husband and winked at Nora.

George looked taken aback for a second but pressed on. "I'll clear these guys for a week from all classes. They'll have to organize buses, waste disposal units, outside latrines, tools, materials etc. beforehand. They'll come in here and gut the place. So you'll have to put everything in the girls' room, cover it and seal it in because the site will be a disaster initially. They'll see how it was all done over a century ago and how strongly it was constructed. I'll have them open the walls for rewiring and plumbing, then insulate the hell out of everything, put up vapour barrier, and then drywall the whole house. And that will include the girls' room because I see that it is still without drywall. And we do not want them growing up thinking that pink insulation is the accepted colour for a young lady's boudoir. They'll have five days to do this and their professors and I will be riding their asses to make sure they meet the deadline."

"There's one little problem, George," said Henry. "A little thing called conflict of interest?"

"Not at all," replied the Dean of Engineering. "You do not teach any of these freshman kids, so you can have no pressure put on you as far as their academic success is concerned. Secondly, 'co-operative education' is standard in most secondary schools in the province and is slowly finding a place in tertiary level schools as well. Thirdly, I'm the boss and I have the full backing of Charley Lee."

"Ah, so. The mysterious and inscrutable Mr. Lee," said Nora irreverently.

"Oh, dear," said Zeke, "My claret seems to have evaporated. I find that happens to me frequently when I'm in the presence of a fine, full bodied vintage. And perhaps I'll seize this opportunity to refresh all of your glasses."

The dinner proceeded and the conversations became free of strain, filled with humour, and occasionally descended into gossip. Henry told some Elmer Knobber tales and revisited his calamitous drop into the septic tank. Nora entertained them with anecdotes of an adolescent Henry and his now-famous and powerful lawyer buddy, Seamus MacPherson, and their drunken encounters with various police forces about Ontario.

Colonel (Ret'd.) George Harper followed up. "I really must tell you about a regimental reunion two years ago when we packed Mel Blackburn's balls in ice," he began, only to be interrupted by Miriam screaming, "You must not tell that story, George!"

But the looks of astonishment and curiosity from the other three convinced him to continue. The laughter continued right through the dessert course. As Nora and Henry were clearing the table, Zeke spoke up. "Miriam, my dear, if you would commit to being the designated driver for yourself and your good husband, I shall break out a flask of the Writer's Tears that I brought along as a sort of hostess gift."

Later, during a comfortable break in the conversation, Nora turned to George. "Will Henry be all right?"

"He will. He may suffer a couple of bruises and abrasions, but he'll emerge triumphant and streaming clouds of glory."

XVIII

As requested the engineers had all brought in their laptops. For the first time Henry was asked what the problem was in the lecture room that prevented them from accessing the internet. He explained that he'd had the access cut off so that the students would have to listen to him and each other and not be surfing porn sites. Some groans and a few chuckles followed this explanation. "However, you can write a document and send it to me and that is what we're going to do today. I want you to write a maximum of one page in which you explain the trick that is being played on the tinker, Sly. I'll be reading these for two things: Your understanding of this basic situation on which the entire play is built, and your sentence and paragraph structure. Don't try to be cute. Write simply and directly. And before you begin, I want to talk about my office hours and the possibility of an early morning remedial writing class."

Henry explained to them the hours in which he would be lecturing and the sign-up sheet that would be on permanent display outside of his office. "If you need or want to see me, write your name in one of the half-hour slots that are indicated and I'll meet you in my office at that time. I know your timetables as engineers are full, so if it has to be before eight in the morning or between five and six in the afternoon, so be it. We'll make it work. Another thing is evaluation. Here's the deal: Do not skip this class. You know that I take attendance. Do the reading that I assign. And put into practice what I'll be teaching you about writing. If you do these three things, I guarantee that you will not get less than a 'B' on this course. And bonus marks will be given if you make me laugh.

If a remedial writing class is needed, we'll set it up on Wednesday. Now go ahead and write me one page of good stuff."

After the class, Henry went looking for Linda O'Connor's office and found her at her desk. He knew that she was offering some remedial work for her Arts students and wanted to pick her brain about the popularity of it and when and where she offered it.

"I'm amazed, actually," she said. "I offer it at eight o'clock on Wednesday mornings and I often get as many as thirty kids or so showing up. And most of the classrooms are empty then so finding a free room is not a problem."

"And what do you offer them?"

"The basics of composition. What a thesis is. What comprises an introduction. The sequence of developmental points. Paragraph structure. Sentence structure and variation. For some of these kids it is totally new ground. They've never been taught it or, more probably, they weren't listening when it was taught. But they need it and now they seem to realize that they really do need it."

"Is anyone else doing this kind of work?"

Linda laughed heartily. "You are a naive one. My colleagues are quick to catalogue the various failings and inadequacies of their scholars. They love bitching about how illiterate they are. Do they do anything about it? Absolutely not!"

Her eyes narrowed and she looked quizzically at Henry. "You've not yet been to the staff lounge have you, Henry?" He shook his head. "You're due. Your education up to this time has been incomplete. Did you bring your lunch?" He nodded. "Then meet me here at noon with your little brown bag in hand and I shall conduct you into the sacred confines of MacKenzie Bowell's Arts Faculty Lounge. And if you have any Guy Fawkes masks or Norma Rae picket signs about, they might ease your entry into this high altar of academic excellence."

Back in his own office, Henry began to read the one-pagers from that morning's class. He read quickly. He was not grading; he was assessing. He was pleased that every student understood the trick being played on Sly, the tinker, and the ruse of the faked play. But there were widespread writing problems. And they were the ones that Linda was addressing in her own remedial class. Only Eric had written a page of error-free coherent prose. Some others, like Adnan, came close. A few were encountering major writing difficulties. But this ain't hopeless, Henry thought, this ain't hopeless at all.

The faculty lounge was on the fourth floor, right next to Dean Whitmarsh's office, in fact. As Henry entered the lounge he first noted that it, too, looked due south and the view was enhanced by a wall of windows that offered a panoramic view of Lake Ontario. It was a long oblong-shaped room furnished with plenty of couches, easy chairs and tables that could lend themselves to dining, card games or college-related work if one were so inclined. At this moment no one seemed to be so inclined. Linda pointed out a couple of refrigerators against the far wall. "I usually keep a container of one per cent milk here, so help yourself. Glasses and plates and such are in that cupboard beside the fridges. People are expected to wash up the dishes and cutlery they use, but I and a couple of others usually end up doing them. I find that little fact interesting, actually."

They were well into their sandwiches when Felicity Barth-Drill approached. "May I join you for a moment?"

"Please do, Felicity. Do you remember Henry Miller from the barbeque?"

"I do," replied Felicity without bothering to look Henry's way. "I wanted to ask you, Linda, if we could count on you to join us at our demonstration at the Air Force base in three weeks. It's critically important that the intellectual elite of this country make their feelings known about the terrible decline into militarism that we are experienc-ing under this government."

"What intellectual elite would that be, Felicity?"

"Us obviously. Who did you think I meant? If we don't speak up in a forceful way we could spiral further into fascism than we already are. Surely you can give up a Saturday to participate in such an important expression of dissent."

"Sorry to disappoint you, Felicity," replied Linda. "But my week-ends with my kids and husband are sacrosanct. I let nothing interfere with them."

Felicity looked contemptuously at her colleague. "You really should get your values straight, Linda."

"Oh, they're straight, Felicity, very straight indeed."

Felicity at last turned to look at Henry. "And what about you? Will you be joining us?"

"Absolutely. It sounds like fun,' replied Henry. "A good old get-together to cheer on the troops, rally 'round the flag, that sort of thing. I wouldn't miss it for the world."

Linda snorted into her glass of milk but did not speak.

"What are you talking about?" fumed Felicity. "We're not cheering on anything! We're protesting against those militaristic bastards!"

Henry feigned a look of puzzlement before he said, "Now I can place you. You're the lady with the foul mouth at the barbeque who had to be escorted away by Dean Harper, aren't you?"

"I should have charged that thug with assault."

"Probably wise not to have," said Henry. "But in answer to your thoughtful invitation, I shall have to decline. I'm actually a great fan of our military, both past and current. In fact I'll be dealing with the entire question of war, soldiering, and conquest in my Shakespeare classes."

Felicity looked at him with an expression of horror, pushed her chair back abruptly from the table, and stormed off.

"Is it not wonderful to see how culture transcends our differences," Linda observed.

"I guess this wouldn't be a good time for me to ask her to donate to the Canadian Battlefields Association, would it?"

"Not at this moment. But I fear, dear professorial colleague, that further opportunities to offend are about to present themselves. I see the Whitmarshes, both dean and hubby, looking this way and they seem to have Malcolm Victor in tow."

"Who's he?"

"He teaches Sociology and he's bound and determined that the good folks at Bowell College shall join the Canadian Union of University Faculties. He'll be wanting to recruit you to the cause."

"I am a most sought-after chap today, aren't I?"

"Jean, Leonard, Malcolm, welcome," said Linda smiling broadly. "We just finished eating and were about to grab a coffee. Do join us."

Coffees were poured, introductions were made, and Jean asked, "How is that early morning remedial class going, Linda?"

"Very well, Dean. I was just saying to Henry that I'm getting as many as thirty kids out for those sessions. In fact, Henry is going to make a similar class available for his scholars."

"You are aware, I trust, Dr. Miller, that there is no compensation for this kind of activity. Why in the name of heaven would you want to waste your time on such a hopeless task?" asked Leonard Twilley. "And for free?"

"Why, Leonard, I would have thought that an idealist such as yourself would have been spear-heading such a movement. Liberating the masses! Raising high the proletariat! Arming our students intellectually for the revolution to come! Would you care to join me in this enterprise? Perhaps we could team-teach."

"I see quite enough of their pathetic scribblings, Dr. Miller, without volunteering for an extra dosage of it."

"Do you not see it as part of our job as teachers to help our students to improve and realize their potential?"

"Not at all," interrupted Malcolm Victor, his thick Scottish burr almost overwhelming the words he spoke. "Our job as teachers is to maximize our compensation, improve our working conditions, and minimize the required number of hours spent in the classroom."

"Are you kidding me?" asked Henry, flabbergasted.

"I certainly am not, sir. And when we achieve our goal of joining the union, these ambitions will be realized. Look at this faculty lounge, for instance. This furniture should be replaced. A person from the cafeteria should be tasked with being here to serve us coffee and to do the cleaning-up afterwards."

"You've done quite a bit of that yourself, have you, Malcolm?" asked Linda, unable to eliminate a trace of venom from her words.

Malcolm ignored her and returned to Henry. "These extra classes that you and Dr. O'Connor are running do not fit in with our future union's guidelines. You really should keep that in mind."

Later, when he had cooled down, Henry would recall that Jean Whitmarsh had said not a word during these exchanges. But right now Linda O'Connor laid a restraining hand on his arm and reminded him of a non-existent meeting with Dr. Ezekiel Silverstein that they had to rush off to. They carried their coffee mugs over to a sink, swished them out, dried them and stored them back in the cupboard. Then Linda escorted the furious Henry out the door of the faculty lounge.

Back in Linda's office, Henry declined another cup of coffee, but accepted an invitation to sit and chat. "So now you see the malaise that Charley Lee and George Harper are hoping to cure."

"Surely the entire faculty is not like those people we just escaped from?"

"They are not. Many of our colleagues are like me actually," replied Linda. "They love their discipline, enjoy their teaching and are devoted to their families. But, unfortunately, they are not ready to do much beyond what they see as their basic job description, and they are certainly not prepared to get their noses bloodied by standing up to people like Felicity Barth-Drill and Malcolm Victor."

"Will anybody be going on this goddam demonstration at the air force base?"

"You bet. When I said that many of them are like me, I did not mean to imply that they all were. Many of them share her hatred of the military, many of them are ultra-socialists or even Marxists like poor old Leonard, and absolutely, many of them would jump into the arms of the union if it meant decreasing their work load or getting spiffy new furniture in the lounge."

"God help us."

"I don't think it's God that Charley Lee and George Harper are counting on."

XIX

The desks formerly occupied by Ms. Leduc, Ms. Reevely and Ms. Lawton remained unoccupied. The rest of the Women's Studies class was present, however. "All right, let's get to it. Does Kate mean what she says in her final speech? Does Petruchio buy into it? What do you think?"

Henry sat on top of the big desk and recognized speaker after speaker. For twenty minutes he did not need to say a word. Gradually the students came to a consensus that if the entire play was a Shakespearean trick, then Kate did not really mean that women should be the self-demeaning hand-servants for men that her words were portraying. They also agreed that Petruchio, no fool, was not being conned into believing that his spitfire of a wife had become his subservient haus-frau. It was Naomi, however, who had not spoken as yet, who reminded them that they were to have thought about a certain follow-up question to Kate's description of a woman's role. This resulted in silence until finally Ikuko Kawasaki tentatively raised her hand. Henry nodded at her.

"Could the question be, 'What if Petruchio were to give a speech about the role of men?'"

Henry beamed at her. "What do you suggest he would say?"

Ikuko started to reply but bedlam broke out. From every desk came input that men should treasure the women they were blessed with, that men did not have to endure nine months of pregnancy, the pain of childbirth, the cooking and cleaning that women were saddled with, that men should get over their bad tempers, their sulky moods, that men should realize how honoured they were to even have a woman. That men should take more baths and showers.

"And let us not forget PMS and periods every damn month!" added Suzanne.

After the laughter had died down, Henry eased himself off the desk and slowly looked around the horseshoe of faces. "So, yes, I do endorse what Kate says. But only with the understanding that I also fully endorse the unspoken speech by her husband. Now what I'd like you to do is to crank up your laptops and in the twenty-five minutes that we have left write a maximum of one page in which you compose this unspoken speech. Use prose, please, not iambic pentameter. I just want to get an idea of your writing skills and styles."

At the end of the class a half dozen young women converged at the desk at the front. When Henry asked how he could help them, they explained that they were a bit confused, not by the play but by him.

"We can't figure you out. You sounded like a chauvinist at first, and now you're coming across as a feminist. Which are you?"

Henry smiled at them. "First of all, I thank you for being so open and asking me about this directly. But the answer is a tad nuanced. Why don't we wander over to the cafeteria and get a coffee. I'm buying."

As they sipped their coffees and nibbled doughnuts, he began to address their question. He explained that he loved being a man, that he revelled in the qualities of maleness. But, he added, he was, and always had been, surrounded by women whose strengths brooked no untoward infringement of their femininity by a mere male. The girls chuckled and he went on. "I cannot abide a man, or a woman for that matter, who is a bully. But on the other hand, I have absolutely no time for weaklings who wallow in their sense of victimhood. And I fear that much of the good to be found in feminism has been hijacked by loonies who see themselves only as victims of a malevolent male patriarchy and fight back by spelling the word 'history' as 'herstory' ignoring the French origins of the actual word. And I see a parallel situation with some men who bemoan the fact that they are not as rich as the famous one-percent and crawl into the nonsensical morass of Marxism and the equalization of wealth regardless of effort or ability."

Henry was interrupted by Ikuko Kawasaki, "Oh look. There are the skipping threesome." The three Mses – Leduc, Lawton and Reevely – had just come into the cafeteria. "I'm going to ask them to join us," and she pushed away from the table.

She was not gone long. When she sat down her face was flushed.

"Well?" asked Suzanne. "What did they say?"

"They called us traitors for being here with Professor Miller."

"And?" asked Henry.

"They said the only time they wanted to be with you was in a courtroom."

"Oh, Lord," said Henry. "This is like the first scene of *Macbeth*." He smiled at his students, "Look it up. I'll see you next day." And he went off in search of Ezekiel Silverstein.

• • •

The semester seemed to fly by. Henry continued to immerse his classes in Shakespearean classics. But he never forgot his words to Paulo the custodian, that the teaching of The Bard required not only passion, but large dollops of merriment. He pushed the engineers hard, yet got a clear impression that they were keeping afloat with their reading. And they seemed to be absorbing the essentials of the plays. They loved Falstaff in *Henry IV, Part 1*, to such an extent that the consensus of the two classes was to blast ahead and do '*Part 2*' as well. "Let's see what the fat old bugger gets up to next," was the way the much tattooed Matt expressed his feelings on the subject.

And Henry had instituted a remedial writing workshop on Wednesday mornings. Because of their jam-packed course loads he met with those interested at seven o'clock in the morning. To his surprise two dozen students showed up for the first tutorial and the number never really dipped below that mark.

What really amazed Henry, however, was the reaction to his suggestion that he would show Kenneth Branagh's film version of *Henry V* at ten o'clock on the second Sunday of October. He assured the engineers that attendance was entirely voluntary, attendance would not be taken, there would be no test. Some seventy of his students appeared, many looking as if they'd been ridden hard and put away wet the night before. Some brought popcorn. Henry suspected that more than a few had smuggled in beer. The film received a standing ovation and as the students filed out Henry noticed that George Harper and Charley Lee were also present in the back row and beaming. When the classes met again the next day the engineers insisted on analysing the influences of Prince Hal's father, Henry IV, the honour- driven warrior Hotspur, and Hal's fat mentor Falstaff on the young, and soon-to-be, King Henry V.

At times such as these Henry could forget about the threat that was hanging over his head like a sword of Damocles. But not for long. Whenever he met with his Women's Studies class, the empty seats in the back row brought his mind back to the trial that was bound to come.

"When the hell am I going to get these charges delivered to me?" he fumed one night as he and Nora were packing clothes for the family's week-long sojourn at the Harpers' house.

"How many shirts do you want me to pack for you?" asked Nora.

"Nora, are you listening to me at all?"

"Every utterance of yours is deathless prose in my ears, O Socratic One. But right now my priority is to prepare this house so that those goddam engineers can come in here and destroy it. My concern for the destruction of you in the Arena of the Emotionally Distraught will have to wait its turn."

"All right, all right. How many days do we have left before we have to be out of here?"

"They're coming in on Monday, but Miriam wants us to move into her house on Saturday so that there won't be a big rush on Sunday night. So we have three nights left to get ready."

"Are you at all worried about what those kids are going to do to this house?"

"Oh, God, I surely am. My only solace is that George Harper, the Pirate hisself, will be riding the ass of everyone involved in this project. But if it works out as he assures me it will, then it's going to solve a whole slew of problems that we had been facing. Speaking of, George phoned me the other day ostensibly to make sure that I'd have this place ready for his wrecking crew. But he asked if you had heard yet from the College's Human Rights Board. I think he's getting as antsy as you are."

"I just wish it would happen. I hate this uncertainty."

"My darling," said Nora, "worrying about it will accomplish zippo. It's out of your control. So just keep doing what you're doing, enjoy your teaching and your students, and get ready for your visit this weekend with Seamus MacPherson."

She stopped talking and they looked at each other in shock. "Aw shit, why did he have to invite himself for this weekend? We'll have to cancel. We'll be swamped," said Henry.

Nora sat down on the bed. "No. Wait a second. Has he agreed to defend you in front of the Tribunal."

"Well he kind of indicated an interest in my situation. Actually, he really indicated his loathing for this kind of Human Rights Board. But he might be inclined to help me."

"So let him come this weekend. We can put him up on Friday night. He's slept in a sleeping bag on a cot before, I imagine. You two go and play golf on Saturday. I won't be needing you by then. And then I'll check with Miriam and he can join us there for Saturday night. He and George Harper have to meet. Remember George's talk on tactics and strategy? Well the time has come to put it into practice."

XX

The women in Henry's fourth-year class were enthralled by the heroine in Shakespeare's *The Merchant of Venice* but less so by Juliet. Portia's strength as opposed to the fluffiness of the fortune seeker she wanted, baffled them. The ease with which Juliet controlled the hormone-ravaged Romeo delighted them. But the complexity of Portia interested them more. They were, Henry decided, ready for one of the two greatest of all of Shakespeare's women, Rosalind in *As You Like It*. But these women students were not yet ready to leave Portia behind.

"How can Portia really be interested in Bassanio?" asked Suzanne. "Except as a boy toy, of course. But she's way out of his league. Look at what he says the very first time that he refers to her." They waited while she flipped pages in her text. "Listen. 'In Belmont is a lady richly left.' Then he says, 'And she is fair.' The guy is a total loser. The most important thing to him about Portia is her money. Then her looks. Why does she sell herself so cheaply?"

"I have no idea," said Henry. "But I've seen it in real life and you have too, probably. It's sad, but some women make terrible choices about the men they want."

"I agree that he does not merit her," said Naomi. "But on the topic of men, I believe that the most admirable man in the play is Shylock. Look at the abuse and prejudice that he has to face every day. And we can all of us identify with that. We have all faced prejudice. Even Dr. Miller has and in this very room. But Shylock perseveres and is a very successful business man. And as far as I'm concerned he is not a monster as some of the critics I've read have judged him to be. Look at what he says

149

when he finds out that his brat of a daughter, Jessica, has eloped, stolen his money and has exchanged his precious ring for a monkey." Again they waited while Naomi found the words she wanted to use. "Here it is. He says, 'It was my turquoise: I had it of Leah when I was a bachelor: I would not have given it for a wilderness of monkeys.' Compare this to that money grubber, Bassanio."

"You know," said Suzanne, "Portia and Bassanio kind of remind me of Dean Whitmarsh and that dweeb she's married to."

Henry jumped in. "Time out. No nasty comments about real people allowed." But he was smiling inwardly.

The discussion continued. Personal experiences of love affairs, of being used by a lover whether a man or a woman, sad tales of friends who had been betrayed by their emotions, all were grist for the lecture room mill on this day. Henry realized that it was the right time to abandon his prepared format and to let this theme get full exposure. Finally, as the end of the hour drew near, he interrupted.

"I want you to consider this question. Is almost all of what you have been talking about a result of a romantic view of love? Don't respond to that now, but think about it. And be ready to present your opinion next day. Remember, however, that your opinion is equal to mine; they are both worthless. What is of value is the judgement you have exercised in arriving at that opinion. And if you'll recall, I had asked you to read the first two acts of *As You Like It* for today. Well we seem to have pursued another tack, but we were not at all off course. So as well as thinking about romantic infatuations, please read the rest of the play. But, spoiler alert, really focus on Rosalind's words and apply them to the question I've left you with today. Now off you go."

• • •

As Annie and Rachel were clearing the dinner dishes that night, Elmer Knobber appeared at the door carrying a six-pack of Lucky Lager beer. Nora rushed to the door and asked the old man to come in.

"Thought I should thank you for your hand with the bales the other day with this beer. I had forgotten how much beer costs these days."

"Why, Elmer," said Henry, "bless your heart. This is right neigh-bourly of you. A six-pack of beer, Nora. If that don't just beat all."

Nora bit her lip and shooshed her daughters out of the kitchen and upstairs to their bedroom.

Elmer watched them go, accepted Henry's offer of a seat, scratched under his left arm and spoke. "I also wanted to tell you that I'm off to Florida in a day or two and would like you to keep an eye on the place."

"Sure, I'd be glad to look in on your house every once in a while, Elmer. Are you towing your trailer down or renting one down there?"

"Any idea what they charge for renting a unit down there? No, I'll pull my own. I'm not going to be robbed by those weasels."

"There will be some changes to this house when you get back, Elmer. We're gutting and renovating it next week."

"Why on earth would you do that? You'll be spending a lot of money for nothing."

"Actually we won't be spending any money, Elmer. But that's another story." He saw Elmer's eyebrows rise sharply. "I suddenly had a thought about your cattle. Who's taking care of them while you're gone?"

"Why you are, man. What do you think I just asked you? And why do you think I brought over this beer?"

"Absolutely not, Elmer. I will not be doing that. I'll keep an eye on your house and that's all."

Elmer glared at Henry, too angry to speak. "And, Elmer, I know it can be expensive, but have you got travel and health insurance for your time on the road and in Florida?"

There was no response. Elmer got to his feet, pulled his old John Deere cap onto his head, threw the kitchen door open and stormed away.

Nora came in from the hall where she'd been lurking, a huge grin on her lovely face. "It's nice to see you and our closest neighbour bonding like that, Henry. You really are a fine communicator, able to transcend generational gulfs at a single bound. Old ones, young ones, why Henry, they all love you."

"Well at least that old bugger isn't taking me to a Star Chamber. You know, Nora, no matter how hard I try to put that out of my mind, I just cannot. It eats at me all the time."

"Are you scared?"

"A bit. I've read about some of the financial awards that come out of these hearings. People have been wiped out. Ours is just a university Tribunal, so it's a lot smaller than those provincial ones, but I could be blocked from getting tenure. I could even be hoofed right out of Bowell. I may wind up tending Elmer's cows as a job."

"But Charley Lee and the Pirate said they'll have your back."

"And if they don't?"

Henry and Nora went upstairs to supervise the brushing of teeth and hair, to read the further adventures of Peter Rabbit to Rachel and the next chapter in *Harry Potter* for Annie, to give hugs and kisses to the girls and then to douse the light.

Nora started to wash the dishes that had been placed in the sink by her daughters, paused, and as she looked out the window at the remnant of sunset asked, "Do you think this may just blow over? That those girls who walked out of your class are just shit disturbers or maybe too lazy to do all the work you've been assigning?"

Henry looked up from the *National Post* he'd started to read. He was quiet for a few seconds but finally responded, "It's possible yet highly unlikely. In George's terms, the girls are the tactical weapon, but the strategy is to be found in Cynthia Kennedy. She won't let this drop. She wants me gone."

XXI

The next day, Matt approached Henry's desk. The arrogant expression that had marked his face in the first meeting of the class had disappeared. "Professor, I have an observation and a question. First of all, that movie was terrific. I had no idea that Shakespeare could be that good."

Henry smiled. "I agree. But we're not alone, Matt. Shortly after it was released, Kenneth Branagh was walking down a street in London and a cockney teenager approached and said, 'Hey, you the bloke what made *'enry the Fift*?' 'I am,' said Branagh. 'Fookin' marvellous it was,' the kid said. Anyway, what's your question?"

"You'd mentioned a blood and guts play you wanted us to read. When are we doing it?"

"Right now, Matt. Let's get to it."

Henry waited until the fifty engineers were seated, then explained that a change of pace was needed. He reminded them that Shakespeare was a businessman as well as an actor and playwright and had to be concerned about drawing full houses. He had competition from a number of fine dramatists, and he had to surpass their efforts or face the possibility of going broke. One such competitor was Christopher Marlowe, a specialist in blood and gore. So, Henry suggested, old Bill decided to out-gross Marlowe. If the penny stinkers wanted blood and guts, Shakespeare was going to give it to them.

Henry turned to the whiteboard and pulled back one of the sliding sections to reveal a few lines he had written there thirty minutes earlier. "Read this," he said.

'Come brother, take a head,
And in this hand the other will I bear.
And, Lavinia, thou shalt be employed in these things:
Bear thou my hand, sweet wench, between thy teeth.'

"What the hell is going on there?" asked Adnan.

"Well these lines are from Act III of *Titus Andronicus*. Right smack in the middle of the play. Titus speaks them to his brother and daughter. The two heads referred to used to adorn the necks of two of Titus's sons. Titus himself has cut off his own hand in an unsuccessful attempt to save his hostage sons. His daughter has been gang raped, and had her tongue cut out and her hands cut off so that she cannot identify her attackers. Now read it again."

This time the room was filled with a mixture of gagging sounds and laughter. Deborah looked at Henry, "Dr. Miller this is truly disgusting."

"I agree."

Eric chimed in, "I think it's funny as hell."

"I agree. The question becomes, 'How can it be both?' Now I'm going to give you a handout with a longer passage. It's from near the end of the play. Titus has captured the two rapists who are the evil queen's sons, and is about to prepare a special dish for this same queen for dinner. Read Titus's words; try not to laugh."

'Hark, wretches, how I mean to martyr you.
This one hand yet is left to cut your throats,
Whiles that Lavinia 'tween her stumps doth hold
The basin that receives your guilty blood.
You know your mother means to feast with me,
And calls herself Revenge, and thinks me mad.
Hark, villains, I will grind your bones to dust,
And with your blood and it I'll make a paste,
And of the paste a coffin I will rear,
And make two pasties of your shameful heads,
And bid that strumpet, your unhallowed dam,
Like to the earth swallow her own increase.
This is the feast that I have bid her to,
And this the banquet she shall surfeit on;

154

And now prepare your throats - Lavinia, come,
Receive the blood; and when that they are dead,
Let me go grind their bones to powder small,
And with this hateful liquor temper it,
And in that paste let their vile heads be baked.
Come, come, be everyone officious
To make this banquet. (He cuts their throats.)'

Henry watched Deborah for her reaction. He saw her read the passage twice, shake her head and then she looked up at him. She gave him a huge smile and winked at him. Henry smiled back.

For the remainder of the class they talked about how one could reconcile horror and comedy, the role of slasher films in the cinema, and Henry guided them back to his basic thesis for the course: the tension in Shakespeare between appearance and reality. At the end of the period, Henry told them that he was cancelling the Friday class because a host of their first year colleagues were going to descend on his home and gut it and he had to prepare for the onslaught. "All in the name of knowledge, of course," he assured them with a grin. He told them to read the entire play for Monday and that there would be a test. He had never heard a class leave a room so much wrapped in discussion of what had just been presented. "Goddam Shakespeare," he murmured to himself.

As he turned to wipe the first passage off the white board he saw a figure pushed back to the door frame by the throng of exiting students. She had placed a hand at her throat defensively as if she were in peril. The engineers paid her no attention and after they had all gone she looked at their departing backs with a bewildered expression on her face.

"Dean Whitmarsh," Henry called, "come in, come in."

The Dean walked down the stairs between the three rows of desks, found herself in the central arena, and looked about her quizzically.

"Welcome to my domain, Jean. I'm delighted to see you here."

"Actually, this is my first visit here, Dr. Miller. I'm afraid I don't get down to this level often."

Henry smiled and looked at her, but said nothing.

"That group of students was certainly excited," she observed. "They were one of your Engineering classes?"

"They were indeed."

"What were you teaching them to have them so involved?"

"Shakespeare."

She looked at Henry with astonishment. "Incredible," she said in a voice so soft that he could almost not hear her.

"Henry, a package for you was delivered to my office this morning by special courier."

"Dean, you probably know what the contents are without my opening it."

"I have absolutely no idea."

"Oh, come now, Dean. The role of ingénue really doesn't become you."

She opened her mouth as if to speak, but there were no words. Henry did notice a flush that began at her throat and rose into her cheeks. Finally she said, "It awaits you upstairs," turned and walked briskly from the room.

When he got home that afternoon he stayed in his truck staring at a few of Elmer's heifers in the next field. Annie had started to run out to greet him, but Nora's voice from the house called her back. Finally he rolled up the window of the cab, got out, slammed the door and started for the kitchen door.

Nora held it for him and handed him an opened beer. "It's started?"

He nodded and handed her the papers he'd retrieved from Dean Whitmarsh's office. She placed them on the table, took the beer out of his hand and placed it, too, on the table, and then wrapped her arms around him for a long time.

Finally she pulled back and looked up at him. "Well, the timing is good. Seamus will be here in two days, and then we all move into the Harpers' house. So, except for Charley Lee, the war cabinet will be all in one place. And we'll be able to plan."

"Yep," said Henry, and kissed her lightly on the lips. "Now give me back my beer."

• • •

In the morning as he waited for his women's class to take their desks, Henry stood in the pit his back leaning against the long desk. The seats filled finally and silence held the room but he continued to stare at the floor of the arena. After a few minutes, Ikuko Kawasaki spoke hesitantly, "Dr. Miller?"

Henry looked up and seemed almost surprised to see forty-seven pairs of eyes staring intently at him. "Sorry," he said. "I'm afraid I'm a bit preoccupied today." He spoke no further but returned their gaze silently for another few minutes. Finally, he said, "All right. I've decided to let you know what is going on. Yesterday I was served with papers from the College's Human Rights Board. I have been charged with racist and sexist comments made in this classroom earlier in this semester. The complaints have been brought by Ms. Pamela Leduc, Ms. Sandra Reevely and Ms. Judith Lawton. They have allegedly suffered shame, embarrassment and emotional stress as a result of my comments. Their case will be brought forward by the Human Rights Board of this college which will assume responsibility for providing legal representation for them at the hearing in front of the Human Rights Tribunal. The responsibility for my defence rests entirely on my shoulders. The consequences for me could potentially be severe."

Again there was a dead stillness in the room. It was suddenly broken, "Oh, for Christ's sake!"

Henry looked for the source and saw that the oath came from a student who had not spoken in class before. He quickly turned and scanned his seating plan to be sure of her name. She was Shauna Herold. He turned to look at her, an eyebrow raised. "Shauna, we haven't heard from you before."

The girl stood up. "This really pisses me off, Professor Miller. And I hope that my language doesn't offend you. But if they had a problem this is a really candy-ass way of dealing with it. I haven't agreed with everything you've said. But the last time I checked you never did ask me to buy your entire shtick. And this kind of crap does more damage to women's rights than some perceived male oinkings." She sat down and then bounced back up again. "And I am not accusing you of being a chauvinist. Far from it." She resumed her seat.

Once more the room was quiet until at last Naomi stood up. "I think I agree with Shauna. Everything she said, actually. And what I'm going to say might be a bit of a stretch, but when Shauna said that this was a cowardly and ineffective way to deal with a problem, she got me thinking. And I found myself thinking about Rosalind in *As You Like It*. Professor Miller, you had asked us to focus on Rosalind's words. I did. This is a woman who would never have gone to a human rights court to resolve her problems. She was much bigger, stronger and smarter than that."

Henry smiled at her, hiked himself up to his usual sitting position on the desk, and said, "Please do continue, Naomi."

And so she did. Naomi outlined how Rosalind had been cruelly used by her uncle, the usurper of her father's realm and how this man, jealous of her father's increasing number of followers in the forest of Arden, had banned Rosalind from court on pain of death. Naomi explained how Rosalind had not complained, but had acted, 'liberating' some jewels so that she would have funds, had put on a man's clothing so that she would not be as susceptible to attack from bad guys in the woods, had departed under the cover of darkness and had quickly found herself lodging and provisions. "This was a woman," said Naomi, "who got up in the mornings and got things done and made things happen. She was not much into tears and being a victim."

"True enough," said Henry. "Somebody talk to us about the love interest."

Hands flew into the air and a dozen women dissected Orlando. Like Rosalind, he too was misused by fate and took action against his lot. "He was one hell of a wrestler," allowed Shauna, who suggested he was also very brave considering what his wrestling opponent had just done to his first two victims.

"I am confused but quite attracted by the fact that he fell in love with Rosalind so quickly," said Ikuko. "And when he falls in love he really goes the distance. I love those horrible poems that he wrote for her and left all over the forest. I wish someone would write poems about me," she added wistfully.

"It went both ways, didn't it," added Suzanne. She went on to review how Rosalind had also been smitten at the scene of the wrestling match. But the line that had struck Suzanne was Rosalind's explanation that her sadness was not just for her exiled father. She looked in her text and read, "'No, some of it is for my child's father.' This makes me think that she's a girl who is ready for some action."

The class laughed and Henry joined them. When they were quiet, he asked, "How bright is she?"

Again the hands flew and quotes were read supporting the fact that Rosalind was highly intelligent, a very fast thinker, and possessed of a 'killer sense of humour', allowed Shauna.

"Prove it," said Henry.

"Okay, give me a second to find it." She started to flip rapidly through the pages of the play. After a few minutes, she shouted, "Here it is. It's in Act IV, scene 1. She's talking to Jaques who reminds me of a boyfriend I once had who thought it would turn me on if he was bummed out all the time and had a death-wish. Listen to this:

Jaques. I prithee, pretty youth, let me be better acquainted with thee.

Ros. They say you are a melancholy fellow.

Jaques. I am so. I do love it better than laughing.

Ros. Those that are in extremity of either are abominable fellows, and betray themselves to every modern censure, worse than drunkards.

Jaques. Why 'tis good to be sad and say nothing.

Ros. Why then, 'tis good to be a post.

"She hammers him and he doesn't even know it," concluded Shauna.

Henry looked at her admiringly, "Bingo! Bingo! Bingo! But tell us, Shauna, what happened to your melancholic boyfriend."

"I dumped him and found a guy who could make me laugh."

"Let's go back to Rosalind's boyfriend. Is he worthy of her?"

"No way," said Ikuko. "But look what she does with him. She educates him. And you know what the best line is? And it really resembles what Shauna just quoted about Jaques. Orlando has just told Rosalind, who is in disguise, that if he can't have her then he will die. And that is just so like a man. And she tells him, 'Men have died from time to time and worms have eaten them, but not for love.' That is just great! So many men simply refuse to grow up. Well, she's not going to accept an immature lover and she's going to teach him to grow up. I love this woman!"

Henry jumped down to the floor, crossed his arms over his chest and gazed at his class. "I am so proud of you women," he said. "And grateful, too. When I got here today I was so low I could have walked under a snake. And right now, thanks to you and the way you have seized on this play, I feel great. So to show my appreciation, I'm going to tell you a personal story about love at first sight and I think it was Suzanne and Ikuko who had referred to it earlier. Years ago I was at a party and saw a girl named Nora. I'd never seen her before. I got pretty tipsy, and I asked her to marry me. She laughed and turned me down flat." His students leaned forward. "I kept asking her and she kept refusing to even consider the idea."

"And?" asked Naomi.

"A friend told me about the fact that King George the Sixth had to ask Elizabeth – who became the Queen Mother – several times before she accepted. So 'once more into the breach' and all that and I asked Nora an eighth time."

"And?" asked Naomi again.

"We have two daughters." The women laughed. "My point is that Shakespeare doesn't write in a vacuum. He writes truth. What he says in this play about men is hard, but it is true. And women can look to Rosalind as a model. Reality and appearance, our old friends, are there of course, because Rosalind is dressed as a man. But great truths are there as well. Now sadly, I have to talk to you about the mid-semester assignment. I think you'll like it and will do fine work. Here it is: Write a maximum of 2000 words in which you assess how one of the major female characters we've discussed conforms or not to the current state of feminism."

"Well, what is the current state of feminism?" asked Suzanne.

"I have absolutely no idea myself," replied Henry. "But surely you all do. You're enrolled in the fourth year of a Women's Studies program. You figure it out. And remember that your opinion is equal to mine in that it's worthless. What I'll be evaluating you on is the quality of the reasoning and judgement you've brought to bear in arriving at your opinion."

A male voice from the back of the room boomed out, "Channel your inner Rosalinds, young women scholars. Educate this poor unlettered man."

All eyes swivelled to the back of the class and there in the seat formerly occupied by the absent Ms. Reevely sat an old man grinning wildly.

"People," said Henry, smiling but shaking his head bemusedly, "may I introduce Professor Ezekiel Silverstein of the Department of History. Zeke, how long have you been sitting there?"

"Long enough, dear boy, to have formed an opinion of the intellectual tenor of this class of academics. And it is of the highest order indeed. I wonder if I might possibly persuade them to enrol in my History classes. The Lord above knows they would bring a welcome infusion of thoughtfulness and analytical thinking to those sorry sessions."

"Oh, I like him," smiled Shauna. "But," she went on, "I have a question for you, Dr. Miller. My boyfriend is in one of your other classes and he was telling me about *Titus Andronicus*. It's the most disgusting thing I've ever heard. But it made me laugh. Are we going to get that play?"

"No. Absolutely not. I put that drama on specifically for the engineers, not for women."

"But there are women in his class. And right now you're being sexist. And that's what got you into your current problems."

"Aha, she's certainly got you there, my dear boy. Well played, young lady. What is your name? And may I join you, Dr. Miller, in your pit?"

"Shauna" and "Yes" answered him at the same time.

"Dr. Silverstein, why are you here?" asked Henry.

"I wanted to see with my own eyes what a racist and sexist moulder of young minds looks like. I do trust that these young scholars have been apprised of your plight, Dr. Miller?"

"Yes, we have, sir," said Ikuko. "And we think it's terrible."

"It certainly is, my dear young lady. But may I remind you that all that is required for evil to prevail is for good women and men to do nothing." Zeke looked about the tiers of desks and smiled. "Now I'm sure that you treasure each wisdom-packed second that you are blessed to spend with my young friend here, but on this glorious autumnal day I feel that you should be outside being seduced by nature. Henry, is there any way that I can prevail upon you to release these brilliant young women from their servitude so that you and I can seek refreshment in the arms of a welcoming pub and devise strategies to rescue your floundering career?"

Henry laughed and waved the class away, but before they left, Suzanne smiled at Zeke and said, "Can you come back again?"

"You evil young girl, tempting an old man. Leave at once."

And they did, streaming rivers of laughter.

As soon as they took their seat in the Bistro, Olive was at their side. "If you will, Olive, a bottle of that cooking plonk you keep in the back room for me. And Henry and I shall help ourselves to the tapas. There'll be no 'Writer's Tears' today, I'm afraid, my dear. Our wits must be razor sharp and our antennae tuned for trouble."

Olive laughed and went for the wine. Zeke turned to Henry, "I have been chatting with George Harper, Charley Lee and your lovely wife, who by the way, is much too fine a woman for the likes of you. But of course, as you are studying Shakespeare's women, you'll be well aware that such an inequality is standard in human matrimonial arrangements. Your lawyer friend is arriving tomorrow, Nora tells me. And you two are ruining a good walk on the golf course, as Sam Clemens would say, on Saturday. That's good. You can fill him in on the background and the players. Be thorough and brief him fully. He must know about why you were hired, and the reaction to that hiring from Dean Jean and the beautiful Dr. Kennedy. He must know about what you said precisely that day in class that led to the dramatic exodus of the three harridans. And he must be informed about the context of your words and the reactions of the women students who remained."

He paused while Olive uncorked the bottle, poured two glasses of the wine, and set the bottle on the table. He smiled at her and then went on." You may want to make specific notes as you cast your mind back to those events. Your friend Seamus must be absolutely clear on the facts before he even begins to organize our defence."

"You said, 'Our defence'".

"I did. Never lose sight, dear boy, of the fact that you will be the star player, but the future of this school depends on the outcome. And the defence is a team endeavour. Now let's get some of those splendid tapas before we continue."

As they ate, Zeke gave Henry instructions. After Seamus and Henry had played golf they were to meet at the Harpers' house where they would be lodged. Charley Lee would be joining them for dinner and the logistics of finances would be explored and resolved. Seamus would reveal his initial plans for the presentation of his defence, witnesses he wished to cross-examine and those he wished to call himself. Charley Lee had stressed that the theme of the defence be made clear during this dinner planning session.

"And when your courage begins to flag, my dear Henry, remember that the opponents want a cessation of such instruction as you are presenting to your classes, the dear old, dead white Bard, and his replacement with such trite lightweight works as *The Color Purple*, whose author by the way advocates the elimination of Israel from its current habitude in the Middle East. Henry, we cannot allow our young people to be so misled. So, again, I urge you: Be strong."

XXII

Nora and Henry awoke the next morning to the sound of a large vehicle backing down their driveway, its reverse beeper blasting irritatingly in order to warn any wayward pedestrians of its slow progress.

Annie burst into their room, "Mommy, daddy, there's a big truck outside and it has three little houses on it."

The little houses were 'Porta-Potties', mobile outhouses for the use of the construction crews about to descend on their house. "Where do you want these units placed?" the driver wanted to know.

Henry remembered that Elmer Knobber was on his way to Florida and had them placed on the west side of Elmer's barn, leaving a satisfactory buffer zone between them and his home. His load deposited, the driver announced that he would return for pick-up in ten days time, bade Henry a good morning and pulled away.

They were just enjoying their second coffees when two even larger and noisier vehicles arrived, each carrying an enormous steel bulk-lift rubbish and waste bin. Again the question, "Where do you want these units dropped?" was posed, options discussed, advice sought and finally one was deposited parallel to the house on the lawn on the west side, the other similarly located on the east side.

As the trucks exited the driveway, Walter Ruttan drove down it and parked out by the woodpile. "George Harper here yet, Henry?" he called. "I told him I'd arrange for him to meet the electrician and plumber here about this time. Say, Nora, do you have any more of that coffee? It sure smells good."

They sat around the kitchen table and Nora asked, "Walter, how did you get involved in this operation?"

"Oh, I guess Henry, here, told George that I was kind of a fixer and arranger, and so George gave me a call, explained what he was doing and told me to get the best plumber and electrician I knew to get in here after the place is gutted, drill the holes, run the wires and plastic piping and then get the hell out of the way so that the insulation, vapour barrier and drywall can all be installed. And I've also got your building permit and arranged for the municipal inspector to swing by this afternoon and then again next week. That George Harper is not a fella to mess with, is he?"

He held his mug out for a refill. "And I almost forgot. He also wants a site for a ditch to be dug for the students to pee into. Doesn't want it near the house. Said that soldiers never foul where they're camped. Must've been in the army, I guess. So where should they dig it?"

Henry directed him to the south side of Elmer's barn, and when Walter returned from reconnoitering the site he was met by George Harper and two men who turned out to be the electrician and plumber. "The kids will be able to do most of this stuff, Nora, but the wiring and plumbing has to be done to code and by fully qualified people. Now take me inside and let's see how we're going to preserve your window trim that you've been working so hard on."

• • •

Seamus MacPherson was late in arriving that evening. "I always forget what a horror show it is to get out of Toronto on a Friday afternoon. Highway 401 was bumper-to-bumper almost to Port Hope."

Nora gave him a hug, "You're here now, Seamus, and we are so glad to see you. Give the man a drink, Henry, and I'll start the dinner. The girls are already in bed, Seamus, but they can hardly wait to see you in the morning."

With healthy tots of 'Writer's Tears' in hand, Henry gave his oldest friend a tour of the house that was about to be gutted. Seamus marvelled at the height of the ceilings, the size of the windows, and the sweep of the central staircase. Henry explained to him the use of the plaster and lath work and how the technique was centuries old. Seamus shook his head in amazement.

"Do you have any idea what a house like this would fetch in the real estate market in Toronto? You guys have made a great decision to keep the essence of it and replace the worn-out stuff."

Nora called them downstairs for dinner. As they ate, Seamus questioned them about the demolition project and the players involved. "It seems to me," he said finally, "that you have to perform extreme surgery on this building in order to save it."

"That about sums it up, Seamus," chuckled Nora, "and it's the same thinking that these four musketeers are bringing to bear on old 'Colon U', dear old Sir MacKenzie Bowell College."

"OK, let's get at it," said Seamus. "Who are the other musketeers? What triggered this mess? Who do you think is pulling the strings? And on both sides, I might add. What's to be gained? What's to be lost? We've got all night, so I want to know everything. And do you have more of that damn fine Irish whiskey?"

Seamus MacPherson kept peppering Henry with questions and early on had begun to take notes on a large yellow pad of legal stationery. He was still probing when at two o'clock in the morning Henry had to declare himself incapable of further cogent thought and retired to join the long-asleep Nora. Seamus remained at the table, reading his notes and occasionally sipping from his glass and gazing reflectively into the candles that had by now almost burned out.

The grilling continued the next day. On the fourth hole when Henry had hit a fairway shot far over the green into a water hazard, Seamus had putted in from forty feet. But rather than gloating, he had asked, "Why is this Dean Jean married to the wimpy Marxist?" And so it went for the entire round. Seamus played well, usually scrambling to score a bogie, while Henry performed his usual mixture of shots, one out of three being adequate, the other two being insults to the beautiful game of golf. Seamus's attention, however, was not focused on the course. Again and again he put questions to Henry that seemed to be irrelevant or trivial.

"Tell me how you became acquainted with this Paolo guy? How did Tony know that Cynthia Kennedy had never been on that basement level?"

Seamus seemed insatiable; the inquisition lasted the full eighteen holes and into the nineteenth where they were enjoying a restorative draft of Sleeman's Red. At last Henry had had enough. "Goddam it, Seamus!" he laughed. "Enough. Enough already. This isn't a complex case. It ain't rocket science. Why do you need all this peripheral information? What the hell do Paolo and Tony have to do with anything? They're our custodians, for heaven's sake."

Over the brim of his beer glass Seamus looked at his friend of almost thirty years and smiled. "You don't know and you don't need to know. But I do. And that's why I'm the big gun lawyer and richer than God and you are a humble and semi-destitute toiler in the vineyard of academe. Now let's saddle up, D'Artagnan, and go and meet the other three musketeers."

When they arrived at the Harpers' home, Miriam and Nora had already fed Annie and Rachel and the two girls were now happily feeding the ducks at the pond in back of the house. Introductions were made, and the seven adults gathered in the living room. Charley Lee began. "As you know, Mr. MacPherson, this is an arranged situation. We had not planned on it coming to pass so soon, but when Dr. Miller was hired and we did our due diligence on him, we realized that the time had come to act."

"I do understand that, and please call me Seamus. I think for our purposes tonight it would be most efficient to use first names, Charley."

"I agree. Are you also aware of what it is we hope to achieve in this situation?"

And so the issue was joined. The discussion lasted beyond cocktail hour, to the dinner table and continued over postprandial port and brandy. It was George Harper, finally, who decided that a summation was required. He spoke of a reluctance within the university to acknowledge the past in Western culture and his desire to ensure that the next generation was educated about the basis of the culture in which they lived; he summarized the tyrannical effect of political correctness run amok in the university community; he emphasized the lack of openness and freedom of expression that was stifling the debate of ideas that should have been the lifeblood of a college of scholars; he referred to the hatred of Israel and the loathing of men that had permeated some quarters of the university; and finally he referred to the growing lack of dedication among the professors to the teaching of their undergraduate students.

"You seem very concerned about openness and freedom of expression, George," observed Seamus. "Tell me, do you envision the teaching of Marxism in your new reformed college?"

"I do," George replied. "And I would hope that it would be a course offered in the first year and taught by someone like Leonard Twilley."

"Ah, yes, Dean Jean's hubby."

"Exactly. And I would hope, then, that a subsequent course in market economics would be taught to these kids as they mature by someone like Zeke, here. I would hope that they would be given an accurate picture of capitalism and not through the prism of ultra-socialists. But, to your question: all topics must be open for examination and debate."

"And 'Women's Studies', George?" asked Henry.

"Same answer. But the topics raised must be subjected to the same analysis and debate as all others. No longer should it be acceptable to simply portray all men as anti-woman."

Charley Lee spoke up. "It is getting late and we must draw our discussion to a close. But first I would like you, Seamus, to outline your proposed defence of this professor sitting at my right. And secondly, I have of course done due diligence on you as well, and know that your billable hourly rate is quite enormous. What are you going to cost us?"

Laughter followed these words, but all eyes became fixed on the lawyer. Seamus swirled the small puddle of cognac in the bottom of his snifter examining it as if to ensure that no fly was doing a backstroke in the amber fluid. He took a sip and placed the glass on the table. "As for the racism charge, we'll be defending the use of empirical historical facts. Japan was a militaristic and imperialistic power and culture in the front half of the twentieth century. To say otherwise is to lie or to reveal abject historical ignorance. As for the sexism charge, we are going to turn the attack against Henry into an attack against William Shakespeare, himself."

"Can we win?" asked Nora.

"These Tribunals are notorious in the legal community. Trying to predict their judgements is a mug's game. But it is worth the effort. And I'm taking this case not solely because Henry is my old friend, but because there is an issue here that is worth fighting for. And it's also a hell of a lot more interesting than defending him for building an illegal septic system."

Charley Lee smiled, then asked, "And your fee?"

Seamus looked directly at Charley, "I am certainly not a material-ist, Charley. But I don't come cheap, either. However, I really think this case is a chip shot. So if by chance we should lose, no fee. If we win, you establish a program in which the history, literature and philosophy of western culture is taught. You endow a chair in this program. And if I may, I suggest it be called *'The Ezekiel Silverstein Chair in Fundamental Western Cultural Thinking'*."

Zeke gasped, looked wildly at Seamus and finally blurted, "You can-not make such a suggestion. I'm flattered, of course, but my dear boy, you know nothing of me. I, I, - - -." And here Ezekiel Silverstein seemed to have run out of words. His mouth was open and his lips moved, but no sounds came forth.

Henry laughed. "Zeke, I've never seen you struck dumb before. It's rather becoming."

Seamus joined in the laughter before he replied. "Zeke, you should know that Charley Lee is not the only one at this table who has done his due diligence. When this Human Rights issue first appeared on the horizon, thanks to a heads-up phone call from Nora some time ago, I put my own operative to work on this school, George Harper, Charley Lee and your own good self. And while you men are not quite an open book to me I have learned many interesting facts about you all. I'm now aware of 'the Pirate's' military record and combat experience and his frustration with the direction in which this school is going. I know something of Charley Lee's business interests, but they are character-ized by a certain opacity, I must admit. But I do know that he shares

George's frustration and desire for change at Bowell." He paused and looked closely at Zeke.

"And you, Ezekiel, I found very interesting. A towering intellect, a brilliant analyst of historical patterns, and the victim of flagrant, academic anti-Semitism. Therefore, I most strongly disagree with your objections to my proposed 'Silverstein Chair'. In fact, I see you as the poster boy for what Charley and George are endeavouring to achieve."

Charley Lee spoke, "You might choose to remember your namesake, too, Zeke. He was disgusted with his Jerusalem in which false gods were being worshipped in the temple. Ezekiel preached the destruction of the city and its rebirth dedicated to the worship of the one true God. I see some parallels here."

Zeke was sitting between Muriel and Nora. He tried to speak but failed. Each of the women placed a comforting hand on his wrists. At last he said, "Please, let us move on. The issue here is the crisis facing Henry Miller. Let us focus our energies there."

The next morning dawned with a chill wind and heavy rain battering the windows of the Harpers' home. The kitchen, however, was a bright if very busy spot, as George Harper cooked breakfast for his wife and their seven guests. He fed Annie and Rachel first as the adults eased into the morning with a choice of apple or orange juice and strong coffee.

"This French toast is better than what you make, Mommy," announced Rachel.

After the girls were finished the adults sat and tied into the same French toast and bacon. "Damn it, she's right," said Nora. "What's the variable here, George?"

"I use challah. You know, the Jewish egg bread. It's great by itself, but it's especially good done this way. What's on the agenda for you all today? I know I have to go into my office to fine tune the house-wrecking mission. But what about you others?"

"I'm afraid I have to go back to Toronto right after this lovely repast," said Seamus. "But it has been fun."

"When will we see you next, Seamus?" asked Nora. "When is the axe going to drop?"

"It's going to be soon. This Tribunal moves quickly. I expect it to be 'show time' within the month. But don't let the miserable weather outside depress you; I feel pretty optimistic."

Henry and Zeke joined George as he headed back to Bowell, Zeke to retire to his home quarters and Henry to work on the course structures for what remained of the semester. "Drive down in your truck, Henry, and we'll use it and my car to carry a whack of supplies up to your house for tomorrow. I've got two cases of safety glasses, a case of face masks, a case of baseball caps, and a raft of hammers and shovels and so on. I can't manage with just my vehicle. Meet me in my office at 3:00 o'clock and we'll load it all up," George said to Henry as they left for their respective buildings.

XXIII

Henry leaned back against the long desk and glared at his engineers. "I told you that I was going to give you a test today, and I certainly am. But first, I want to know who spilled the beans about *Titus Andronicus* to my Women's Studies class. Come on. 'Fess up."

A sheepishly smiling Adnan haltingly put up his hand. "It may have been me, sir. In an unguarded moment."

"'It may have been me, sir,'" sneered Henry. "Be bold, Adnan. Tell the truth with ringing conviction. Enough of these skim milk utterances, as Hotspur would say."

"'Twas I, Dr. Miller." Adnan started to laugh. "I confess all and throw myself at your feet and plead for mercy."

"Are you the rogue who has introduced laughter into the glum life of Ms. Shauna Herold?"

"Me again."

"Do you realize what you have done, Adnan Gupta? I was teaching a class of ladies who would not have looked out of place as novitiates in a convent, and because of you they are now howling for the horrors of Shakespeare's most disgusting play."

Stephanie broke in. "You're calling that crew a bunch of nuns?" her voice rising in incredulity.

Henry merely cocked an eyebrow at her and turned back to Adnan. "Well?"

"Sir, let me explain. You have no idea how few debutantes fight to break into my social calendar." This admission was met with some ribald chuckles. "So I found myself in the pub – and being a devout Muslim,

I don't drink alcohol...really... and got talking to Shauna and started telling her about the bloody stumps, the baking heads and all that and she started to laugh. Really hard. I figured I was on a roll, making her laugh and actually discussing Shakespeare in the student pub. So don't blow my cover, Dr. Miller, don't let her know what a loser I am."

"In actual fact, Adnan, I am in your debt. You've done me a huge service and made my job a great deal easier. I'm teaching Shakespeare and a lot of people are most upset about that. But now, not only are my students talking about him in the pub, but they're asking for more plays. So I owe you. And, Adnan, you are not a loser. You are very much the opposite."

"I have a question," announced Matt. "Are we going to have any more of those Sunday screenings? That last one was very much cool."

"I have a request." It was Adnan again. "I am the world's biggest fan of Al Pacino. He did Shylock in *The Merchant of Venice* on Broadway a while back. Could we get it?"

"And while we seem to be in a frenzy of request-making," said Deborah, "I feel that it is really sexist of you to deny us these plays you're doing with your nuns that deal with strong women. Why can't we do the same plays? And for that matter, why can't they get to see Falstaff and Prince Hal and Toby Belch? Surely," she added with a big smile, "you didn't design these courses with our genders in mind?"

Henry leaned back against the desk and did not answer. He was deep in thought and the silence developed into several minutes.

Finally, it was broken by Eric. "You've got a lot on your plate right now, Dr. Miller. Make it easy on yourself. Just make the courses the same. That seems to be where the consensus is headed."

Henry looked at his class. "I'll give you my decision on Wednesday. But right now open those laptops; you've got some writing to do."

• • •

Late that afternoon as he stood in the Harpers' kitchen trying to pat Nora's bottom without being observed by Miriam, Henry asked, "Do you think I'm sexist?"

Nora brushed his hand away and looked him directly in the eye. "Yes, I do. Not often, only occasionally, and usually without any trace of recognition that you're being sexist. And I believe that's the way it is for most men. Most guys are not malicious bastards to women; but most men are, more or less, sexist."

Henry's face became crestfallen and he slumped into one of the kitchen chairs. Miriam had come into the kitchen in time to catch Nora's words, and looking at Henry she said, "Don't get unduly upset about this, Henry. Nora is absolutely correct; but it stands to reason, doesn't it? For millions of years women were subjugated, often brutalized, and it is only in relatively recent times that their worth as something other than sexual relief agents for men became understood and acknowledged. And for that milestone change in human relations we all owe much gratitude to the feminist movement."

"What brought this on, Henry? Surely you haven't just recognized what you're being charged with?"

Henry told them of the perceived gender decisions he'd made in structuring his courses: How some of his women students wanted other characters than only strong females, and how one of his women engineers had pointed out that they were being denied any women characters at all with the sole exception of Kate the Shrew. He shook his head in frustration.

Miriam took over the sautéing process that had been occupying Nora and she sat beside her husband and took one of his hands in hers. "Henry, my darling, you were being unconsciously sexist. But it is a simple problem to fix. Go in front of all three classes and tell them of your error in judgement and fix it. They'll love you for it and it shouldn't be hard to fix."

"Eric, my future architectural engineer, suggested I simplify my life and make both courses the same."

"Kid's a goddamned genius," boomed the Pirate's voice as George Harper strode into the kitchen on his way to the fridge to grab a beer. "Of course, he is one of my engineers, isn't he? So it stands to reason. Just do what he suggests. Problem solved. You want a beer, Henry?"

Henry did not get a chance to respond as Miriam let out a shriek, "George Harper! Look at you! You're completely covered in plaster dust and it's going to blanket my house. Get outside," she yelled, "and don't come back in until you've peeled off those ghastly work clothes and had a shower under the hose."

"Damn fool," she muttered to Nora. "He's been working at your house all day and he dares to come in here looking like that."

• • •

Nora had been right. As Henry explained the change of course content the next day to his women's studies class he felt a sea change in the room's atmosphere. The tension that he had become used to seemed to evaporate to be replaced by a sense of something like harmony. "So you see, because of some of you being very open with me I now do see that I was being semi-blinded by gender. And I now do see that you women have the right, maybe even the need, to see some of Shakespeare's most memorable men in some of their worst and best moments. And absolutely, the engineers could benefit from an exposure to Rosalind and Cleopatra and other great, strong women."

"Dr. Miller," said Suzanne, "I think you're actually getting it."

"Are you sure you're married?" asked Shauna. "You could be my trade-up from Adnan."

The laughter that followed was interrupted by a knock on the door at the top of the shallow stairs behind the third tier of desks and Paulo the custodian hesitantly poked his head around it.

"Sorry to intrude, Professor Miller, but the Dean said to bring this to you right away." Paulo walked down the stairs and handed an envelope to Henry.

Henry tore the envelope open and read the contents. As he placed the letter back into its envelope, Naomi asked, "What date is the trial beginning?"

Henry looked at her quizzically.

"You're not good at keeping your emotions out of your face, Professor. It's much like reading a book. So don't keep us in suspense: When is it happening?"

He looked at her and chuckled. "This Saturday at 10:30 is show time."

Seamus contacted Henry that he would arrive at George and Miriam's house late on Friday night and that they should drive to the campus together the next day as he assumed parking would be at a premium. Seamus arrived after the household, except for Henry, was sound asleep. He enquired after Henry's week and was filled in on the progress in Shakespeare by the classes and the demolition and reconstruction of the old farmhouse by George's engineers.

"So great progress on both fronts. You must be very pleased, old chum."

"I am, Seamus, but I'd be a liar if I didn't say my mind was elsewhere."

"Well, Henry, we'll be in the thick of it quickly tomorrow morning – actually, it's later this morning, isn't it – and you'll find your nerves will steady down and you'll be fine. So go to bed and let's get an early start."

XXIV

The concern about parking turned out to be well-founded. The campus and streets leading to it were jammed with cars. Henry's space was a reserved spot and nobody as yet had taken it.

"What the hell is going on, Seamus?"

"This is getting a lot of attention, old buddy. You're about to become a celeb."

Henry looked at him blankly. "Have you not read the papers?" asked Seamus. The blank look continued. "Your friend, Charley Lee, he of the many unknown interests, apparently called in a few tickets and all three of the national papers are covering this case. The lefties are viewing it as an attack on progressive gender-neutral values, and the righties are hailing it as an affirmation of core conservative principles. The one in the middle is flapping its gums as usual on both sides of the situation. The tabloid paper ran a great headline, 'Bard Being Banned?' I don't know how old Charley got the lefties to spend money on covering it. The other two owe him big time for his advertising. He said he'd back you to the hilt, and when he found out I was coming pro bono I guess he decided to spend his money in other ways. Let's go in."

The case was being heard in the main lecture hall on the first floor of the Management Studies building. It seated 200 and was filled to overflowing when they arrived. As Seamus arranged his brief case and files on the defense desk he looked to his left and smiled at a woman who was similarly occupied. "Seamus," she smiled back. "I'm so pleased that we'll be involved in this case together."

"Johanna, this is my client, Dr. Henry Miller; Henry, may I introduce the eminent counsel, Ms. Johanna Ferrelle." Henry reached around Seamus and shook hands with Ms. Ferrelle. He was impressed with the strength of her grip. She was a middle-aged woman, about fifty, of average height. And she was impeccably dressed, navy blue blazer and matching slacks, cream coloured blouse and a small strand of perfect pearls adorned her neck. Her smile seemed genuine and her face showed warmth.

"Seamus," she went on, "This is going to be a very interesting case. So please don't spoil it by plunging too deeply into your bag of Bay Street tricks."

"Johanna, old friend, against you, my task seems Herculean." They both laughed and turned to the front as the entrance of the Tribunal panel was announced.

The panel arrived from behind the stage preceded by a small coterie of Tribunal personnel, one of whom instructed all present to rise before the presence of such majesty. The lead member of the group of three seemed unimpressed by this required obeisance, smiled and waved for all to be seated, waited for silence and then spoke.

"Ladies and gentlemen, good morning to you all. This case has obviously sparked interest in this community and beyond. I see some old friends from our prestigious daily papers are in attendance, note pads ready, pencils poised. I have only one word of caution: Given the nature of this case I shall tolerate no disturbances of any kind within the walls of this theatre. Those who ignore this stricture will be immediately removed.

"Let me introduce to the concerned parties and to this audience the Tribunal panel that shall be hearing the testimony presented. On my left is Mr. Jeremy Swan, a senior undergraduate student representing the Students' Council here at Bowell College. On my right is Professor Isabel George, a full Professor in our Faculty of Arts and Humanities. And I am Dr. Samantha Raymond, also a full Professor at Bowell and I hail from the School of Management or Business, if you will. I shall serve as Chairperson and Adjudicator of these proceedings and all comments, questions and observations will be made to me.

"The nature of this case is serious. A professor has been accused of racist comments and sexist course content. His chance of achieving tenure could well be decided by this case. The situation also brings to focus the issues of freedom of thought, freedom of debate, and freedom from abuse. The complaints were initially taken to the college's Committee of Rights and Grievances, were considered to be grave, and consequently were forwarded to this College's Tribunal of Rights and Grievances. The panel was selected and now sits before you. The legal counsel for the complainants is Ms. Johanna Ferrelle. The legal counsel for the defendant, Dr. Henry Miller, is Mr. Seamus MacPherson. For efficiency's sake, please address me simply as 'Madam'.

Again she smiled benignly at the audience. "Let us begin, shall we. Ms. Ferrelle, if you please."

The eminent counsel stood, walked around her desk and placed herself directly between Henry and Professor Raymond. "Madam," she began, "this case is, as you described, a most serious one. Professor Miller's reputation is at stake as well as the viability of his achieving tenure in the future. I have no doubt that Dr. Miller is a man of integrity and decency. But these qualities are not what we are examining today. We are here to address outdated modes of thinking towards ethnicities other than our own; we are here to address regressive attitudes towards women; we are here to determine if this college shall be an institution of progressive thinking or one that reverts to an archaic philosophy that has lost its relevance in a world that advances with startling speed. So we shall certainly not impugn Dr. Miller's character, but we shall certainly call into question his judgement."

Henry took a pad of yellow legal paper and scrawled on it, "Why the hell are you so friendly with her?" and shoved it towards Seamus who read it quickly, made a brief note and shoved it back. "She ain't the enemy!" it read.

Ms. Ferrelle continued. "Some have categorized this Tribunal as a sort of 'Star Chamber', a form of 'Kangaroo Court'. Nothing could be further from the truth. This Tribunal represents the finest traditions of our university heritage. This Tribunal is being asked to weigh the values of legitimate areas of study against the dangers of over-zealous extremism. Like the Senate of this country Canada, itself, this Tribunal acts as a chamber of sober, second thought. We shall show that there is danger here and that it must be addressed."

She turned, smiled at both Henry and Seamus and resumed her seat. Professor Raymond gestured to Seamus who stood but stayed behind his desk and said, "Madam, I have no opening statement. Perhaps we can proceed to the calling of witnesses."

A murmur followed this and the attending journalists scratched busily at their notepads, some shaking their heads in disbelief, others nodding sagely.

"Very well," spoke the Adjudicator. "Ms. Ferrelle, your first witness if you please."

When the first witness had been sworn in, she was seated and the questioning began. "Would you tell us your name, please."

"Sandra Reevely."

"You are a student at Sir MacKenzie Bowell College?"

"I am."

"What program are you enrolled in?"

"I am a fourth year student in Women's Studies."

"Is there a compulsory English Literature component in this program?"

"Actually, we have to take a literature course in each of the four years."

"Therefore you have taken three such courses before this year."

"That is correct."

"Were you successful in these three courses?"

Ms. Reevely smiled smugly and replied, "Three straight A's."

"Well done," acknowledged Johanna Ferrelle. "Did you register for the fourth-year literature course before this semester began?"

"Of course."

"Was this course different from the preceding ones?"

"It was."

"In what way?"

"First of all, it was being taught by a man."

"Professor Henry Miller?"

"Yes."

"Why was this unusual, Ms. Reevely?"

"Simply because all of our previous professors had been women."

"Did you find the course content different from what you had expected?"

Seamus was on his feet. "Objection. Leading the witness."

Professor Raymond looked at her two partners briefly, then replied, "Not really. We'll let the question stand, Mr. MacPherson."

"Ms. Reevely? Was the content different?"

"Yes. He was going to have us reading Shakespeare for the whole semester."

"But Shakespeare is a renowned playwright. What was different about studying him?"

"Well, of course, he's a very famous writer. But all of our previous courses had dealt with women authors."

"So you were surprised by this course selection."

"Yes, ma'am, I was."

"Was there a specific incident on that first day that caused you distress?"

"At the end of the class, yes."

"What happened?"

"He gave us a sealed envelope and told us to read it at home that night."

"What was in this envelope?"

"It was a speech, I guess, from one of Shakespeare's plays."

"Did you find it offensive?"

"I really did."

"What did it say?"

"It said that women should be subservient to their husbands, should always do what their husbands said, and should always be in a good mood and smiling so as to not offend their husbands."

"And this caused you emotional stress?"

"Yes, ma'am, it did. I was in tears after reading it."

"Did anything else in that class cause you duress?"

"He made a racist comment about the Japanese being imperialists."

"Did you remain in Dr. Miller's course?"

"No. I left at the end of the first class."

"Why was that?"

"I felt that if I remained I would be condoning his racist and sexist views."

"And you left knowing that this was a compulsory course."

"Yes. A woman has to take a stand in the face of such patriarchal abuse and I was willing to face the consequences of my actions."

Johanna Ferrelle turned and looked at Seamus. "Your witness, Mr. MacPherson."

Seamus approached the witness stand, placed a hand on the railing that separated the stand from the rest of the courtroom and smiled at Ms. Reevely. She did not smile back.

"Good morning, Ms. Reevely. I have just a few follow-up questions that you can help me with. During the three previous Literature courses that you got A's in – and congratulations, by the way," again Seamus smiled at the witness who again scowled back at him, "did you study any male authors?"

"Of course not."

"Nothing by George Eliot?"

"I've already told you, no male authors."

"Actually, Ms. Reevely, George Eliot was a woman, and she wrote a classic nineteenth century novel entitled *Middlemarch*. It's possible that you might actually enjoy it. But let me pose a further question: Do you feel that you missed anything by not studying even a single male writer?"

"Absolutely not."

"Why is that?"

"The purpose of a Women's Studies program is to study women. So we read women authors, and learn about women's history, and women's culture."

"Do you think there might be a male author somewhere who could cast a light on the problems faced by women over the ages?"

"No, I do not. All the problems faced by women have been caused by men. I really don't think any man has anything of value to say to me."

"Even the greatest writer of all time?"

"Who?"

Seamus smiled encouragingly at Ms. Reevely. "Shakespeare?" he suggested.

"He's a man, isn't he? And I've already told you, no man has anything worthwhile to say to me."

"And if that male author were a homosexual?"

Johanna Ferrelle was on her feet. "Madam," she implored.

"I withdraw the question, Professor Raymond."

"You state, Ms. Reevely," Seamus continued, "that no man has anything of worth to say to you. I shall try not to take that personally."

"I don't care if you do take it personally."

Seamus raised an eyebrow in the direction of the Adjudicator who interjected, "Ms. Reevely, Mr. MacPherson did not ask you a question. You will restrict yourself to answering his direct questions only. Your editorial comments are out of order."

The witness was now glaring at Seamus. He smiled benignly at her and continued. "Ms. Reevely, during the past three years at Bowell College have you taken any history courses?"

"We get lots of history in our regular Women's Studies courses."

"Do you indeed? Have you studied World War II?"

"Why would we? It was just another patriarchal blood bath."

"Was it indeed? Ever study the world history that preceded World War II?"

"No. We studied the subjugation of women by men through the ages."

"The reason I ask, Ms. Reevely, is that Dr. Miller there has been charged by you, among other things, with racism. In your brief time in his classroom did you hear him make any racially biased statements?"

"Yes, I did. He wondered why we'd think he was an imperialist if he didn't look Japanese."

"I'll ask you again: In your study of women's subjugation by men through the ages did you ever consider the war aims of the Japanese military in the three decades preceding World War II?"

"And I'll tell you again: No!"

"We're almost finished here, Ms. Reevely, and I do thank you for your patience. But one question keeps bothering me. The course taught by Dr. Miller was a compulsory one. Did you need it to graduate?"

"Yes."

"So you were willing to sacrifice your academic career to bring to light what you see as the transgressions of Dr. Miller? You were prepared to fail your program?"

She hesitated, and finally said, "Not exactly."

"I'm confused. What do you mean, 'Not exactly'?"

"We were told that we'd be taken care of."

"Really?" said Seamus, eyebrows arched towards his forehead, eyes wide with amazement. "And who told you that you'd be taken care of?"

Ms. Reevely did not answer, but looked desperately at her lawyer. Johanna returned her gaze calmly, then began to write notes on her legal pad.

"Please answer the question, Ms. Reevely," instructed the Adjudicator.

"I forget."

Again Professor Raymond was about to order her to answer the question but was stopped by Seamus. "Madam, I quite take Ms. Reevely's point and accept that she has suffered a lapse of memory. And at this point I have no further questions of this lady." The benign smile flashed again before he turned his back on Ms. Reevely and returned to Henry's side at the defense table.

Johanna Revelle studied Seamus's face for a long moment, her brow furrowed. At last she stood and asked that the next witness, Pamela Leduc, be called. The same litany of questions was put to Ms. Leduc as had been asked of Ms. Reevely. But Johanna did probe deeper on one issue.

"Ms. Leduc, did you experience any personal repercussions from this admittedly brief experience in Professor Miller's classroom?"

"Yes, I did."

"Could you specify for us, please."

"I felt degraded, stressed and very apprehensive about my academic career. But my principles as a woman demanded that I take a stand."

"Your witness," said Johanna and returned to her table.

Seamus quickly established the same responses he'd heard earlier: No formal history had been studied, nor had any male authors. But then he changed tack.

"Ms. Leduc, when Dr. Miller began his first class with you he opened the proceedings by saying that the students could ask any questions they liked about him. Is that your recollection?"

"I guess so."

"Did you have any question for Professor Miller?"

"No."

"Did you say anything at that time?"

"I don't remember."

"Oh my, my, my," chuckled Seamus. "We do seem to be experiencing an epidemic of faulty memories, don't we? Let me see if I can help you. Did you not say, 'I don't think there's any need for questions. I've heard all about you.'?"

"I don't remember saying that."

"Ms. Leduc, I can produce a parade of your classmates who are quite sure that those were your words. Would you like to reconsider your answer?"

"I might have said something like that," she mumbled.

"Well, you have certainly piqued my curiosity. Given that Professor Miller was new to the school, indeed in only his second day of teaching here, from what source had you, and let me use your own words here, 'heard all about' him?"

The young woman looked with desperation at her lawyer who returned her look coolly and said nothing. Then Ms. Leduc turned to the panel, "Do I have to answer that?"

"I'm afraid that you do," replied the Adjudicator.

Ms. Leduc turned back to Seamus and snarled, "I was talking to a faculty member."

"Indeed. Let's change direction now for a moment. Because you have left this compulsory course you will not graduate. Is that not so, Ms. Leduc?" There was no answer to this and Seamus gently prompted, "Ms. Leduc?"

"I was told that I would graduate regardless."

"Were you told this by a faculty member in a position of sufficient responsibility to make such an assurance?"

"Yes, I was."

"Was this faculty member the same person who told you – and again I'll use your own words – all about Professor Miller?"

"She was."

"And her name, Ms. Leduc?"

A long pause ensued, but finally the witness said, "Dr. Kennedy."

"Were you and Dr. Kennedy quite close?"

"She had taught me two courses."

"Was that the extent of your relationship?"

"I don't know what you mean."

"Were you and Dr. Kennedy sexually intimate?"

Johanna was instantly on her feet, but before she could object, Seamus said, "I withdraw the question."

He smiled at Johanna, turned to the panel and said, "And I have no more questions of this witness, Madam."

"Mr. MacPherson," snapped Professor Raymond in a tone that had not been heard that morning. "I am appalled by that question. And your withdrawing of it is cavalier and ineffective. If you do not have evidence to support such allegations you will not make them. Do you understand me, Mr. MacPherson? Have I made myself quite clear, sir?"

"Madam, you have. And I apologize to this Tribunal. It shall not happen again."

"See to it. You will please be more careful with your questions. Now I believe that we have time for one more witness before we break for lunch. But we shall take a ten minute break now. Please try to be back in twenty minutes, people."

Linda O'Connor corralled Seamus and Henry and guided them to her office where a fresh pot of coffee was steaming. "It's going to get somewhat more interesting now," Seamus said. "We caught Johanna napping a bit this morning, but she'll be coming at us hard with her questioning of the lovely Ms. Judith Lawton."

"How did you catch her napping?" asked Linda.

"Those girls had not told her that a deal had been cooked up with Dr. Kennedy. And when I put that last question about intimacy, Johanna was ready to explode. She's a terrific lawyer, but she does not like being jerked around. And these girls have not been open with her. So she'll be out for blood. It'll be fun."

The courtroom reconvened thirty minutes after the break had been called. "Thank you all for your promptness and cooperation, ladies and gentlemen," Professor Raymond said with a smile. "Ms. Ferrelle, let's begin."

Judith Lawton proved to be a more energetic and voluble witness than her classmates. Her responses were punctuated with hand gestures, changes in the volume of her voice and the eye contact she made with the panel and spectators in the courtroom. She ignored only Seamus and Henry.

After the usual catalogue of establishing questions, Johanna asked, "You came back for the second class with Dr. Miller?"

"Yes, I did."

"Had any other students chosen not to return?"

"Yes, two friends of mine refused to go back."

"Did that surprise you?"

"Not at all. After reading the assignment that he had given us ---"

"By 'he' you are referring to Professor Miller?"

"I am. After reading the assignment that Professor Miller had given us, I was interested to see how many girls would go back."

"And did only two not attend the class."

"That's right. But there were quite a few who were considering dropping the course."

Seamus was on his feet. "Objection, Madam. Speculation."

"Sustained. Please answer only the question put to you, Ms. Lawton."

"How would you describe the atmosphere in the classroom that morning?"

"People were angry. Some said the passage we'd had to read was chauvinistic. One girl called it crap. Forgive me, Madam, I'm just quoting."

"Were there other statements by Professor Miller that you found offensive?"

"Yes. On top of his comments the day before about the Japanese and Germans, he suggested that we could write a Master's thesis on the benefits of colonialism, and suggested that India should not have gotten its freedom from the British and he also started praising capitalism to the skies."

"Ms. Lawton, why did you return for the second class with Professor Miller?"

"I wanted to see how bad this man was going to make the situation."

Professor Raymond glanced expectantly at Seamus who looked on placidly and kept his seat.

"Did it get worse?"

"Yes. He began to analyze the passage he'd given us the day before.""

"I have here a copy of this passage. Is this what you were given by Dr. Miller?"

Ms. Lawton took a few seconds to read the piece, handed it back to Johanna and said, "It certainly is."

"What is there in this passage that you find offensive?"

"It advocates the complete subjugation of women by men. It's disgusting, it's insulting and I think it's criminal."

"Had you encountered such writing in any previous courses in Women's Studies?"

"Never!"

"Did you ask Professor Miller directly if he endorsed the sentiments in these lines?"

"I did."

"And his response?"

"He said, 'I do.'"

"And how did you interpret this statement?"

"I thought it was blatant sexism."

"How did you respond?"

"I walked out and slammed the door behind me."

Johanna turned and nodded at Seamus, "Your witness."

"Ms. Lawton, where are these lines to be found?" he asked.

"Apparently in one of Shakespeare's plays. That's why I won't read him."

"You left the class before Dr. Miller and your classmates read the first two scenes of *The Taming of the Shrew* did you not?"

"I wasn't going to stay around to listen to any more of his crap!"

"Ms. Lawton," began Professor Raymond, clearly not amused by this statement, but she was interrupted by Seamus.

"Madam, if I may, such a minor outbreak of colloquialisms is surely acceptable in order to evidence the depth of one's feelings, of one's passion. Let us not be overly harsh in our condemnation of what are, after all, mere words." Professor Raymond rolled her eyes, but nodded at Seamus who continued on.

"So, Ms. Lawton, you were, and I suppose still are, totally ignorant of the fact that absolutely nothing in this play is to be accepted at face value. And that includes Kate's speech which you find so offensive. In fact, Kate's words, ironic as they are, must be seen from a position some 180 degrees from what she is literally saying. You were not aware of this?"

Ms. Lawton opened her mouth as if to speak but no words emerged.

"You were not aware that Professor Miller was teaching this play from a completely feministic point of view?"

There was no response. At last she said, "That's impossible. He's a man. A man cannot understand feminism."

"Are you suggesting that all men, because they are men, are the enemies of women?"

"I'm not suggesting that. I'm stating it as a fact."

Seamus gazed at her for a long moment. Finally he said, "Apart from being sexist, Professor Miller is also accused of being a racist. Do you believe that he is racist?"

"I certainly do."

"Can you recall for us the remarks that led you to this belief?"

"One of us said that he was probably an imperialist and he said that couldn't be because he didn't look Japanese."

"Do you recall who accused him of imperialistic beliefs?"

"No, I do not."

"As a matter of fact, Ms. Lawton, it was you."

She scowled at Seamus furiously.

"Were you aware then that his comments about Japan and imperialism were defended by one of your classmates as being entirely accurate from an historical point of view?"

"Oh, come off it. You know who did that?"

"Yes, I do know. It was Ms Ikuko Kawasaki."

"Well, what did you expect? She wouldn't say 'you know what' if her mouth were full of it."

"Why would she not, Ms. Lawton?"

"It's obvious. She's Japanese. She does what she's told. They're raised that way."

The stillness in the courtroom was palpable and Seamus did not utter a sound to disturb it. Slowly Ms. Lawton began to realize what she had just said and she put her fingers to her lips.

"I didn't mean - - -" she began, only to be interrupted by Seamus.

"I think it best if you let me do the speaking and you restrict yourself to brief answers, don't you?" She glared at him.

"Let us consider this question of rape that so upset you that you had to flee the classroom and abandon your hopes of timely graduation. Were you also unaware that the sentiments expressed in this series of Shakespearean lines were clearly not in any way to be construed as systemic or institutionalized rape, and that this opinion was also expressed by one of your classmates, one that you have known for the last three plus years?"

Ms. Lawton shook her head. "What do you know about rape?" she stormed. "Our culture is based on rape. Why don't you spend some time at a women's shelter and see what rape is all about? You're just ignorant."

"In my other life, Ms. Lawton, I do a lot of pro bono legal work for a women's shelter situated not far from my office in Toronto. I have seen the effects of rape and they sicken me. But that is not the point at this moment. Were you aware that while this classmate I just referred to was in Africa she, her young sister and aged grandmother were all brutally and systematically repeatedly raped?"

Tears began to flow down the witness's cheeks and Seamus returned to his desk, plucked a few Kleenex sheets from the box there, and handed them to her.

Johanna rose, "Madam," she began.

"I concur with what I suspect my learned colleague is about to propose," said Seamus. "Perhaps, Madam, we should take this opportunity to excuse us all for a much needed lunch break."

The Tribunal panel had been assigned a small wood-panelled office where they could confer and indulge in snacks or luncheon. And it was here that they reviewed the morning's testimonies and questioning. Jeremy Swan explained that as a member of the College's Students' Council he was the recipient of a great deal of campus input about issues, but especially about professors. "And what I've heard about this guy Miller is pretty positive. I just didn't find those students this morning very convincing."

"I disagree, Jeremy," said Professor George. "In fact, I disagree quite strongly. Those women have taken a stand based on principle. It seems to me that Professor Miller is something of a bully. He finds himself in a spot of trouble and he calls in the high-priced powerful help from Toronto. And I don't find Mr. MacPherson's attitude or line of questioning at all compelling. What about you, Samantha. What's your thinking at this point?"

"I'm simply not sure. Miller is involved in something much greater than 'a spot of trouble', however. But I abhor that question about sexual intimacy. So right now, I'm just going to wait and see."

• • •

The group that convened for sandwiches and coffee in George Harper's office was, with the exception of Seamus MacPherson, not a happy gathering. Both Charley Lee and George felt that a strong defence had not been mounted by their lawyer. Linda O'Connor and Ezekiel Silverstein looked worried. And Henry looked shell-shocked.

"Goddam it, Seamus," said George, "you've been treating these students with kid gloves. When are you going to go at them, draw some blood?"

"I must agree," added Charley. "We have the future direction of this school at risk here and so far I do not see any sense of urgency from you, Seamus. So far I do not see any reason to feel confident about Henry's future let alone the hope of a sea-change in the ultra-liberal direction that Bowell is being led."

Seamus looked at Zeke, Linda and Henry for further input and seeing none asked, "What kind of sandwiches do we have on offer here?" He examined the tray, selected an egg salad concoction on a whole wheat bun, took a large bite and started to chew with vigour.

"Goddam it again, Seamus," snarled George, "can you give me one reason why I should go back in there this afternoon and waste my time the way I did this morning?"

The lawyer finished another large mouthful of his sandwich, dressed his coffee with cream and sugar, and as he stirred the mug announced, "I really prefer honey to sugar in my coffee." He took a sip, placed the mug on the table and turned to George.

"Dean Harper, I am going to ask you to put on your colonel's hat for a moment. When you were leading young men into combat in Afghanistan did you locate the enemy and immediately order your troops into battle urging them to 'Go kill the scumbags'?"

"No, of course not."

"What did you do?"

"I went through an entire process first: reconnaissance, probing patrols, air strikes and then artillery to soften the bastards up."

"Why did you not just send those superbly trained soldiers of yours directly into the fight."

"Casualties. We'd take too many casualties."

"So as Hamlet said, 'The readiness is all' and the readiness takes precise preparation, does it not?"

"Come on, Seamus, get it out. Where are you taking this?"

Seamus smiled, took another healthy bite that almost finished the sandwich, and smiled at his audience as he chewed. "I am preparing my readiness," he finally stated. "Look at where we are. We've established that these students have been educated, if I can accurately use that term, with a most narrow focus. We've established that the fix was in. They were to smear Henry and suffer no academic repercussion. We know who was responsible for all of this, the mastermind as it were, Cynthia Kennedy, and the suggestion of an illicit teacher-student relationship has not been established, but made a factor. The current witness, the lachrymose Ms. Lawton, has revealed herself as a closet racist and a hater of men. Not a bad morning's work."

"Indeed you are a Daniel, my friend," observed Zeke, "but where are you going now?"

"This afternoon we are going to expand the horizon to encompass the problem of evil and its presence in all times and in all places."

"Fine, fine, fine," said George. "The preparation makes sense. But tell me when the shooting starts."

"Monday, with Jean Whitmarsh, and finally with the dangerous Cynthia Kennedy, herself. Be patient. But don't go away."

XXV

"Now Ms. Lawton, I do hope that you have quite recovered from the stresses of this morning."

The witness stared back at Seamus glumly.

"But I'm afraid I must take us back to the horrible tale of rape narrated by your classmate, Ms. Naomi N'Kuma. Do you know Naomi well?"

"Not really."

"Yet you've been classmates for the last three-plus years, have you not?"

"I suppose, but we didn't really socialize together."

"Pity, that. She is a remarkable woman."

"Madam!" Johanna was on her feet. "Where is this meandering line of questioning going? It strikes me as irrelevant."

The panel cast quizzical eyes at Seamus.

"With the Tribunal's permission, I'd like to illustrate that this Shakespearean speech that has allegedly caused so much anguish is actually a love song of the greatest beauty. But to do so I must provide a context of the ugly reality of too much of our lives."

The panel exchanged glances and Seamus was told to proceed.

"Were you aware, Ms. Lawton, that Ms. N'Kuma was a citizen of Kenya at the time of the gang raping we talked of this morning."

"No."

"Would you be surprised to hear that her assailants were black Islamic Somalis?"

"Madam!" snapped Johanna.

"I must be given some leeway, Madam, to establish the universality of the brutality that has been and continues to be the fate of far too many women. These first three witnesses have clearly illustrated that their education has been restricted to the narrowest focus conceivable. And if I am to adequately defend my client, faced with charges of sexism and racism, I must be allowed to introduce the topic of race into my questioning."

The panel conferred and grudgingly allowed Seamus to continue. "But exercise great caution, Mr. MacPherson."

"Let's explore another topic, Ms. Lawton, the literature that you've read during the Women's Studies program. Women authors only, of course. Did you read *The Color Purple*?"

"Yes. I loved it."

"So did I, actually, Ms. Lawton. And I also am a big fan of the movie version with Oprah Winfrey. In fact I confess to being a fan of so-called chick-flicks. What was the author's name?"

"Alice Walker."

"Just so. Again, would you be surprised to learn that the woman who wrote such a beautiful story is filled with a vitriolic hatred of Israel and Jews in general?"

Ms. Lawton seemed to regain some of her former spunk. "So what's wrong with hating Israel? Look at how they treat the Palestinians."

"It is a topic with great potential for debate, Ms. Lawton, I agree. But debate, in its purest form, sees two rational yet conflicting points of view being civilly and intelligently argued. And Ms. Walker refuses to acknowledge that Israel is the only functioning democracy in the Middle East region with a most aggressive free press and a very high level of tolerance. In fact she urges its extermination. Tell me, Ms. Lawton, do you have any gay friends?"

"You've been wanting to ask me that all along, haven't you?" she snarled. "What you really mean is: 'Am I gay'?"

"Ms. Lawton, you cannot exaggerate the lack of interest I have in other people's sexuality, yours included. I find my own sexuality quite sufficient to keep my mind occupied without the clutter of other people's preferences. What I am asking is, would you recommend that an openly gay friend of yours travel to any country in the Middle East other than Israel? It's a rhetorical question, actually. But the key point is this: an author such as Ms. Alice Walker can write a beautiful tale and yet be personally filled with ugliness. Is the gender of the writer of any consequence?"

"Of course it is. A man cannot understand women. Only a woman author can do that. And Alice Walker is a woman of colour who is also a great author."

"Let me be very clear about what you are saying, Ms. Lawton. If an author composes a work that is powerful, beautiful and addresses the human condition, then that work can stand by itself with no regard to the hateful and venomous personal opinions that the author may hold in other arenas of life?"

"Yes, I agree with that."

"And such an example would be the literary work by Alice Walker in *The Color Purple* as opposed to her political views, wouldn't it?"

"She's a great female author and I really do not give a damn about her political views or about Israel either."

"I quite take your point, Ms. Lawton. Now let us look at another great author, the one at the centre of this hearing. I am speaking, of course, of William Shakespeare. Is it not possible for his work also to stand by itself regardless of whatever political views he may have held or the configuration of his chromosomes into an XY pattern?"

Ms. Lawton's face was reddening with fury. "He's another dead, white male. He has nothing to say to me. He has nothing to say to any woman." She was almost shouting.

"May I bring you a glass of water, Ms. Lawton?" asked Seamus gently.

"You can bring me nothing. I'm sick of being bullied and brow-beaten by you," she stormed. "You're typical of every man." Her face was fuchsia and she glared at the lawyer with rage.

Seamus retreated to the desk, turned and leaned against it, his legs thrust out in front and his arms crossed over his chest.

"Is that why you hate Professor Miller, Ms. Lawton? Is he just another typical male forcing a male agenda onto you?"

Henry Miller looked past Seamus to see Johanna Ferrelle start out of her chair, her mouth open as if to speak, pause, look piercingly at Seamus and slowly resume her seat.

Henry leaned in close to Seamus, "Why is she not objecting or something?" he whispered.

Seamus turned his head only slightly, never taking his eyes off Ms. Lawton. "I've told you already; she is not our enemy," he murmured.

He plucked two more tissues from the box of Kleenex and approaching the witness stand, held them out to the now sniffling young woman. She took them, dabbed at her eyes and then made a pass at her nose as well.

"I am afraid, Ms. Lawton, that I must very, very briefly follow up that last question which, by the way, you have not answered. First: Is the reason you object to the proposed study of Shakespeare that he was a man?"

Ms. Lawton continued to dab at her eyes and nose but did not respond.

"And finally, is the reason you would like to see Professor Miller denied the opportunity of tenure at this college because he is a man?"

Seamus did not wait to see if there was going to be an answer. He turned to the panel and said, "Madam, I have no more questions of this witness."

XXVI

The ride back to the Harpers' house was much more convivial than had been the atmosphere at lunch in George's office. Ezekiel had chosen to ride with Henry and Seamus in the Chevrolet rather than join the dean of Engineering in a trip to the job site, the deconstructed house of Nora and Henry Miller. And in the back seat of the car Zeke was ebullient. "Seamus, my young friend, you are a Daniel, a Daniel I say. The light is beginning to glow around the unjustly accused yet again. It is like the day I first spied him stepping out of the sun to lead us on to more fruitful paths."

Seamus turned to Henry, "What the hell is he talking about?"

"Don't ask," laughed Henry.

Dinner was pleasant but not at all like some of the more raucous affairs that had been experienced at that table. "There's still more work to be done, but I'm feeling a lot better about it than I was earlier," said George.

"Don't get too confident yet," said Seamus. "We've still got two essential witnesses to go. And they're going to be very tough."

"What are you talking about?" said George. "I meant the Millers' house. We'll take a trip out there tomorrow, Nora and Henry, and I think you'll be surprised and pleased with what you see."

"You know, Seamus," said Nora, "this Tribunal isn't the only crisis in our lives at the moment. I trust George, but our house could be a pile of rubble when we see it next. Of course, so could Henry's current career at Bowell as of Monday evening. Why don't you come with us tomorrow and view the great demolition."

"Not me. Sadly, I'll need all day to prepare. Miriam, is there a room here that I could hole up in tomorrow? All I need is an internet connection and frequent mugs of coffee and you won't see me until night. But, Nora, do bring back a complete report on the once and future house."

It was a small convoy that pulled into the driveway to the old farmhouse. Miriam, George and Zeke in one car; Nora, Henry, Annie and Rachel in another; and they had been joined by Linda O'Connor and her entire family in a large van and Megan Fiorini in a brand new Mercedes convertible. The vehicles pulled into a circle opposite the old summer kitchen which had remained unchanged.

But once they had walked through the kitchen door Nora's mouth fell open. She didn't speak as she slowly proceeded through the kitchen into the living room, dining room, family room and central hall. She proceeded up the stairs and into each of the three bedrooms and two bathrooms and finished in the girls' bedroom. She finally turned to Henry and attempted to speak, but instead broke into tears. Henry took her by the shoulders and pulled her to him. She seemed to be crying into his chest for a long time until Henry realized that she was no longer weeping but laughing. He pushed her out to his arms' length and looked at her in total confusion.

The sight of his face, so perplexed, caused her to laugh still harder until finally she stopped for breath and managed to say, "Look what they've done. It's all new. It's wonderful."

No matter where they looked, nothing remained of the old plaster and wall coverings. The baseboards, door frames and window casings had all been removed and were stored in the summer kitchen. Electrical wires protruded from walls and ceilings in the precise spots where Nora had envisioned chandeliers, wall switches and outlets. In the kitchen and bathrooms copper and plastic pipes grew out of walls and floors indicating the future location of sinks, showers, baths and toilets. And miraculously, not a speck of dust or dirt could be found on any wall or floor.

Megan Fiorini shook her head in admiration. "This is a Georgian designed house. They are jewels and you've saved this one. It's irreplaceable and you've given it a whole new life."

George began to speak, "You've now got R20 insulation in every outside wall, sound buffer insulation in every interior wall, and R40 in the attic and under this ground floor. It's all been covered with vapour barrier and all sealed. You're tighter than Toby's - - -"

"George!" interjected Miriam. "That's enough. Now I've brought a lunch and there's more than enough for everybody. But where shall we all sit?"

The picnic table was carried in and extra chairs from their place of storage in the summer kitchen were pressed into service. Cold chicken, potato salad, raw carrot and broccoli pieces appeared, as well as chocolate milk for the youngsters and several bottles of chardonnay for the others. Paper plates and plastic glasses appeared and the empty rooms echoed with the sounds of chatter and laughter. George became deeply involved in conversation with Nora.

"Here's what I suggest. You really must stay for one more week at our place, because I've already arranged for the floor finishers to come in tomorrow morning. It'll take them three days to cut through the umpteen layers of paint and linoleum and stain that are everywhere, and then to put on a thin coat and then two full coats of urethane finish. This floor here in the kitchen is maple and hard as granite and the dining room is oak. All the others are pine or fir. They'll glow like honey. You'll love them."

"What about the walls? The drywall still needs to be taped and sanded. And that'll make a horrible mess of the new floors."

"Way back, I told you that I had a deal for you if you let me use your husband as a sacrificial lamb. And part of the deal is that on Thursday I've got some Portuguese guys coming in to do the taping. These guys are so good there's almost no sanding and what there is, they ensure leaves no residue. I found them through Paulo, the custodian at Bowell. Nobody can tape better than the Portuguese."

"George, I am so in debt to you."

"Well, there is a bit of a monetary cost attached to this. You and Henry will have to pay for the floor strippers and drywall tapers. Can you do that?"

Nora laughed and threw her arms around him. George spoke into her blonde hair, "And don't forget that the electrician and plumber have still got to finish. And they may want to be paid too."

"And what else?"

"I'm guessing you may want to paint these bare walls. Can you two do that yourselves?"

XXVII

At precisely nine o'clock on Monday morning, the presiding Chairperson of the panel motioned for proceedings to begin. The witness was sworn in and took her seat in the box.

"Could you tell us your name, please," asked Johanna Ferrelle.

"Jean Elizabeth Whitmarsh."

"And what is your position here at Bowell College?"

"I am the dean of Arts and Humanities."

"Would you give us a brief summary of your responsibilities in that role."

"I am ultimately responsible for the courses offered, the curriculum that is contained in those courses and the instructors who teach those courses. Everything that pertains to the program that we offer eventually must clear my desk."

"Were you involved in instituting the Women's Studies course?"

"I was not the driving force behind it, but I supported it wholeheartedly and without reservation."

"Who, then, was the driving force behind this course?"

"That would have been Dr. Cynthia Kennedy."

"Why are you such an enthusiastic backer of Women's Studies, Dean Whitmarsh?"

"To answer that question properly I should have to go back to what I see as the mission of this school in general and the Arts Program in particular."

"And what is that mission?"

"I firmly believe that this college should be offering the best in progressive education to enable our students to make a difference in a society beset with terrible problems that affect so many of our citizens."

"And how does the Women's Studies course fit into this vision?"

"Well, what could be more relevant than the study of the ways in which women have been deprived of reaching their potential over so many centuries? I want our young women to know where they have come from so that they'll know where they should be going."

"Is that why the history component of the course centres on women's issues through the ages rather than the more conventional study of wars and political movements?"

"Of course."

"And again, Dean Whitmarsh, is that why the literature component centred exclusively on women authors?"

"And again, Ms. Ferrelle, of course."

"I have looked at the syllabus for literature and the works studied are drawn entirely from the 1920's on to today. Is this a flaw in the curriculum? Should the students not be given the opportunity to examine great works from the past as well?"

"One does have to make choices. There is such a vast body of work to draw on that it would be impossible not to ignore some areas of literature. Perhaps quite a few areas, actually. We decided to focus on current and recent works."

"But how do you explain the complete absence of male authors?"

Henry turned to look at Seamus whose eyes were riveted on the witness but whose right hand was busily making notes on his large yellow legal pad. Henry turned back to the dean.

"And again I say to you that one has to make certain choices. And there is such a large body of work by such fine women authors that we felt no need to intersperse male writers among them. But if I may add, when one studies Engineering, for example, one's courses all deal with subjects relevant to Engineering. This is a Women's Studies course and its content should rightly be concerned with women."

"There was no bias, therefore, against male authors."

"Absolutely not."

"Dean Whitmarsh, did you play a role in the hiring of Dr. Henry Miller?"

"Yes, I did."

"What was that role?"

"I reviewed the applications for the position that was available and selected Dr. Miller from among them."

"What about his application stood out for you?"

"He had a substantial teaching background and his doctoral dissertation suggested a strong interest in the area of women's issues."

"Were you surprised when he informed you that he would be teaching Shakespeare to the fourth year class assigned to him?"

"Stunned actually. I am not at all convinced that works that are 400 years old have an immediacy that I see should be a central part of our progressive mandate."

"But you let him carry on?"

"There was no choice really. We needed an instructor for that class and we had run out of options."

Johanna put her questions for another half hour, but eventually turned and with a smile said, "Your witness, Mr. MacPherson."

"Professor Raymond, may I suggest that we take a brief comfort break at this time?"

"You may and we shall. I think our ten minute recess worked admirably on Saturday and so I shall call for a ten minute interval and do, please, be back here in twenty."

Seamus spied Charley Lee in the room and made a beeline for him leaving Henry to find a washroom and then seek a fast half-cup of coffee in Linda O'Connor's tiny office. While she found the sugar and packaged whitener for him, she rhapsodized about the house tour the day before. "Even my fifteen-year-old loved it. He kept marvelling at how old it was."

"Yeah, George's kids did a great job last week. And their supervisors, of course. My stone mason friend, Walter Ruttan, actually told me a couple of weeks ago that if we had not bought it and done the proposed renovation work, that the place might have to be bull-dozed. It was in that bad shape."

"Well, Henry, you and Nora have done a wonderful thing. Are you nervous about Seamus's cross-examination of Jean?"

"I'm nervous as hell about the whole damn thing." He finished his coffee. "I'd better get back."

The large lecture room settled down, the Tribunal panel seated themselves and the Adjudicator nodded at Seamus who approached Jean Whitmarsh in the witness box.

"Good morning, Dean," he said. "I have a few points from your testimony earlier that I'd like your help with for clarification."

She nodded at him warily.

"Did you state that if one is studying Engineering, then one's courses would all deal with subjects relevant to Engineering?"

"I believe I said something like that."

"Oh you said exactly that. And if that is so, then why are two classes of third year Engineering students studying English literature with Professor Miller?"

"It's compulsory."

"Quite so. Yet it has no connection to the field of Engineering. Why, then, is it compulsory?"

"I'm not really sure."

"But, Dean Whitmarsh," and Seamus made a pass through his notes, found his quarry, and continued, "you have stated that everything that pertains to your program must clear your desk. Surely you must have approved this English course for Engineering students and must also have okayed the fact that it is a compulsory credit. Is this not true?"

"Of course it is," replied Jean, her voice beginning to rise. "It's perfectly reasonable for them to take it and for it to be a compulsory subject."

"And what, pray, would that reason be?" asked Seamus quietly.

"They have to have exposure to something outside of their area of concentration. Otherwise we'd be simply a training school, not a university. They have to have some sense of breadth in their studies."

"Ah," Seamus responded. "But that reasoning, with which I happen to agree, by the way, raises a question in the curriculum of the Women's

Studies courses. For example, the field of historical study, you testified, focuses on only women's issues through the ages?"

"Correct."

"Dean Whitmarsh, one of the charges being brought against Dr. Miller by three senior students in the Women's Studies program is that he made racist comments in class. These comments referred to the topic of Japanese imperialism. Yet not one of those students had the remotest idea of the issues involved in World War Two or of the world history in the decades preceding that terrible conflict. Not one of these students had any idea of the imperialistic and militaristic ambitions of Japan in those years. They had been taught no history other than women's issues. Can you explain why they would level such a charge against Professor Miller with zero historical knowledge to support it?"

Jean hesitated, reached for the glass of water that had been provided in the witness box, took a sip, and finally said, "I imagine they were aghast that he would make such a statement based on skin colour."

"Skin colour!" Seamus exploded. "Do you yourself, Dean Whitmarsh, have any idea of the crimes against humanity committed by the Japanese armies in those years against the Chinese and the Filipinos? Or are we to ignore a very sensitive and ugly topic because the people in question have identifiable facial features?"

There was no response, but Seamus did move the Kleenex package to the railing on which he had been resting his hand.

"Let us move on, shall we?" he said. "You testified, Dean, that for similar reasons the literature component of these courses focused exclusively on female authors, did you not?"

"I did."

"You also stated that - and let me check my notes and quote you here - there was a vast body of work to draw on. And you, and again, I quote, 'decided to focus on current and recent works'. True?"

"Yes, it is. I said that."

"Was one of those works the novel *The Color Purple*?"

"Yes."

"Why was it selected?"

"The author is a renowned black woman."

"Why do you mention her colour? You just pilloried Henry Miller for that very same sin."

"Well, she is black. It's a fact," shrilled Jean.

"It is a fact indeed, Dean. And, sadly, it is also a fact that this black woman is a vitriolic anti-Semite who has advocated the destruction of Israel. Were you aware of this fact, Dean Whitmarsh?"

She did not answer. After a few seconds she instead reached for the tissues and wiped her eyes and then blew her nose. Seamus waited patiently for her to finish and then restated his question.

"Were you aware that she was a racist?"

Jean nodded. "I suppose that I was aware that she had some strong views about Israel."

"And so with what you described as a vast body of work to choose from, you chose to include an author filled with hatred? Was that because she was a woman, and a black woman at that?"

. "We feel that women authors of colour are not given their fair due; they receive too little recognition."

"That is a partial explanation only. Was she included because she was not a man?"

Jean stared at Seamus and her lip trembled slightly. She took another sip of water before she answered. "That she was a woman was a factor. But that was not the entire reason. I know where you want to go with this line of questioning and I reject it."

"And why is that?"

"The novel can stand by itself. It is a superior piece of work, a real accomplishment that merits study."

"Regardless of the politics of the author?"

"Absolutely!"

"Regardless of the gender of the author?"

"Yes!"

"Then why could not Shakespeare as well be included in the curriculum? His are recognized as the greatest literary works of all time. Why would you be" – and Seamus again referred to his notes – "'stunned actually' to see that Dr. Miller intended to teach this icon of letters to this class of senior women students?"

Jean flushed, struggled to find the words, and finally said, "The man's writing is 400 years old. He's out-of-date. He has nothing to say to today's women."

"And, to use your words, you want the curriculum to have an immediacy that is a central part of your progressive mandate?"

"That is correct."

"The fact that Shakespeare was a man is not a part of your reaction to his inclusion?"

"Of course not."

"Dean Whitmarsh, let's take a look now at the procedure used for the hiring of Professor Miller. You said that you reviewed the applications and selected him. Correct?"

"Yes."

"Which of his qualifications stood out for you?"

"He had very positive reviews of his teaching skills and Bowell is essentially a teaching college."

"What else?"

"His academic background showed a strong interest in women's issues and literature."

"Indeed. Did the fact that he was a man have any bearing on his being offered the position? Please think carefully, Ms. Whitmarsh, before you answer."

"No. He was the best candidate."

"In fact, Dean, he was the only candidate, was he not?"

Jean gasped and took a sharp intake of air. "Where did you hear that?"

"From the Chair of the Board of Regents, Mr Charley Lee. Was he lying to me?"

Jean glanced at the members of the Tribunal, then looked plaintively around the auditorium as if seeking help.

"Dean Whitmarsh?" prodded Seamus.

"He was the only candidate."

"Did Dr. Miller place any conditions on his accepting the post?"

"Yes. He wanted us to fast-track his road to tenure. He wanted tenure after one year if his teaching evaluations were above average and if no issues had been raised against him."

"Is this unusual?"

"It is actually. But at a small college such as ours there are precedents."

Seamus turned to the Tribunal. "Madam, at this time I should like to place into evidence a body of affidavits from over 100 of Professor Miller's current students which attest to their regard for his teaching skills and success. I might add that the comments range from 'very good' to 'the best teacher I've ever had'. These were submitted to me as emails and I have reproduced them here in hard copy."

He turned back to the witness. "It would seem that one of the two conditions for tenure is well on the way to being met, wouldn't it? Now please keep in mind that the proceedings of the Board of Regents are not held *in camera*. Was the fact of Dr. Miller's maleness an issue?"

"Yes, it was," she said, almost inaudibly.

"With whom?"

"Dr. Cynthia Kennedy. She objected strenuously."

"Let me summarize here, Dean Whitmarsh. A professor in your faculty, whom you hired, has been charged with racism and sexism, and his chance for tenure is in jeopardy. He is teaching a recognized genius in the analysis of the human condition, William Shakespeare. Yet he is being pilloried for not adhering to a course content that is based to large extent on race and gender. Dean Whitmarsh, do you not see the irony here? Do you not see the hypocrisy here?" Seamus paused before he continued. "But you need not answer those questions, Dean. They are rhetorical."

Jean's eyes overflowed.

"However, I must insist that you answer this: Despite the fact that you are the dean, and therefore the person responsible for the Arts and Humanities department, are you under the sway of someone else? Are you being controlled by Dr. Cynthia Kennedy?"

Jean Whitmarsh bent over, her hands to her face, her sobs resounding through the room.

"Madam," said Seamus, his face showing a deep sadness, "I am finished with this witness."

"We'll break for lunch now," said Professor Raymond, "and resume at two o'clock."

Johanna Ferrelle quickly approached Jean and assisted her to the door behind the stage at the rear of the auditorium where the Tribunal panel was just disappearing. Then she came directly back to the desk where Henry and Seamus were huddled in quiet conversation.

Seamus looked up, "Johanna, you have been surpassingly silent. What is going on? You're giving me carte blanche."

"I would very much like a glass of chianti, Seamus, if such a thing could be made to happen."

"Join us. We're going for lunch at the dean of Engineering's office. We can chat privately and without any observers."

XXVIII

"Chianti?" asked George Harper with surprise. "Did you take me for a chardonnay woman, Dean? Yes, chianti if you have it."

"I know that I don't. Fiorini, you have any of that good Italian wine in your office stash that I'm not supposed to be aware of?"

Megan Fiorini laughed, slipped out the door, returned promptly with a bottle of chianti, poured a large measure and handed it to Johanna. "Ms. Ferrelle, would you like us all to leave so that you can confer privately with Seamus?" she asked.

Johanna looked at the group which included Megan, Linda O'Connor, George, Charley Lee, Seamus and Henry. Her eyes paused on Ezekiel Silverstein. "You are the only one I don't have at least a passing knowledge of."

"Allow me to introduce myself, gentle lady: Ezekiel Silverstein, Professor of History, scourge of Marxists, and self-styled Merlin and mentor of our accused criminal there." He smiled at Henry.

"Merlin, eh? I may need some conjuring skills this afternoon. So, Megan, in answer to your question, you may as well all stay. What I have to say is unconventional, but not without precedent in the annals of lawyerly cooperation. It is, however, highly confidential and I'd ask that what I am going to discuss stay within the confines of this room. I also realize that seeking executive session privilege from seven people is going against any reasonable expectation. Nevertheless," and she looked at each member of the group, "if your paramount concern is the future of this college as a viable institution, then you will honour my request. Would any of you rather leave?"

No one did, and Johanna began. She explained how furious she had been on Saturday after the three student witnesses had been examined, that she had been misled by all three young women about the charges, and that she had not been told of the 'arrangement' that had been made to safeguard their credit requirements despite dropping the compulsory English course.

"Ah, the three weird sisters stirring their cauldron," observed Zeke.

Linda quickly shushed him, "Be still, old man!"

Zeke smiled and obeyed.

Johanna went on to clarify that she had originally thought the case was a fairly conventional instance of a reactionary male parading his anti-female sentiments. "And, frankly, there is absolutely no place for that on today's campus or anywhere else."

But as the day had worn on she realized that she was not seeing male insensitivity, but female intransigence. "This bothered me very much. I am a committed feminist, as Seamus knows, but the feminism that I espouse is one based on equality with males in all spheres, and one based on rationality and even-handedness. What was going on here resembled a rigged quiz show with the prize being a totally feministic approach to the liberal arts program. True feminism abhors such a state."

Johanna continued at length. She had, on the Sunday after, called a meeting with the three witnesses, informed them that they had polluted the client-lawyer relationship by withholding from her the most essential facts of the case, and explained that from that moment on, their relationship would no longer be based on lawyerly confidentiality.

"How did they respond to that?" asked Henry.

"They just shrugged. They seemed totally unimpressed. However, I got their attention quickly enough."

She had gone on to tell the three women that the case they had instigated had little or no chance of success. "When you three were being cross-examined," she had said, "I was able to watch the faces of the Tribunal panel. You lost at least two of those people. Your credibility is shot; your case has gone south. It is finito, over, dead in the water. And you people sitting here around this table know that if there had been a trace of hope it vanished with the performance this morning by Dean Whitmarsh."

"What'd they say?" asked Megan Fiorini.

"Well they sure quickly lost their super-cool attitude. And suddenly the penny fell and Judith Lawton asked about their lost credit for that compulsory English course. I told them that they could kiss it goodbye. One of them started to cry, I think it was Lawton, and the other two looked devastated."

Johanna went on recounting the long interview with the three. She had said that she understood their fierce defence of women, that she herself was a feminist, but that boundaries had to regulate the conduct of the movement or it lost its moral bearings. She pointed out that their condemnation of Dr. Miller had been precipitate and that in fact the man was teaching Shakespeare with a feministic and entirely legitimate interpretation, one supported by some of the most acclaimed literary critics in academe including the profound Harold Bloom. She finally had revealed to them that, years ago, as a young undergraduate at an Arts college in a prestigious Ontario university, she, too, had been tremendously influenced by one of her female professors. The relationship had grown until finally they had become intimate. At the end of the term, the professor had left on a full year's sabbatical and Johanna had never heard from her again.

Johanna had paused and looked at each young woman in turn. Then she resumed her words to them. "I was shattered. But I can put myself into your positions. You must admit that you have been used, haven't you?"

"Why don't you ask her," said Sandra Reevely pointing at Pamela Leduc. "She was Kennedy's squeeze."

Johanna lifted her glass of chianti, studied it for a moment, and then put it back down on the table. She looked hard into Seamus's eyes. "I asked Leduc if that was true and she nodded. I told them that there might be a way I could present their problem of insufficient credits to graduate to the proper authorities at the college, but only if they cooperated with me."

"'What do you want?' they asked."

"I want you all to sign a written statement confirming that what you have just revealed to me is true. That Dr. Cynthia Kennedy was going to use her influence to allow you to graduate if you launched the charges against Dr. Henry Miller, and that she was also engaged in an intimate relationship with Pamela Leduc. And here's the signed document." Johanna tossed a sealed envelope onto the large meeting table. "Kind of like Henry's first reading assignment for these girls, isn't it?"

The quiet that ensued finally was broken when Seamus said, "Whatever is in that envelope won't have any legal legitimacy at all. You know that, don't you, Johanna?"

"Of course I do. But it could be quite an effective stage prop this afternoon, don't you think?"

Charley Lee spoke up, "What direction are you going to take, Seamus? This is our last shot at getting meaningful improvement for our school. You had better be at the top of your game."

"I understand, Charley. But Johanna, I wish that I was as sure of the panel as you are. I'm afraid, Henry, that I'm going to be calling on you after we finish with Dr. Kennedy. This is not quite the chip shot that I'd predicted." He glanced at his watch. "We'd better get going. It's almost show time."

• • •

Cynthia Kennedy looked stunningly beautiful as she walked down the aisle to the witness stand. She was dressed in dark chocolate pants and blouse with a burnt orange jacket. Her brunette hair shone. She took her oath, sat down, glanced impassively at Seamus and Henry and then turned her attention to Johanna Ferrelle.

After the initial perfunctory battery of questions, Johanna asked, "What is your role at Bowell College?"

"I am a tenured full professor and in charge of the Women's Studies program. I also serve as faculty representative on the Board of Regents."

"What is your history with the Women's Studies program?"

"I created it seven years ago and have been integrally involved with it ever since."

"What do you see as the mission of this program?"

"To explore the realm of womanhood now, in the past and in the future."

"Do you see a role in this program for any male influences?"

"Absolutely not."

"And why is that?"

"It strikes me as perfectly obvious that 'male influences' as you call them have been responsible for all of the ills of society since humankind began. So why should they be allowed to appear in a branch of study that is focussed on women?"

"Dr. Kennedy, would you care to elaborate on these societal ills that men are responsible for?"

"With pleasure. I can list so many, but let me give you just a few: wars, colonialism, religious intolerance, imperialism, capitalism, wealth inequality, racism, misogyny. These can all be traced to the activities of men. Need I go on?"

"I think not. Therefore, when Dr. Miller was appointed to the position he currently holds you were not supportive of the decision?"

"I was totally against it."

"Did you make your views known?"

"I certainly did. As I told you, I serve on the Board of Regents and I argued strenuously before that body against this man being hired."

"But you were not successful."

"No. They relied on some nonsense about gender imbalance on the faculty to ensure that a woman was not chosen."

"Was your relationship with Professor Miller cordial?"

'No. And it became even less so when he announced what he proposed to teach."

"Shakespeare?"

"Shakespeare. Yet another dead white European member of the patriarchy that has been subjugating women for millennia."

"I feel compelled to say that he does have a certain acclaim as a playwright."

"That is because women have never been given a proper platform to show their own writing skills. Shakespeare has nothing to say to the women of today."

"When the three students laid the charges of racism and sexism against Dr. Miller, were you supportive?"

"Once I had seen the material he had distributed and heard from several sources what he had actually said in the classroom, I was fully behind them."

"In your opinion, should Dr. Miller be granted tenure at this university?"

"Absolutely not."

"Dr. Kennedy, I thank you for your time and for your cooperation this afternoon."

Cynthia Kennedy, for the first time, looked nonplussed. "That's it?" she asked.

"Yes it is," replied Johanna who then turned to the panel, "I have no more questions for this witness."

She turned and as she walked back to her desk she smiled and said, "Your witness, Mr. MacPherson."

Seamus strode to the witness stand, his face set in a stern look. "Dr. Kennedy, were you aware that at the time of Dr. Miller's appointment there had been no other applications for the position?"

"I suppose that I was aware of that fact," she replied hesitantly.

"Interesting answer, Doctor. You 'suppose' that you were aware of a fact. The reality was that no other applications existed save Dr. Miller's. Is that true?"

"It is, but it should have made no difference," Cynthia Kennedy snapped.

"And why, pray, should that be?"

"There should have been further requests for applications to be made. We had time. There was no need to rush into hiring him."

"Dr. Kennedy, were you willing to keep advertising the position until finally a woman submitted her interest in the post?"

Cynthia glared at Seamus who returned her gaze placidly. "Yes, I was," she snarled. "That position should have been filled by a woman."

"Was there a gender imbalance in the Arts faculty, Dr. Kennedy?"

"I don't know what a gender imbalance is."

"Were there, are there, many more women on the Arts faculty than men?"

"There may be more women than men, but I do not see that as being 'many more'."

"What would you consider to be the perfect ratio of men to women on this faculty?"

Cynthia hesitated, started to answer and stopped. Finally, she said, "I'm not sure what a *perfect ratio* would be."

"Would you accept a ratio of 100% men to no women?"

"Of course not. Don't be ridiculous, please."

"Would you accept a ratio of 100% women to zero men?"

Cynthia's eyes blazed at Seamus. "It's a simple question, Professor. Would you accept such a ratio?"

"As a matter of fact, I would. It would be refreshing to see a program administered and taught by women without the malevolent influence of men to hinder them. The results would be wonderful."

"You see no problem in such a hypothetical arrangement?"

"I do not."

"Do you acknowledge that William Shakespeare was and is a funda-mental and foundational pillar in our cultural structure?"

"I certainly do not agree with that. Our cultural structure that you refer to needs to be totally restructured."

"And that restructuring would include the removal of Shakespeare's works from the ideal college program that we are discussing?"

"If necessary, yes it would. Where are you going with these bizarre questions?"

"'I'll try to make that evident, Doctor. The two most evil philoso-phies of the last century also eliminated history and insisted on total subservience to a single political view. I refer, of course, to fascism and communism. They, too, wanted to disconnect their subjects from the presence of a real past and the presence of a real culture. How would you distinguish your views from the practices of those two systems?"

"Are you comparing feminism to fascism?" Cynthia exploded.

"No, indeed. I do not consider you a feminist. I think you espouse a form of totalitarianism and it certainly is not feminism. How do you think your all-woman system should be categorized?"

Cynthia turned to the panel. "Do I have to put up with this kind of abuse?" she cried.

"Mr. MacPherson, could you ramp down the inflammatory tone somewhat, please," said the Adjudicator.

"Of course. With the panel's permission, I should like to quote an acclaimed British medical doctor and essayist who wrote not long ago about Aldous Huxley and George Orwell and their universally recognized portrayals of dystopias, *Brave New World* and *1984*. In his essay, Dr. Theodore Dalrymple said, 'For both Huxley and Orwell, one man symbolized resistance to the dehumanizing disconnection of man from his past: Shakespeare. In both writers, he stands for the highest pinnacle of human understanding, without which human life loses its depth and its possibility of transcendence.' Would you still leave Shakespeare off the syllabus, Doctor?"

"I would. And I point out that you refer to three males, no women, in your little sermon."

"I did, yes. And as you raise the subject of women, were you aware, Dr. Kennedy, that Professor Miller's course was called *Shakespeare's Strongest Characters: His Women*?"

Cynthia scowled at him, but did not reply.

"Were you aware?"

"Yes, I was. But it made no difference," she snapped. "He should not have been there."

"Did your campaign to have Dr. Miller removed begin even before he set foot in his classroom?"

"What are you suggesting?"

"I am no longer suggesting, but stating, that you coerced a small band of malleable young women to seize upon the slightest pretext to lodge a complaint against Dr. Miller, to leave his course on a quasi-point of principle, to put their successful completion of program at Bowell in jeopardy, all on the understanding that you would see that no penalty accrued to their actions."

"This is disgusting. I did no such thing." She was on the edge of her seat, straining forward, her hands clutching the railing of the witness stand, her eyes wild.

Seamus turned to his desk, picked up a sealed envelope and holding it in the air approached Cynthia Kennedy.

"Inside this envelope are three signatures affirming the truth of what I just said. And they affirm something more: The unacceptable relationship of a person in a position of responsibility with an undergraduate student. Would you like me to break the seal on this envelope and read its contents, Dr. Kennedy?"

"You lousy chauvinistic pig," she screamed. "I'd do anything to stop the likes of you having anything to do with my program." She stopped, a small drop of spittle showing at the corner of her mouth, and seemed to realize what she had just admitted.

Slowly Seamus looked away from her to the panel. "I am now finished with this witness." He walked back to the desk, sat, and stared at his hands, his chin almost on his chest. Henry did not speak to him.

Finally, Professor Raymond asked if there were any more witnesses to be called. Johanna shook her head. "No, Madam."

"Just one, Madam," said Seamus. "I know that Professor Miller has been present for all the preceding testimony. Nevertheless, I should, with your permission, like to call him to the stand."

"Carry on, Mr. MacPherson," she replied.

Once Henry was in the stand, Seamus approached him and said, "For the official record would you please identify yourself and your position at Bowell College."

"My name is Henry Miller, I have a doctorate degree in English literature and I am currently a lecturer in that discipline at Bowell College."

"You understand the gravity of the charges against you?"

"I am acutely aware of the seriousness of the allegations against me."

"Are you also aware that this situation might possibly have been avoided had you chosen not to instruct your students in Shakespearean dramas?"

"Yes."

"Do you regret not selecting a different course of study given the current situation?"

"No, sir, I do not."

"Would you please explain for this Tribunal why you feel so strongly in this matter."

Henry took a deep breath, looked down at his hands and finally turned to face the panel. He began to speak slowly, but gradually his pace quickened as he warmed to this topic which was so dear to him. As he delved into the areas which he had taught to his students he almost forgot that he was in a court-like situation and he became again the professor whose lessons had earned such rave reviews from his three classes. His passion was clear and contagious.

Seamus quietly backed up to his desk, leaned against it, folded his arms and watched the faces of the three people who would decide Henry's future. They were enthralled. Nor were they alone in their focus on the man speaking. The entire auditorium was still and soundless. Seamus let Henry continue for what seemed a long time but was only twelve minutes. Finally he interrupted.

"If I may stop you there, Dr. Miller, I feel that you have amply responded to my request. And I have no more questions for you. But perhaps Ms. Ferrelle does."

"Madam, I have only two."

Johanna stood behind her desk but did not approach the witness stand. "Professor Miller, would you categorize William Shakespeare as a feminist playwright?"

"Absolutely."

"And secondly, would you characterize yourself as a feminist?"

"Without question, I am."

"In response to what I have just heard, Madam, I have no further questions."

XXIX

"**R**achel, go and pat Zeke's bottom. He's crying and maybe that will put him back to sleep. And pat his bottom gently, please."

Nora turned back to the enormous hip of beef that was slowly turning on the spit that she'd last seen at the Harpers' barbeque in August the preceding summer. The coals in the trays beneath the meat were white hot and as she reached in to gather drippings from another metal tray designed for that purpose, the heat caused a ribbon of perspiration to appear beneath her customary ponytail.

"Let me do the basting, Nora," said Henry. "You should still be taking it very easy."

"Back off, Teacher Man. This is the only job that's been left for me to do. And while I appreciate your concern for my well-being, Henry, it has been six weeks, and remember that it was the easiest of the three deliveries that I've had." She stood up and put a hand to his cheek. "I'm fine, Lover, I really am."

They stood with their arms about each other and watched the gigantic roast slowly turn brown, its juices flowing in small streams about it.

"You know, Henry, we could have got the coals going and the meat on the spit ourselves. The Pirate didn't have to show up here at six o'clock to do that."

"True 'nuff. But you know George; he's military right through and perfect preparation is essential to him."

"'The readiness is all,' as that gloomy Dane said."

They looked toward the driveway as a white panel truck pulled in, the words 'The Bayside Bistro' painted on both sides. "Here's Olive and the chef with all the other goodies for this sybaritic extravaganza. How Zeke got them to agree to this I'll never know."

"Quite an achievement," said Nora, "given that he's only six weeks old."

"It was him, was it? Silly me. I was under the impression that this had been orchestrated by the President-Designate, one Dr. Z. Silverstein."

"Henry, get over here," shouted George Harper, his hand on the huge carved mahogany post used to draw draft beer from the keg sitting in icy contentment in what had once been a washing machine. "It's almost one o'clock, the buses will be here soon, and these keg lines need to be tested."

Henry glanced at Nora, who laughed, and said, "Have one for me, Sailor. I'm going inside to check on your son."

George took two glass steins from the ice, filled the first and threw all the foam onto the ground, then held it at an angle and slowly let the amber fluid rise inside the mug. He repeated the procedure, handed one to Henry, took a long sip, smacked his lips, and pronounced, "Now that is what I call a tasty drop!"

The two men enjoyed the beer for a few minutes, then George said, "It was really nice of you to invite those first semester English classes to this shin-dig."

"Yah, well most of them have already headed for home. About a nano-second after the last exam, actually. But a few are still around and the free beer and food will drag them out here."

"Sounds like the faculty," laughed the Pirate. "Speaking of faculty, some of them won't be too pleased to be sharing a bus and barbeque with flesh-and-blood students. Entirely undignified, don't you know. But tell me, Henry, why did you invite those three classes particularly?"

Henry drained the last swallow from his mug, refilled it and did the same for George. "I owe those kids, George. They were the ones who sent the emails to Seamus. And they orchestrated that themselves. One of your Engineering guys quarterbacked it. Lad by the name of Eric. Those emails probably saved my sorry ass."

The sound of two approaching school buses interrupted Henry and they watched as a combination of students and faculty descended onto the lawn near the rotating beef. Henry turned back to George, "You know, the situation with the mixture we see over there might not be too bad. We are, after all, without some of the players who blessed us with their presence last August at your place."

"That's true, Henry. And just before the thirsty hordes lay siege to my keg here, I must tell you that we've had a really well-qualified applicant for the new Foundations of Western Civilization program. Charley Lee was telling me. And irony of ironies, she's from Yale. So some of that old professor's ideas may be bearing fruit here at Bowell. What was that old guy's name?"

"Professor Donald Kagan."

Henry busied himself pulling glasses of draft without stopping for the next thirty minutes. When he at last had quenched the initial thirstiness of his guests, he pulled one for himself and surveyed the scene. Ten picnic tables were crowded with happy diners; a much longer table loaded with salads, pickles, cold vegetables, fruits and desserts was in the attentive care of Olive, Zeke's favourite waitress; yet another table presented a variety of decent plonks, both red and white, the latter cooling in a washtub filled with ice, as well as plates and cutlery. And Paulo and Tony, having removed the hip from the huge skewer had let it rest for twenty minutes and were now merrily carving and serving the roast beast.

Three customers appeared, their glasses empty. "Adnan, Eric, I didn't even notice you guys before. And Shauna Herold, as I live and breath. I am so glad that you three came. But wait a second here. Adnan, you told me you don't touch alcohol being the devout Muslim that you are. What are you doing hanging around a beer keg?"

Adnan held out his empty glass so that Henry could sniff it.

"Ah, coca-cola. Lips that touch wine shall never touch thine."

"Now hold on, sir. I may be devout, but I'm not fanatical."

They all laughed and Henry said, "I know that you two chaps will be back for your senior year in the fall; but what will you be up to, Shauna?"

"I got accepted into Osgoode. I'm going to study law."

"Were you influenced by Portia?"

The young woman laughed. "Somewhat. But mostly I was influenced by those two lawyers at your Tribunal hearing. I was knocked

out by their intelligence and the civility they showed to the whole pro-
ceeding, even though they were on opposing sides. That's where I see
myself."

"And speaking of the devil," said Adnan, "look who just wheeled in."

"I'll be damned. I didn't know he was coming."

"Thought I might find you draped over a keg," laughed Seamus,
nodding at the three students. "You might as well pour me one, Henry."

"Shauna, here, was so taken by your lawyerly talents she's going
into law this fall."

"Well, both you and Johanna Ferrelle," said Shauna. "How is she?
What is she up to?"

Nora had approached, holding the baby, and Seamus gave her a
peck on the cheek. "Johanna's doing well, Shauna. Busy as hell. But
she's going on a cruise in a few weeks. Eastern Mediterranean. Starting
in Istanbul and ending up with a week in Israel. She deserves it and
she's really looking forward to it. I'll tell her you asked."

Seamus put his hands out for the baby. "Hi, Zeke. You are one of the
reasons I came to this depraved event. I wanted to see my godson and
you are a beauty. You done real good, Mom," he said to Nora handing
the infant back.

"Thanks, Seamus. What else did you want to see?"

"Well, among others, I wanted to see the house now that it's been
finished. Henry has told me that it is gorgeous. And I also want to see
that goddam septic system that caused me so much effort in keeping
your moron husband out of the slammer."

"Come with me, sir, and I shall show you all," said Henry. "Eric and
Shauna, you're in charge of the keg. Don't let Adnan have a drop."

The two men strolled to the top of the gently rising mound situated
on the western side of the driveway. "This is it, Seamus. The sewage
and grey water gets pumped under the drive to this wee hill where it is
disseminated and that's all there is to it."

"And that guy from the Department of Health wanted to destroy
the trees and the front of your house instead of this," marvelled Seamus
more to himself than to his buddy. "Incredible. But, Henry, why is this

hill so pock-marked? And you've done a lousy job of spreading the grass seed."

"Ah, thereby hangs a tale. I had this perfect. I'd raked it repeatedly, spread the seed exactly right, had then spread just the right amount of topsoil to barely cover the seeds, and very gently rolled it all. It was perfect. It only had to start growing."

"Okay, so what happened?"

"We woke up one morning about three o'clock to this really loud mooing noise. I went outside to investigate. Elmer Knobber's fence was down and every cow and heifer that he owned was standing on my perfect septic hill. I got them all back into the field, but it took me a couple of hours, and the hill was as you see it. I was not a happy person."

"Where is old Elmer? I thought he'd be over here scoffing the free beer and beef."

"There is a God, Seamus, and occasionally She reveals Her face. Elmer took off to Florida pulling his trailer. I'd asked him if he had out-of-country health insurance and he just looked at me as if I were nuts. He got down there, had a heart attack, was in the hospital for some time, had to be flown back and when the bill finally came in, it was for just over $80,000. I think that's what killed him, not his heart. So the lad from the next farm over bought Elmer's land from the estate, fixed the fences and is planning to fix and save that wonderful old barn over there."

Seamus chuckled and drained his glass. "I really do want to see your restored house, Henry. Honestly. But right now, if you'll excuse me, I see Megan Fiorini over at the cooking sherry. I think I'll go and compare my divorce history with hers."

Nora was still chatting with the three students. "Osgoode?" she mused. "That's associated with York University. Isn't that where Jean Whitmarsh and her husband are teaching next year?"

George Harper had returned to see if the keg had run out and if the second one needed to be connected. "Yup," he answered to Nora's question. "York is not entirely unfamiliar with devotees of politically correct silliness among its faculty. She and Leonard will fit in well."

"And I am bursting with curiosity, George, what has happened with the lovely Dr. Cynthia Kennedy?"

George smiled at Nora. "She worked a deal with Charley Lee. She's off on a full year's sabbatical. But she's scheduled to be back with us after that year away."

The buses loaded up at four o'clock and the frolickers were bundled in and carried back to the school campus. The clean-up crew, supervised by Paolo, Tony and Olive, made short work of the tables and chairs, extra food, garbage, and plates, knives and forks. Only enough to feed the dozen or so people staying at the house was left. Everything else disappeared into The Bistro's panel truck and was soon on its way back into town. The protective screen was placed over the still-hot coals, and that was that.

Muriel Harper and Zeke had finally arrived as had Linda O'Connor and her husband. Henry gave Linda a hug and smiled, "Welcome indeed, Dean O'Connor. And Zeke, should I call you Mr. President or My Thrice Gracious Liege?"

"Either," replied Zeke, "so long as you prostrate yourself fully on the ground before me as you say it."

"What's up for you this summer, Zeke?" asked Linda.

"Well, I am rather excited about it, I must confess. I'm going on a cruise through the Eastern Mediterranean that ends up with a week in Israel."

Henry started to say something but was stopped by a sharp jab in his back from his wife. Just then, Annie and Rachel rushed up and gave the old man hugs around his long legs.

"Uncle Zeke," gushed Annie, "I've been reading about Merlin. Did you know that he didn't grow old the way we do? He started old and grew young. Isn't that wonderful?"

"It is my darling. Truly wonderful." He stopped and looked around him at the circle of friends. "Let me propose a toast. To Now, which is ever The Beginning."

Made in the USA
Lexington, KY
09 August 2014